Juarez Justice

Juarez Justice

JACK TROLLEY

Carroll & Graf Publishers, Inc.
New York

First edition 1996

Carroll & Graf Publishers, Inc.
260 Fifth Avenue
New York, NY 10001

ISBN 0-7867-0356-3

Library of Congress Cataloging-in-Publication Data is available.

Manufactured in the United States of America.

For Miss Stanley,
who is smart and funny,
and every bit as beautiful,
as Catalina De Lourdes Venezuela.

Acknowledgments

My thanks to San Diego's Reader, *and two of its contributors, Luis Urrea and Edith Moore, who first sparked my interest in El Pozo del Mundo, The Hole of the World, and also to Albert Zuckerman and Robert Goldfarb, who are my agents and my friends, for encouraging me to look into it, and always to Kent Carroll, my publisher, for his caring help with the final cut.*

A poor politician is a poor excuse for a politician.

—Mexican Proverb

Juarez Justice

One

There always was a woman, Donahoo thought. In his line of work, you'd think there'd always be a corpse, but no, a woman. There always was a woman and sometimes there wasn't a corpse. Sometimes it was missing and you had to go look for it and sometimes you couldn't find it. There was absolutely no telling what a killer might do with a corpse. She might grind it up and serve it to her friends as Bridge Mix.

In this instance, though, the corpse was, or had been, in plain sight, and the woman in the case was very beautiful, with a proud profile and a long neck, two things he much admired. She also had dark, slanted eyes and a full mouth. The lips pouted like little cocktail sausages. Her name was Catalina.

"She is one of us," Torres had said mysteriously, as if he had a gang or something, a little after making an elaborately casual introduction, all in Spanish. "Miss Catalina De Lourdes Venezuela. It is my pleasure to present Sergeant Tommy Donahoo, and his partner, Investigator Cruz Marino. They are police officers from San Diego. Here to assist me in a matter."

This while, after coming into the bar, she had paused, ever so briefly, as if to let her dark, slanted eyes adjust to the gloom, clutching a white plastic supermarket bag with red printing, LEY's. She was wearing a plain blue dress with white piping at the collar and plain blue flat-heeled shoes. She might not have been wearing anything else. No lines showed. Donahoo had noted the eyes and the sausage lips and the long, faintly auburn-tinged black hair piled in a careless bun. The full bust and wasp waist and flaring hips and the impossibly long legs.

Torres had not said that the matter involved murder. Cruz had briefly translated, "He says we're cops," and then, together, they had said, "Senorita," and then she had merely smiled and gone away, vanishing through a tattered dirty cloth that served as the door to the kitchen. To disappear, but sure to return at some later date, Donahoo thought. He was positive of that. Somehow, he knew. It was more than just a guess.

"Pretty girl," Donahoo said. He thought he should say that, and anyway, it was true. She looked special. In another, better time, a kind of Rita Hayworth, waiting to be discovered.

Marino translated and Torres shrugged and pulled on his Dos XX, as if a task had been completed, now he could relax. He made yet another inspection of the bar although he seemed familiar with it, in that he knew the thin, sickly bartender, Luis. It was called The Desperate Frog, located in the border district known as Calle Primero, or First Street. There was a linoleum-covered bar, a few spindly tables and chairs, some weathered bullfight posters and dusty piñatas fashioned mostly after cartoon characters, Popeye the Sailor and Daffy Duck and a marvelous work-of-art Pluto, and no customers, just them, Donahoo and Cruz Marino with their host, Carlos Torres, Captain of Detectives, Grupo Homicidios, Baja California Policia Judicial del Estado, showing them the City of Tijuana. El Pozo del Mundo, The Hole of the World. Sodom on the Border. Disneyland Calcutta. The most celebrated bastion of chaos in the western hemisphere. With a government so corrupt it approached burlesque. In a country that treated its people like a renewable resource. Even now they were out there fucking. More would be along soon.

They were parked out front, illegally, having arrived in Torres's wheezing Chrysler LeBaron, which had Baja plates and may have been stolen in the United States—it had a California emissions standards stamp under the hood. Donahoo had taken the trouble to look the second time they stopped to fill the radiator.

"Later, we'll go to the dump," Torres said, and Cruz Marino, rolling his eyes, translated, and Donahoo said nothing, although, as far as he knew, the dump was not connected to the case under review. Nor, for that matter, again as far as he knew, was The Desperate Frog. Donahoo also thought that actually the case wasn't presently under review. Torres had been diligently avoiding discussion of it. He had suggested, upon picking them up at their motel, that instead they first get the feel of the place, meaning Tijuana. The file presumably was in his attaché, a small aluminum box which might be used to carry rings for sale, or perhaps a dismantled sniper's rifle, depending on one's calling. Donahoo thought that you could never be sure here. You could never be sure anywhere, of course, but you could be less sure here.

"Tell him okay."

"You're kidding."

"Tell him yes."

"Jesus Christ."

"Sí, Capitán," Donahoo told Torres, thinking that something else he'd do later, he'd have a talk with Marino, who had several fatal flaws as an interpreter. He injected himself. He made judgments. He left things out. Donahoo was trying to pick up as much Spanish as he could. So far he had picked up *capitan* and *El Dompe*. He had *si* and *gracias* from previous visits. *Fucking gringo*. The essentials.

"What are we going to the dump for?" Marino demanded, a question that went both ways. He was in the middle, the short, plump one of the three of them bellied at the bar, close to the street door, the better (Donahoo thought) to have met Catalina De Lourdes Venezuela. "What's at the fucking dump?"

Well, for one thing, not garbage, Donahoo thought. They didn't appear to be collecting it. But again he said nothing. His mind was on Catalina De Lourdes Venezuela and how she might be—correction, *was*—a part of Carlos Torres's hidden agenda. He could barely contain the urge to spring up and crash into the kitchen. Catalina, he was certain, would be gone, the back door swinging. She had put in an appearance, that's all. Made her presence known.

Torres said amiably, "What you're going to see," this in reference to what was at the dump, and, without waiting for Marino to translate, ordered three more Dos XXs.

Marino started to protest, "We're on duty . . ." and Donahoo whacked him sharply with an elbow. He got out his money. "Tell him it's my turn and my pleasure."

"*Mañana*," Torres said, pushing it away.

Donahoo wondered how fluent Torres was in English. Probably very. But it was hard to tell. They'd been together a couple of hours and Torres had yet to react to Cruz Marino's complaints and comments unless they were in Spanish. Now, he had seemed to understand, immediately, that he, Donahoo, wanted to pay, but he had been careful not to respond until he saw the billfold.

"Today I am your host."

"*Gracias*."

Donahoo accepted the beer, his third for the morning, they'd had warm Coronas at their first stop, another empty dive, Caramba!, and thought that Torres *had* to know English. For a senior police officer in Baja, it would be a prerequisite, surely. So why would Torres pretend ignorance? Then Donahoo was reminded that Spanish wasn't a prerequisite for him, even though, by all measures, it ought to be. Hardly a day passed when it wouldn't be helpful to him on the streets of San Diego, where, in normal circumstances, he headed up the SDPD's elite Squad 5, also known as SCUMB, for Sickos, Crackpots, Underwear and Mad Bombers. He had almost decided to take a course when the futility of it overwhelmed him. To be truly efficient, he'd also need Mandarin, Korean, Vietnamese, Thai and Cambodian. Every boat brought, as Lewis, captain, Investigations, maintained, mostly honest, worthy, hard-working people, but also at least one impenetrable slope prick sonofabitch. Still, if he knew Spanish, he wouldn't be saddled with Cruz Marino, Donahoo realized, and he wouldn't be at such enormous disadvantage with Carlos Torres. Nor, if the moment came, *when* the moment came, would he be plunged into a terrible fix with Catalina De Lourdes Venezuela. Catalina, being *one of us*, might, like Torres, (a) not know English, or (b) pretend not to know English. The idea was unsettling for him. He was already having flights of soaring fancy. Had no idea where to start about taking an interpreter to bed.

They drank their beer and chatted and Cruz Marino dutifully translated all of it, finally coming, *finally*, Donahoo thought, to his, Donahoo's, reputation as the best homicide detective south of Seattle, which was in no way true, but nevertheless his reputation. In truth, he was merely the luckiest. It was luck—pure, sheer luck—that had solved The Purple Admiral Murder Case, The Stardust Donut Shop Murder Case, and The Babes in the Woods Murder Case. It was luck that extinguished the Balboa Firefly and luck again that stopped Manila Time. All big, big stories in the *Union-Trib*. His picture plastered all over. His name spelled right. He was being modest. "Luck."

"Yes, well, whatever," Torres said, Marino translating furiously. "Luck, fate, skill. It doesn't matter. Just that it works and that it's on our side for a while. Let me say again how pleased we are that you agreed to come."

Donahoo had to grin around his beer. *Agreed?* What had happened, actually, was that Saperstein had called him in and made a long police chief speech, something about mutual dependency, better communications, improved relations, hands across the border and cutting through red tape, all of which meant that he, Donahoo, was being loaned, indefinitely, to Grupo Homicidios, to help solve Tijuana's most baffling high-profile slaying in half a century, the brutal dagger-in-the-heart rape and murder of socialite Deedee Hernandez, who had been found with a photo of Elvis Presley stuck in her pussy. "A crotch shot," Saperstein had said, and Donahoo had pointed out that he didn't speak Spanish, and Saperstein had said that's why Investigator Cruz Marino would be going along, because he did. Saperstein was a primo con. He'd shit in your hand and say it was a Hershey kiss. Oh, and Lewis had added, looking wise, "When you solve it, tell them they solved it, Tommy." He, Donahoo, had thought that if he was smart enough to solve it, he was smart enough to know that, but he hadn't said anything. Lewis was just being careful. He was a careful guy. They had driven down that morning. They were staying at El Greco. Sharing a room with kitchenette.

"You are going to need it," Torres said now, meaning luck or whatever. He paused, deep in thought, hunched between huge shoulders. He was staring at, but not seeing, his Dos XX. He obviously saw something else. Probably, because it was about time, something to do with the murder of Deedee Hernandez. Donahoo frankly knew very little of the case, except that it was a week old, unsolved, although there was a material witness, Pedro Juarez, held in the Tijuana Jail. He knew the victim was a prominent and popular beauty active in several charities. He knew her rich, handsome husband was a doctor, specializing in the reconstruction of limbs, particularly hands. He knew that one was dead and that the other wasn't a suspect, yet. That's about all. While the murder had made a big splash in Tijuana, it had caused hardly a ripple in San Diego, and possibly would have passed unnoticed if it were not for Elvis. Many things crossed the border, but not social standing, Donahoo mused. Torres muttered, "How do you define a myth?"

"Something that attempts to explain the unexplainable."

Cruz Marino was interpreting all this.

"Well, yes, that will do, I suppose. In any event there is the myth of a man found hanged in an empty, overheated room, dangling from a light fixture, four feet off the floor, and there is nothing he could have climbed up on, no tipped chair or anything of the sort, and all doors and windows locked from the inside, and there is no other possible way of exit/entry, such as a fireplace, and the only clue is a spot of water."

Donahoo waited. He had heard this one. It was a grade school problem.

"Ice," Torres pronounced with satisfaction. "He stood on a block of ice." He drank some Dos XX while Marino translated. Then, "This has never been revealed to the prying media, which, obviously, will never give us any peace, but we have the same problem in the peculiar death of Deedee Hernandez, Sargento. Door, windows. All locked from inside. And—it could mean nothing or everything—some spots of water."

Donahoo was suddenly interested. He looked around. There was only the bartender, the very thin, very sickly Luis, deep in a newspaper, probably out of earshot. He kept his voice low anyway. "What are you suggesting?"

Torres answered with another question. "That she may have fucked herself?"

Marino had by now suspended disbelief.

"Possibly," Torres answered. "A neat trick. But why not?" He also shot a quick look at Luis. He spoke in a hush. "Her husband is a doctor. The house is full of medical books. Somewhere they must tell how much damage forced penetration is apt to cause. Photographs showing tears and bruises."

Now Donahoo was fascinated. He couldn't help it. "Semen?"

Torres shrugged. "Saved from the day before. Spit into a wine glass. Who's watching?" He said, "Myself, I always have my eyes closed then."

"But not the doctor's semen, obviously?"

"No."

"And not Pedro Juarez's?"

"No. They were both kind enough to volunteer samples. Well, maybe Juarez didn't volunteer."

"So tell me. How does this clear Hernandez and not Juarez?"

"Juarez would have had a fucking accomplice?"

"But not Hernandez?"

"I love how your mind works."

Marino said, "I want to go home."

Donahoo considered. A woman rapes herself with an icicle. And now for the hard part. She *falls* on it? He was sure that in those medical books there would be ample instruction on which ribs to go between to pierce the heart. He didn't think someone could do it though. It was . . . what? Showing off?

"Deedee, she, uh, didn't lock up after the killer left?"

"No. The coroner insists that she died instantly."

"And the blood placement suggests that?"

"Yes. No trail."

Donahoo considered. Huh, he thought. "How long have you had this theory?"

"It's not a theory."

"What is it?"

"A nightmare. The Deedee Hernandez Nightmare Murder Case."

Donahoo put a big, reassuring, stick-around hand on Marino. He didn't want him running off at the good part.

"The doctor and the Presidente, they are like this, huh?" Torres said, shoving a large finger up his nose. "Very tight. Brothers." He left it there for a longish time. "The doctor, and, therefore, the Presidente, won't be satisfied until we produce the wife's rapist killer. They are not interested in the disgrace of a macabre and revolting suicide. You see the problem?"

"So you haven't discussed suicide with the doctor?"

"Not a word."

"Despite the door and windows being locked from inside?"

"He says there's an explanation."

"Did he say what it was?"

"No."

Donahoo returned to his beer. He wondered what the fuck this was and where it was going. For a moment, just an instant, he thought it might be some elaborate practical joke, and that Saperstein might suddenly burst out of Popeye the Sailor, yelling, "Surprise!"

"Tell me more about Pedro Juarez," Donahoo said, although he felt sure that he didn't want to know. "Is he a material witness, or is he a suspect?"

Torres became distant. A faraway look. He rolled his Dos XX between oversize palms. "Both, I suppose. In Mexico . . ." The faraway look remained. "In Mexico, there are suspects, and then there are suspects. When Colosio—the candidate for Presidente?—when Colosio was assassinated here, there were twenty suspects, all of them in jail at one time or another, but in the end, there was just the one suspect, the man who killed him in front of a dozen witnesses and the TV cameras."

"So he's not a suspect?"

"I didn't say that."

"Then he's a standby suspect?"

Torres looked at him. "I didn't say that either."

Oh, Donahoo thought. He was sure that's what was said. "He's a material witness. Why?"

"The Tijuana police arrested him near the Hernandez residence shortly after the body was discovered. He was in possession of a monogrammed handkerchief. The letters, DD. For Deedee Hernandez."

"And that's all?"

"What do you mean?"

"Not the family silverware?"

"No."

Marino was tiring. Donahoo said, "What else should I know about Pedro Juarez?"

That faraway look. "He's a troublemaker."

"For who?"

"Politically. He asks embarrassing questions."

"What party does he belong to?"

"The National Action Party. PAN."

"Isn't that the party in power here?"

"The party in office. Not necessarily in power."

Donahoo thought he wanted to go home too. He also thought that Carlos Torres didn't look like a capitán of detectives in Grupo Homicidios. He was too large and outwardly sane for that. Donahoo thought he belonged on a horse or perhaps climbing telephone poles. Some enterprise that permitted him to lord it over without that appearing too obviously intentional. On the ground, it couldn't be avoided. He was six two, as tall as Donahoo, and heavier by thirty pounds; he'd be two hundred and fifty, easy, and surprisingly hard for an older man. There was no guessing his age. He could be fifty and he might be sixty. That kind of guy who hides the truth in a thousand contradictions. Sharp eyes in brown crinkled skin. He talks slowly, but he's fast? My little Mexican brother, Donahoo thought, only he's not so little, and he's starting to scare me. Cruz Marino, the forlorn, complaining midget between them, was an easy read in comparison, often mistaken for a Jew who looked like an Arab but merely an Italian trying to pass as a Mexican. Your Basic Man, blessed with a choirboy's face and only slightly balding, Donahoo thought, not unaware of the ironies, which were too many to list at the moment. He said, "I don't like my tits pulled."

"Pardon me?"

Donahoo repeated the statement and this time Marino translated more carefully.

Torres smiled. He showed all of his hard white teeth. "You want to know where this goes? It goes wherever you want to take it, Sargento."

"Does it?"

"Yes. You weren't asked here so that we could put roadblocks in your way. Quite the contrary, you will have every assistance. There is no road you can't walk. No pisshole you can't look down. I have that on the very highest authority."

Donahoo looked at him. Carte blanche? He doubted that. The Mexican cops he knew were proud and independent and crooked as shit. Torres, whom he didn't know, not yet, hadn't shown any sign that he was unique among them. He might, under pressure, ask for help, but he wasn't going to let a gringo dick walk over him. Donahoo thought that he knew how it would work. Torres would say one thing and he'd do another. He'd find some way to chart the course. And it wouldn't be straight.

"The Presidente himself," Torres said softly, finishing his beer. "He knows your reputation. He wants only that you solve this murder."

Donahoo wasn't satisfied. "Oh? How does he know of me?"

"He can read."

"And he believes that shit?"

"No. But I suspect, like all of us, he saw shreds of truth, Sargento, which is perhaps more than he saw at Grupo Homicidios."

Marino, sweating, translated all this, not drinking his beer because he was on duty.

"Well, I've got to water the flowers," Torres announced. He went down to the rear of the saloon, his cowboy hat bumping the low-hanging piñatas, creating little clouds of dust. He flicked Luis's newspaper as he passed. Donahoo caught only one word. "Hialeah."

Marino said, "Well, what do you think?"

Donahoo shook off the question. He watched Luis get up and follow Torres. They went into the toilet together. Then, moving quickly, Donahoo went to the dirty cloth, pulled it back.

Catalina De Lourdes Venezuela was gone. The kitchen was empty. The back door was unbolted. The white LEY's bag was a crumpled diaper on a counter. In and out, like a stork, Donahoo thought. He went back to the bar.

"Well?"

That question again. Donahoo was busy with others. Torres and Jesus, the bartender at Caramba!, they, too, had gone to the toilet together. Not long enough for anything indecent. Torres might be fast, but not that fast, Donahoo thought. Still, it did give pause.

"Catalina, did you like her?" Torres asked when, again promptly, he returned, and after Marino had translated, Donahoo said, "The girl? I liked what I saw," and Torres said, "What did you see?" and Donahoo told him, all this being translated accurately, for once, by Marino, "I think temptation."

Torres didn't answer. His eyes went flat. Donahoo knew when he said it, it was the wrong, if not the incorrect, answer. But he couldn't resist. His whole life, he had preferred victory to pleasure. He wanted Torres to know what he knew, that Catalina had been there by arrangement, to show herself, *one of us*. It was a small thing to be aware of but it was something. He would have preferred to know everything, what exactly he was being recruited for, and why. The other thing he knew, that it was extremely unlikely. He would bet first on Saperstein popping out of Popeye. He said, "Well, off to El Dompe, Capitán?"

TWO

El Dompe was at Colonia Sausto Gonzalez, a barrio slum south-west of the city, close to the ocean. Donahoo saw the seagulls first and was to see the children last. Babies, some of them. The seagulls, when they rose together, disturbed, were like a gray sheet against the polluted sky, shaken by some mythic cleaning lady laboring behind the rise. They briefly blotted out the horizon, then fell back too soon. Donahoo wished the sight would last longer. So far it was the nicest moment of the tour.

"Did I know her?" Carlos Torres said, asking the question of himself without any prompting. He was still talking about The Deedee Hernandez Nightmare Murder Case. Once he had gotten started, he couldn't stop. Working with one hand, he opened his aluminum attaché, withdrawing a photograph. He shoved it past Marino to Donahoo. "No, not really. But I had briefly met her on several occasions. Most notably, at a ball honoring her charity work, I brushed, again briefly, against her angel wings. It was like being in heaven."

Marino, riding up front with him in the LeBaron, where it was easier to serve as interpreter, looked at Torres strangely as he repeated the statement.

Brushed her wings? Donahoo, watching the seagulls fall, accepted the photograph absently. He wondered if Marino had gotten that right. He was going to challenge it but decided to take advantage instead. It might be the opportunity he was waiting for. He repositioned and said, "Of all my wounds, it is my mind that remains the most open."

"What?" This from Marino.

Donahoo was watching Torres in the rearview. The smile was faint but there. No translation would be necessary. You fraud, Donahoo thought. He said, "Tell him."

Marino did so. Donahoo meantime looked at the photograph.

13

Deedee Hernandez in a royal pose. She was in a purple gown, seated on a thronelike chair, and she was very alluring in a severe, dark way. She looked more interesting than fun.

"Yes," Torres said solemnly. "Her beautiful white wings." The LeBaron had veered. It didn't turn. It veered. They were now aimed more directly at the sheet of seagulls settling atop the vast, dimly smoking landfill that was Tijuana's central garbage disposal site. "They are awarded annually by the Tijuana Guardian Society of the Poor to the person who, in the society's opinion, has made the most significant contribution, in the past year, toward the betterment of the deprived. Instead of a proclamation or plaque or other bauble, the recipient is presented with full-size wings, fashioned from the feathers of white doves, which cleverly attach to their shoulders, and they get to wear them at the society's annual ball."

Oh, Donahoo thought. "It must make the winner a standout on the dance floor."

Torres nodded, still solemn. "Yes. The way the wings are constructed, they lift when one twirls, so one seems to just fly around. Thousands of feathers are used, glued on by volunteers, much as for a float in your Rose Bowl."

"And when did Deedee Hernandez win?"

"A year ago last March."

"And what for?"

"El Dompe."

"The dump?"

"Yes. El Dompe was her main charity."

Marino asked the question on his own behalf. "How can a dump be a charity?"

"That's what you're going to see," Torres told him, which was what he had basically told him at The Desperate Frog. He glanced back at Donahoo, his expression saying your friend is young, with much to learn. "That is why we are going there."

Marino missed the rebuke. He was busy lighting up. Departing the bar, he had discovered a cheap, satisfactory cigarette, Pacifico. A pack cost one-sixth of what he normally paid for his Marlboros. He said, "Does it have anything to do with the murder?"

"Not that I am aware." Torres again glanced at Donahoo. "But that's why we have new blood on the case. Perhaps your Sargento will see some connection." Torres paused briefly, waiting for

Donahoo's attention, which came with the mention of his rank, then said, "Tell him this: What I do know, the Tijuana Guardian Society of the Poor was formerly Society of the Poor and Oppressed, but shortly after Deedee was honored, they dropped the oppressed part, presumably under pressure, although no one will admit it. The executive director says the name was too long for the letterhead. What I suspect, Deedee, because of her prominence, brought official attention to the society. I can see a government admitting to its people being poor. But I doubt it wants to own up to oppression."

Donahoo, watching the seagulls, was suddenly, uncomfortably, alert. "I hope we're not getting into politics here. What are you suggesting? That Deedee may have offended someone in authority?"

Now Torres didn't turn back. "That would be an easy thing to do, I suppose. But no, I'm not suggesting it. I'm simply stating a fact. The society used to be for the poor and the oppressed. Now it's simply for the poor. And that this happened after she became involved."

"But she wasn't involved. She was just honored."

"To be honored is sometimes to be involved."

"Explain that."

"Well, the society would have to ask her permission to honor her, would it not? And what if she put a price on that? 'Yes, but only if you change your name?' "

"And you suspect that?"

"No. I am not suspecting here. I am, at your request, *explaining*. How someone being honored could become someone involved."

"Why wouldn't the society tell her to go to hell?"

"Because it needed her name more than it needed its name. Remember, Deedee is, was, very social, very wealthy. There was a potential at work. If she took an ongoing interest, she could bring a lot of rich friends, a lot of money, to the Guardians."

"And what happened?"

"It had started to happen."

"And then she was murdered?"

"Yes."

Donahoo considered. He knew nothing, absolutely nothing, about Mexico. He knew the cops, some of them, perhaps a lot of them, were crooked. He knew, if the press reports were true, that the politicians, some of them, perhaps a lot of them, were crooked. He also knew that he wasn't looking for trouble. He had enough of that on his side of the border.

"Questions," Torres said, as if filling in time. "So many questions." He nudged Marino, reminding him of his duty, which was to translate, not pick tobacco off his lips. "The one that persists for me: Why would Deedee Hernandez kill herself? In a land of need, she wanted for nothing. She had everything. Wealth, power, position."

Donahoo picked up the gentle rhythm of the man. "Her husband shared that with her, did he?"

"Yes, the doctor," Torres said. "It all stemmed from him, of course. He is the one from the important background. Without him, or someone like him, even with her great beauty, she would not have, could not have, attained any significant position in society. Nor any significant wealth either. It is a man's world."

"Truer here than in most places?"

"I haven't been most places."

Yes, well, neither had he, Donahoo thought, but, like the Presidente, he could read. He considered mentioning this and decided against it.

"Which reminds me of a story that illustrates the difference between our societies," Torres said cheerfully. "An American and a Mexican are trying to impress each other. The American complains that it costs too much to keep the family pet. The Mexican says, 'What's a pet?' Score one for the American. Then the Mexican complains that his maid is lazy, and the American says, 'What's a maid?' "

Donahoo thought that was true. He personally had never had a maid, and he doubted that Cruz Marino had had one, either. He used to have a cleaning woman come in once a week. That was as close as ever he got. Torres, on a captain's pay, however meager, could have a maid in Mexico, though. Perhaps two maids. Donahoo thought of his cat, Oscar, who was not a pet exactly, but still fell into that broad category. He had a pet and not a maid. That was one of the differences all right.

Donahoo said, "So what are you saying?"

"Nothing."

The LeBaron veered again and started, with difficulty, to climb. They had left the boulevard and were on a side road winding around the landfill, which clung, like a cancerous growth, across what had to be at least twenty acres of mesa tops and canyons. Donahoo caught a smell of it, rich in turned earth and rotted food and foul smoke.

"Deedee Hernandez's other world," Torres said, and Marino's translation sounded doubtful. "She would come here twice a week, Tuesdays and Saturdays, driving up by herself, in her Mercedes. She was passionate about it. Some would say she was obsessed, I suppose. Myself, I see it as penance."

"She had so much?"

"Yes, and the dump people, they have so little, they have garbage."

Donahoo waited. Now the LeBaron, wheezing, was at the crest, and when it made it, the seagulls moved again, en masse. They lifted together, not so high this time, the gray sheet merely shifting, adjusting to the car's presence, but still high enough to blur the landfill's view of the ocean. They drifted down again in a handclap.

Marino said, "Fuck."

Donahoo thought that this might be what Hell looked like. The fly-infested landfill held its own heat, fueled by always-burning fires, and the acrid smoke curled from cracks in the earth, spreading a cloying, noxious haze. He knew it was permeating his clothing and skin. Already his eyes and nasal passages were burning.

Basureros, trash pickers, moved through the smoke like condemned beggars, poking with their poles, filling their bags. There was an army of them. Men, women. The elderly. The crippled. And, on the fringes, some children too. Babies, some of them, Donahoo thought. They were toddlers.

Beyond, presenting a post-apocalyptic vision, the colonia's makeshift hovels, fashioned from plywood, cardboard, tar paper and other scraps, were fitted into the sides of the canyons, held in place by old tires stacked as retaining walls. There was no sign of electricity. Probably no running water. The sewage would run raw.

Donahoo said, speaking of Deedee Hernandez, "Is that a common thing? For people to come here and try to help?"

"As penance?" Torres frowned. "I don't think so. Not by Mexicans, at any rate. Perhaps it explains the gringo missionaries and their followers. They come here once a week in their vans and hand out surplus food and donated clothing and bathe the children and give them toys."

"You sound critical."

"I express the opinion of others. That it makes these people dependent and lazy. And so they will never crawl out of this place. They will stay here and accept charity and never progress."

Torres stopped the LeBaron in a hard-packed clearing at a good distance from the scavengers and garbage trucks and tractors and the clouds of dust. He got out and leaned on the hood. He lit a cigarette. Marino followed after a while, doing the same. Donahoo stayed in the car. The windows were down. He could hear.

"It is all organized," Torres said, Marino translating. "A private company has a concession to operate the place. It charges a small fee for dumping and a small commission on sales of recycled material. Scavenging is permitted and is in fact encouraged. Maybe two hundred families make their living scavenging here. Mostly they are migrants who can't find other work. It's hard, dirty labor, but it pays okay. A man can make as much as at a regular job. Maybe a few dollars a day more. If he gets lucky."

Donahoo stayed in the car. He felt adrift in a sea of filth. The scavengers, carrying burlap sacks and plastic bags, were digging into the fresh piles left by the garbage trucks, sifting for anything that might have some value. Others picked through a brightly colored swamp of rotting fruit and vegetables.

Torres was still telling the story. "The scavengers must sell to a designated middleman, and there is only one buyer permitted here for each major scavenged commodity, such as glass, aluminum cans, or scrap metal, so in fact a monopoly system exists, and the scavengers are always complaining that they don't get a fair price, but the argument is this is the only way to maintain order." He paused to look around. "There are some who think that the scavenger's economic position is somewhat better than the typical worker's. There's no boss. He works his own hours. Also, if you ask a man why he is here, he will ask you, 'What is the alternative?' and he will say, 'It is better than the life I left behind.' "

"That rotting food," Marino said. "They eat it?"

"It's better to eat slop than die hungry. And what they can't eat they give to the pigs."

Donahoo said, "What are the children collecting?"

"Broken glass. Bits of broken, colored glass."

"To be used for what?"

"To be reclaimed, mostly. But there are many purposes. Jewelry, for instance. And stained glass decorations."

"Church windows?"

Torres looked at Donahoo, who was still in the backseat of the LeBaron. "Not especially. What I think, more probably, Tiffany lamps, for matrons in your Mission Hills."

Yes, Donahoo thought. *But do they know who collects the glass?* He thought the priests might know. Not the matrons. The priests. He said, "What did Deedee Hernandez do?"

"She campaigned against this. The children."

"Was she successful?"

"For a while."

Donahoo waited.

"The very small children, for a while they were not permitted to work," Torres said finally, flicking away his cigarette. "And hours were restricted. A normal working day. And when the smoke was too bad, they had to stop. That kind of thing."

"For a while?"

"You will recall that she died."

Donahoo accepted that. He was here, he reminded himself, to solve a murder, and if he knew *why* Deedee Hernandez was killed, then he might figure out *who* did it. They said motive was everything. It wasn't true. But it was true often enough.

Marino pulled deeply on his Pacifico. He wanted to leave. "Is that it?" he asked Torres.

"No," Donahoo said. "The children. Who do they belong to?"

"Poor people."

"Who need the pittance they earn?"

"Yes."

"But a poor person didn't kill Deedee Hernandez?"

"No."

"Nor any scavenger here?"

"I would not think so."

Then why are we here? Donahoo wondered, but he didn't ask the question, because he thought for sure that the answer, whatever explanation might be offered, would be false. Like the murder, he was here to figure it out himself. Torres was merely a guide. He was not The Answer Man. There wasn't any. He, Donahoo, was the closest they had to that, and he was not very close. Down the road, he might be closer. Perhaps even close enough. But not now. Not yet.

"You said she arranged for some adoptions."

"Yes."

"Were there hard feelings?"

"No. Just gratitude. They were true orphans. The natural parents were dead. No known relatives."

Marino took a last pull on his Pacifico. He wanted to leave.

Donahoo tried to think. He wanted it all covered. A rich woman. A rich, *beautiful* woman. Driving a Mercedes. Twice a week, Tuesdays and Saturdays, she comes to this smoky, scavenger-ridden hell. Mixed cripples and small children collecting broken glass. To see a lover? Donahoo didn't think so. To make some other kind of illicit contact? Drugs, perhaps? No. Hardly.

"The autopsy," he said anyway. He hadn't yet inquired. "Any traces of drugs?"

"No. Just Dispan-Doble. It is a kind of diet pill. Dispensed over the counter."

"Can we go?" Marino said.

Yes, I suppose, Donahoo thought. Later, he would speak to Marino. He wanted to tell him that he, Donahoo, was the Sargento, and that he, Marino, was merely an *investigador*, and in this instance, not even that, but a lowly translator, who could be replaced by a machine. They had computers that could do that now, translate conversation, it was a modern world, full of advances, marvelous inventions, magic.

Torres pushed in behind the wheel of the LeBaron. The motor caught after a few tries. They made a wide, bumpy turn, cutting through the smoke, and then started back down the hill. The seagulls paid no attention.

Donahoo glanced back. The last thing he saw was a small child with a tin pail. Some would say a cute little beggar.

Three

El Greco was in Zona Norte in downtown Tijuana, on Avenida Niños Heroes, down the street from Catedral de Virgen Guadalupe. The cramped neighborhood and its red-light district were a few blocks and another world away from the brassy carnival of tourist-trap Calle Revolución, which was what most Americans thought of, if they thought of it at all, when they thought of Tijuana. In Zona Norte the streets were narrow, the shops small, the people . . . what? More resigned to their fate? Certainly less intimidating, Donahoo thought.

He noticed it everywhere. The hawkers merely smiled and gestured. They didn't scream, "Hey, big spender!" The beggars held out their cups. They didn't shake them. The whore on the corner just stood there. The only thing that moved was her tutu skirt. And only in the breeze.

Marino wanted to go home. "It's a half hour away."

"Yes," Donahoo admitted. "But the lineup at the border is longer. And it won't thin out till after your bedtime. The Titanic sank faster." He waved goodbye to Carlos Torres's wheezing LeBaron. He wanted Marino's company. "And, anytime, at a moment's notice, something could come up on the case, it is that kind of case. Face it, you're here for the duration, Cruz. You can go home on the weekends."

"I've got a girl."

That's healthy, Donahoo thought. He wished he had one too. He'd have her come down for a visit. The thought prompted several not-so-fleeting images. His ex-wife, Monica. His one true love, Presh. And the one who got away, Rosie the Snake G-String, The Wham Bam Ice Trail. It also reminded him of the record player, which was still in the trunk of his car, the Toronado parked in the slot in front of their room at El Greco. He stopped to get it, along with the one record that traveled with it, "I Wonder Who's Kissing

Her Now." He checked to be sure that their guns were in their oilcloth packs. His own Colt Python. Marino's .38 Police Special. Torres had asked that they be discreet. Guns were against the law in Mexico. Denied to the citizenry and visiting cops.

Marino was saying, "She's gonna wonder."

"What?"

"This close. Why I don't come home."

"You're a cop," Donahoo gritted, thinking that was becoming more and more doubtful. "Tell her you're on a case. You can't discuss it. What's easier than that?"

Marino stared. He wasn't convinced.

"Cops have got it better than anybody," Donahoo said. "Firemen, they can say they were at a fire, but that can be checked. A bus driver? He's got a shift. It's over. Shoe salesman? How often can they take inventory?"

"Jesus."

"Count your blessings."

Donahoo unlocked the motel door and pushed inside their dingy room. The powerful odor of an industrial-strength disinfectant washed over him, and, beneath it, never to be obliterated, the musty smell of time. He dropped the Deedee Hernandez Nightmare Murder Case file on his bed. He put the record player on the dresser. He plugged it in.

Marino picked up the record, an old 78. "What's this?"

Donahoo took it back. "A record."

"You're gonna play it?"

"If I get drunk."

Marino looked at him. Donahoo put the record back on the scarred bureau, which was spotted with cigarette burns, carved initials. He wished he was down here with somebody else. Spick Gomez, he'd be perfect, he knew the lingo, he'd accept the situation, the conditions. The place was fucked. That's why Gomez had left, a long, long time ago. Palmer, he'd be okay, too. Because he wouldn't care. He would just do the job. Montrose? No. Spook, he would be angered by it all. He would want to do something about it. He would be distracted. Cominsky? No. He was too fucking crazy. Donahoo went through the men on his squad and decided he would rather be with Gomez or Palmer. He was changing his mind about Marino's company. He didn't want to be with Marino. The guy wore bookkeeper shoes.

Donahoo said, "What's her name?"

"Theresa."

"How long have you known her?"

"Two years."

"You're engaged?"

"We're gonna be."

Donahoo thought about that. Marino, he'd be pushing thirty, but he still had a baby face, a fat schoolboy's soft body. He wasn't physical and he didn't seem all that sharp either. He was just a squishy lump of a guy who barely made the grade. He didn't look like he was ready for the obligations and duties of holy matrimony. A name like Theresa, it would have to be holy. Maybe that's why Marino had a Bible?

"She's Catholic?"

"Yeah."

"How about you?"

"A bit."

Donahoo almost smiled. Me, too, he thought. He had started out whole, and now, after a lifetime of the nonsense, he was a tattered, doubtful, anxious—not frightened—bit Catholic.

Marino was getting angry. His dark, liquid, Sal Mineo eyes moved to the record. "What's her name?"

"Slut," Donahoo said, making the choice without thinking. He was talking about Rosie.

"A lost love or something?"

"You could say that."

Donahoo went into the kitchenette, which also served as a kind of hallway, leading to the rear door. It had shallow metal cabinets and a tiny, one-tap sink. There was a rattling countertop fridge, a rusty toaster oven, a stained electric fry pan. He had tested them. None worked very well. Fifteen dollars a night.

"You wanta watch the news?"

"Sure."

Donahoo found a glass and got some ice. He poured himself a drink. Old Crow, he'd brought it down. He wondered again at how Saperstein had chanced upon El Greco. Saperstein had made the reservation—he'd made the call, in front of them—after giving them the assignment. "Here's where you oughta stay . . ."—he'd said that. Later, Donahoo had asked his immediate superior, Lewis, captain, Investigations, and Lewis had said that Saperstein, years ago, had been on some sort of bilateral commission, it took him to conferences in Tijuana, and maybe that was how it happened, that Saperstein had gotten to know El Greco. "The kind of thing you'd look for in Saperstein's past," Lewis had said.

Yes, and find, Donahoo decided. Saperstein's past was a favorite topic because Saperstein's future was an even more favorite one. It was widely accepted and understood that the police chief had enormous ambition. He wanted to be mayor, and, after that, governor. He wanted to be a senator, or, if the timing was right, he might skip that, head directly for the White House. He would, of course, run on a law-and-order platform, so it was necessary, especially necessary, that he be ab-so-lute-ly squeaky clean. When Saperstein's past was examined, there would be nothing, *nothing*, questionable. His expense accounts would be models of restraint. When, at taxpayers' expense, he stayed at a motel, it would be a very fucking cheap motel.

"There's no cable."

Yes, and no color, Donahoo noticed, leaving the kitchenette with his drink. He had not made one for Marino. He had not offered to do so. If the guy wanted to drink, he should have brought his own stuff down, or got something when he bought the Pacificos. He'd had ample opportunity on the tour provided by Torres. There were liquor stores everywhere. There was one on the corner.

Marino whacked the TV. The blurred picture became wavy lines. It stayed that way after several more whacks.

Donahoo settled on his bed with the Deedee Hernandrez Nightmare Murder Case file. In Tijuana, if you threw a rock, it would hit either a taxicab, a farmacía, or a liquor store, he thought. It would hit a hawker or a beggar or a crooked cop. It might hit a whore. He looked at his watch. It was five after six. Lewis ought to be home.

"I don't believe this."

What? Donahoo wondered. That they were staying in a shitty motel because Saperstein wanted to be president? Or that the television set couldn't handle forty whacks? He put his drink aside and opened the file. He tried to picture Lewis. He wondered what he was doing, exactly.

Nombre, Deedee Guadalupe Hernandez. *Edad,* 33. *Ocupación, ama de casa,* housewife. Donahoo struggled that far and decided to look at the pictures. Deedee Hernandez, he realized with a shock, appeared in death very much like she looked in life, bequeathed with the same effortless serenity.

"We're working?"

"Yes."

Donahoo went through the photos in order. As she was found, on her back, the bedcover gathered at her waist, her dark hair flared, an ugly red blotch staining the bosom of her white, oddly plain cotton nightgown. Full body shot, the bedcover drawn aside, the nightgown pulled up, her long, slender legs spread, a folded piece of paper—that's what it looked like—poking from her vagina. The piece of paper removed and unfolded and revealed to be a photograph of Elvis Presley. A head shot, three-quarter pose. Taken at the height of his career. When he really was The King.

"We, uh, gonna eat or something?"

"Maybe later." Donahoo wondered about Lewis. Did he watch the six o'clock news? He didn't want to disturb Lewis in the middle of the news. He wanted his undivided attention. He said, "Elvis. What the hell do you make of Elvis?"

Marino didn't know. He said, "It frankly beats the shit."

"Me, too," Donahoo admitted. "The Latins, they've got their own singers. Why not Julio Iglesias? Help me here. Did Xavier Cugat sing?"

"Yeah," Marino said, meaning that there were Latino singers. "But Elvis, he was like the Beatles, international. He knew no boundaries. Hell, they put him on a stamp."

Donahoo doubted that had anything to do with it. "They put everybody on a stamp. I bought a stamp the other day, Ruth Benedict was on it. Do you know who Ruth Benedict is?"

"She's an anthropologist."

"You've seen that stamp?"

"No."

"Then you got lucky. Most people, they wouldn't know." Donahoo closed the file and passed it to Marino. "They've got a fish on a stamp. Read it to me."

"Now?"

"Yes."

Marino took a deep breath. He was going to protest but changed his mind. He was going to get on his bed but changed his mind about that too. He took the easy chair that wasn't all that easy. He made a face as he settled into it.

God, what a wuss, Donahoo thought. He wondered how Marino got through the academy. Probably, probably solely, because he was bilingual, he decided. Times were changing. So were the crooks. A cop had a real advantage if he could talk to them. There were occasions, a lot of occasions, when he, Donahoo, felt like he was working the wrong side of Star Trek. He didn't have a Nuclear Automatic Transitor Two-Way Language Translator Pack. He couldn't communicate.

Marino passed on the name, age, and occupation stuff. He began, "Nature of death, probable homicide."

Donahoo closed his eyes. Probable. The woman has a hole in her heart and the fucking weapon is fucking gone. He said, "How is that possible? *Probable?*"

Marino didn't answer. He wasn't supposed to. He continued to read. "Police were called by a maid when the deceased failed to respond to repeated knocks and inquiries at her bedroom door. Investigating officers had to force the door, which was bolted from the inside, as were the bedroom windows."

"Bullshit."

"Subsequent investigation determined that there was no other possible exit."

"More bullshit. Are we still on the initial report?"

"Yes."

"Who are these guys?"

"Who?"

"The first officers on the scene. Uniforms?"

Marino looked. "I don't know. Cocos and Marquisa."

"Homicide?"

"No indication."

"Make a note," Donahoo said. "I want to talk to them. Cocos and Marquisa. Have Torres arrange it."

"When?"

"As soon as possible."

"Tonight?"

"No, tomorrow. Tonight you are reading me the file, okay? I want to hear all of it, like I was reading it myself, word for word."

Marino sighed. He got his Pacificos.

"The smallest detail. Don't leave anything out." Donahoo saw Marino's expression when he reached for his Old Crow. It was a child's. Full of anger, resentment, and, Donahoo thought, self-pity. "Understand?"

"Yes."

"Read the part about the security."

Marino found it. "First floor only. Silent alarm."

"And it didn't go off?"

"No."

"Well, maybe the silent alarms here really are silent."

"I guess."

Donahoo reminded himself that it had been a long time since he had worked with anyone so young. He was used to seasoned officers. The men on his squad were his own age or a few years junior. With the exception of Cominsky, who was crazy, they had the maturity, experience, and, what was the word?—was it acceptance?—that only time on the job could bring. Marino, by comparison, had made investigator only six months before, and had yet to work a major case. Perhaps he should make allowance for that. "The maid? What's her name?"

"It doesn't say."

"Ask Torres. I'll want to talk to her. The no-name maid."

"The husband," Marino said, reading. "Dr. Jorge Hernandez. He was away at the time. A medical conference of some sort. Mexico City."

"When did he leave?"

"It doesn't say."

"I'll want to talk to him, too," Donahoo said. "Make a note. Tell Torres." He sipped at his Old Crow. "Why Elvis?"

"It beats the . . ."

"Yes, you've said that," Donahoo said. He put his glass aside and looked at Marino. "But if you could learn why, you would solve the murder, Investigator. Elvis is key. He wouldn't be there if he wasn't."

"I don't see how."

"I don't expect you to."

Donahoo saw by his watch that the news would be almost over. It was a good time to call Lewis. He got his cellular and punched in the number. He indicated to Marino that he should turn off the TV. There was still no picture. Just the wavy lines. But the audio was clear. Some type of situation comedy. A lot of canned laughter.

Lewis answered with a gruff hello. He had a year to go before retirement. He got crankier with every day.

"It's me," Donahoo said, pushing up straight. In his mind's eye, he saw Lewis, an old, fat guy, a big belly, his pants rumpled, his shirttail hanging out. "You gotta minute?"

"Yeah. Go ahead."

"I need a favor."

"What else?"

"Yeah, well, this is an easy one," Donahoo said. "Torres? The captain, Grupo Homicidios? The guy who requested me?"

"Yeah?"

"He's been talking poor boy to me all day. He's got a one-man crime lab for the whole fucking state. His identification kit is all worn out. Especially the mustaches. It's very sad."

"Yeah?"

"Well, what I thought, maybe you could round up some of our outdated stuff to give him, okay? Things we're not using anymore. Or are planning to throw out."

"The voodoo shit stuff?"

"That kind of stuff."

"So we can donate them?"

"So *I* can donate them."

"You're the hero?"

"Yes."

"Why?"

Donahoo got his Old Crow. He said, "Lewis, I'm here in a shitty motel, El Greco, because Saperstein wants to be president. I'm here with Investigator Marino, he's got a girlfriend named Theresa, she's Catholic, and his greatest claim to fame is, he can speak Spanish, there's a beggar in the gutter outside, he can speak Spanish, you know what I mean?"

"So?"

"So are you gonna do it or not?"

Lewis was silent for a while. "Okay."

"Thank you," Donahoo said, and he clicked off.

Marino was staring at him. "That's how you think of me?"

Donahoo said, "What makes you think I think of you?"

"Oh, wow," Marino said, blinking. "I didn't . . ." He started to say something and he stopped. He got a better grip on the file. He started reading. "The autopsy report . . ."

Donahoo waved it off. He was tired of hearing about Deedee Hernandez. Actually, he was tired of himself. He didn't know what the hell was wrong with him. It wasn't just being pulled off his regular duty to work on a bullshit case in Tijuana. It was more than that, deeper. He was suffering . . . what? A general malaise? He ought to make allowance.

Marino put the file aside. He pushed up, with effort. "I think I'll get something to eat."

Donahoo showed him his glass of whiskey. He was going to stay and drink. He'd probably skip dinner and just go to sleep. He showed him all that with just a gesture.

Marino said, "I haven't got a key."

"Leave it unlocked."

"You, uh . . ."

"Think that's wise? Is that what you were gonna say?"

"Yeah," Marino said. "That's what I was gonna say."

Donahoo grinned. It took so little to make him happy, he thought. Sometimes, just a little spunk. A glimmer. He dug around in his pockets and found the key. "Don't be too late. We gotta big day tomorrow. Torres is gonna show us more of the city."

Marino looked at him, taking the key. "Why?"

"I dunno."

Marino got almost as far as the door before he stopped. "That fucking dump," he said then. "Those little kids working there. I felt like throwing up. I don't even know if I can eat." He stood waiting for some comment or observation. "What kind of a fucking country is this?"

Donahoo went into the kitchen. What was the question? How could anyone eat when babies were hungry? Was that it? "Well," he said. "Cruz, you know, there are babies hungry all over the world, the solution is not to stop eating, the solution is to do something about it."

He waited. The door opened, and closed. He looked, and Marino was gone. He said, softly, "You stupid Catholic fuck." He made himself another Old Crow.

Later, after several more, and before Marino returned, he played the record.

I wonder . . . who's kissing . . . her now.
I wonder . . . who's teaching . . . her how.
I wonder . . . who's looking . . . into her eyes,
　　breathing sighs . . . telling lies.

It didn't get any better. The TV still showed only wavy lines. The ice ran out.

Donahoo knew what the problem was. People, pure and simple. He read the papers and he watched the box. Mexico's problem and particularly Tijuana's problem. Tijuana's population was increasing by ten percent a year. The country's interior spilled out a constant flow of unemployed migrants, many of them hoping for work in the *maquiladora* industry, plants assembling components brought into Mexico duty-free, then exported back at a reduced tariff rate. But while the *maquiladoras* might provide some jobs, it was only a relative few, and nobody provided affordable housing, so the migrants had to live in shacks or on the street, and meanwhile the infrastructure couldn't keep pace. No job. No place to live. No welfare system. People got desperate. So they kept on going. They ran the border.

Saperstein had tried to put his police chief finger on it. "Mexico is exploding. Let me tell you a little story. The wife and I once spent our vacation—this was thirty years ago?—in a little village down in Mexico, they had an interesting practice, and, it turns out, they still do. Sunday afternoon, everybody goes down to the square, the boys and girls go through the rites of courtship, the old folks watch. The kids who are already dating, 'chosen,' as it were, or engaged, walk in one direction around the square, and those who are still looking for a partner, they walk in the other direction, indicating they are available to hook up. You with me so far? Well, thirty years ago, there were maybe two hundred young people walking around in circles in that little village on a Sunday afternoon, but now—a generation later?—the wife and I go back, and, conservative estimate, it looked like a mob in a French election, it made me dizzy just watching. There were *thousands*. Thirty years from now? Another generation? You won't be able to count 'em, Tommy, and they'll all be coming here, looking for a job."

Lewis had buffed that up with his version of the real skinny. Lewis, when he walked them out to the Toronado, the captain, Investigations, he had said, "Rosa Parks, that little old black lady down in Birmingham—she wouldn't give up her bus seat to a white man?—you always heard a lot about her, but you never heard much about him, did you? What ever happened to that guy? I hear they buried him standing up. You wanta know the future? O.J. got off." Lewis had put them in the car. "Okay. You really wanta know the future? Early in the morning. You walk down to Tenth and Broadway. You catch a Number 30 express bus going north to paradise. Get on and listen carefully. If you hear a word of English I'll tattoo it on my forehead. Those ladies, most of 'em still of childbearing age, will be getting off in La Jolla, Tommy.

They're cleaning ladies, working in the mansions, but their kids won't, there aren't enough mansions, and—the point?—none of 'em are ever going back to Tijuana. Those rich folks keep it up? La Jolla is gonna be Pasadena." He had waved them good-by. He was kind of running alongside. "Okay. What you should really be worrying about is Canada. Quebec is gonna separate. It's just a matter of time and then we've got the fucking Balkans a fucking inch from Minnesota. Those frogs finally get their own country? So now they're doing nuclear testing in the Saint Lawrence Seaway. Get outa here, willya? I don't wanta see you till you're back."

I wonder . . . who's buying . . . the wine.
For those sweet lips . . . I used to . . . call mine.

Donahoo thought that there were a lot of things that he ought to do, and one of them, he ought to make allowance. He shouldn't have told the kid that Elvis was key. What if Marino believed that kind of donkey doo? He might mention it to somebody. After all, like Saperstein, he had his reputation to worry about, Donahoo thought. He wasn't running for president. But he was running.

I wonder if she . . . ever tells him . . . of me.
I wonder . . . who's kissing . . . her now.

Four

There are several Tijuana jails. The truly infamous one, remembered in nightmares and cherished in song, is the municipal, or city, jail, housed in a four-story, fortresslike red brick building at Eighth and Constitución in downtown Tijuana. Most of the prisoners are serving short terms, 15 to 25 days, for relatively minor infractions, such as public intoxication and disorderly conduct. But some mentally ill are kept there for longer periods; it is a dumping ground for them. And some prisoners are kept there a long time in the hope, some think, of driving them insane.

Torres took Donahoo and Marino there at mid-morning, which, he admitted, was a bad time, because with each new day the prisoners came to a new realization of their plight, and by mid-morning they had not yet adjusted to it—not, perhaps, that they ever fully did. Torres also pointed out that there never was a good time.

"This is your first visit to the Tijuana Jail?" Torres asked, Marino translating.

"Yes," Donahoo said. "Once, a few years back, I almost made it. I changed lanes on Calle Revolución, not signaling, and I didn't have my registration, and the cop said he'd have to impound the car, and then they'd have to search it, and it would take awhile, and I'd have to wait in the jail, but I gave him twenty dollars and he said, you know, thank you very much."

"He was accommodating?"

"Yes, very."

They went through a revolving door fashioned of steel bars and into what a visitor had once called the lowest rung of Dante's Inferno. The guards knew Torres. They exchanged looks. One of them said, "Capitán." That's all.

In the dank dark, Donahoo was aware of the stench first. Vomit, excrement. Piss and B.O. It hit him like a body bag even before they reached the sour rot of the garbage-littered courtyard. Briefly, in disbelief, he put a hand over his face, trying to block it out.

Torres led them straight into it. "You will get used to it," he said, smiling, and Marino, wide-eyed, translated.

Donahoo doubted that. He would have insisted on leaving if it wasn't so important that he talk to troublemaker Pedro Juarez, the material witness, the standby suspect (or so he thought). He thought that there were several ways that Juarez could have come into possession of a handkerchief monogrammed DD. He could have taken it—a sort of souvenir?—after killing Deedee. The real killer could have given it to him. He could have found it in the street, after it was dropped by someone. Deedee, the killer, or, perhaps, a maid. Yes, a maid could have taken it and lost it. Or, this also was possible, the cops could have said, "Here, Señor Juarez, you wanta blow your nose? Have a hankie." One, two, three, four. "Where did you get this hankie?"

There were those possibilities, and others. Donahoo wanted to hear what material witness, standby suspect, troublemaker Pedro Juarez thought were the possibilities, if any. Torres had said Juarez had stopped talking. Juarez hadn't said anything, not of consequence, before. Still, he had stopped talking, formally.

"Watch your step."

"I will."

The pockmarked concrete floor was slippery with standing water and rotting food. Orange rinds, banana peels, scraps of buns. White noodles in spirals. Donahoo stopped amid the tossings, slowly looking around, appalled. The courtyard rose about eighty feet to a corrugated iron roof. Antiquated fans and vents labored in it. Four tiers of cells, reached by iron stairways, laced one wall, marked A, B, C, and D. A, the lower tier, was impossibly crowded, the prisoners like worms struggling in a jar. Two dozen men in 10 × 10 cells.

"Juarez is on C," Torres said, leading the way. "A is the drunk tank. Down at the end, there also are some long-term men, so they are not so crowded, sometimes two to a cell, sometimes alone. B is for minor crimes. The women are at the end. C is for the mentally ill, the homeless. Persons who have no families." He paused at the foot of the mucky metal steps. "D is empty. I don't know why. Perhaps because it is so far for the guards to climb? Watch your step."

Donahoo was still trying to sort it all out. "Why is Juarez on C? He isn't mentally ill, is he?"

Torres said, "No. But perhaps someone has a premonition?"

The stench grew stronger as they climbed. The clogged toilets buzzed with flies. Excrement coiled on the cell floors. The prisoners surged to the bars, hands outstretched, yelling and asking for food.

"Aren't they fed?"

"Yes, but in effect, only once a day, and only a soup made from spoiled vegetables, so it causes most who eat it to become ill."

"So how do they survive?"

"There is a commissary where prisoners with money can buy meals. Or friends or relatives can bring them food."

"And if they have no money? No friends or family?"

"They can eat dirt."

Now they were at Tier C. It was worse here. Fresh excrement. Vomit. The body odor hung like a ripe corpse. Donahoo tried not to look. They passed a gibbering idiot, a ranting beggar, a naked fool. They came to Pedro Juarez.

"You have a visitor," Torres announced.

Donahoo was afraid of what he might find. He looked instead to the next cell. A child-sized, emaciated woman was curled on the floor, wrapped in filthy rags. She raised empty eyes. Her chapped lips made an empty sound.

"He is from San Diego, Sergeant Tommy Donahoo," Torres said, Marino making a halting translation. "He is the head of a special squad there, it is called SCUMB, for Sickos, Crackpots, Underwear and Mad Bombers."

Donahoo looked now. For a moment, the cell seemed empty. Just the bunk bed and the toilet and, on the wall, near the door, two photographs, both of the same woman—who, if not beautiful, couldn't be ignored. She had a strong, broad Indian face. The mouth a slash across most of it. Eyes so dark they were black.

Juarez, huddled in the shadows where the bunk cornered into the wall, made hardly any impression at all. He was small and still, thin arms wrapped around his knees, shaved skull set there like a melon.

"Scumb?"

"Yes."

Juarez raised his head. He looked something like the woman in the photographs. The Indian face, although not as strong, and the mouth more feminine, and the eyes not quite so black. There was the resemblance though. He said, in good English, "Why the underwear?"

Donahoo gave his standard, copyrighted spiel. "I dunno. It just shows up as a key element in the evidence sometimes. Panties, garter belts. Corsets. In maybe one out of five of our cases, roughly twenty percent. Sometimes those teddies. Bras. The most popular, 38 double Ds. Some kind of underwear. We don't know why, but it's a fact, yes."

Juarez stared. "That's interesting."

Donahoo shrugged. He wasn't sure whether it was or wasn't. It was Palmer who had identified the phenomenon, and Montrose, by comparison with the casework of other units, who had proved it. It was Cominksy who thought it was interesting. But then Cominsky thought a gearshift knob was interesting.

Juarez unfolded like a sick cat. He half-fell off the bunk and approached the bars. He was wearing a black shirt, a blue leatherette vest, oversize gray jogging pants, latticed leather sandals with rubber-tire soles.

"What do you want?"

"To talk to you," Torres said, Marino translating, and Donahoo thought that Torres had made another slip. Juarez had asked the question in English.

Donahoo put a restraining hand on Torres's arm. "Pardon. Let me."

Juarez was staring with his not-quite-so-black eyes. "What is your interest?"

"An increasing one," Donahoo said. "Initially, frankly, none at all. But I am starting to get interested." He thought it must be like underwear. If you wore it long enough, it grew on you. "The police here asked me to assist on the case."

"The police?"

"Torres here."

Juarez was staring. "Why?"

"I have a reputation."

"He is a famous homicide detective," Torres said, Marino translating. "He has solved many difficult cases. He is too modest to say so himself, but he has become, in fact, a legend."

"*Mierda.*"

"It's true."

"He means, I think, the reason why you asked me to assist,"

Donahoo said, hoping he had that right. "He doesn't think it was to help him. He thinks it was to convict him. He doesn't trust you." Donahoo saw Torres stir. "Of course, he doesn't trust me either. That's the problem."

Juarez was staring.

"Let me talk to him, alone," Donahoo said, making it sound like an order. "Leave me with him. Both of you."

Torres said, "I can't do that."

"I'll find you when I want you," Donahoo said. He told Marino, "The *capitán* is going to show you more of the slimy underbelly of Tijuana. You may wish to take notes."

Torres considered. Donahoo wished that Torres would say get fucked, and then he, Donahoo, could go home. It would mean that Juarez, who was probably innocent, would probably be charged with the murder of Deedee Hernandez, but still he wished that Torres would say it. Please, Donahoo thought.

Torres said to Juarez, *"El también tiene suerte,"* meaning that Donahoo was also lucky, and moved away, pushing Marino ahead of him. They walked along the tier toward the stairway.

Juarez smiled. The first time. Then he said, "That's an interesting routine. Has it ever worked?"

"Do you know why you're here?" Donahoo asked. "They haven't got anybody else." He said, "That is a very dangerous reason to be here."

The smile blinked off. "I know that."

"Yeah. But do you know how to get out?"

Donahoo took off his jacket and turned out the pockets. He took off his shirt and turned around in a circle. "I'm not wired." He stepped forward, so that his legs were against the bars. "Pat me down."

Juarez looked at him.

"Do it."

Juarez ran his skinny hands over Donahoo's ass, crotch and legs. A light but knowing touch.

Donahoo put his shirt back on. "The murder. Did you do it?"

"No."

"Do you know who did it?"

"No."

"Do you know anything about it?"

"No."

"Do you have an alibi?"

"No."

Donahoo leaned against the bars. He thought that he'd be here for a while. Deedee's DD handkerchief really bothered him. It was what they called rubber evidence. If it didn't work, it could be snapped back, and while it might sting a little, no one got hurt, not the suspect, and, more importantly, not the cop. It wasn't like a smoking gun or a bloody glove. Once they were introduced, they stayed. But a hankie? Well, a hankie, especially this hankie, it could come snapping back, no harm done, because there were so many innocent explanations, and all you had to do was accept any one of them.

"Where were you?"

"When?"

"At the time of the murder."

"Sleeping in my bed."

"With whom?"

"No one."

"So only you can account for your whereabouts?"

"Yes."

Donahoo sighed. He thought that a man who has himself as a witness is a fool. "How did you get the monogrammed handkerchief?"

"I don't know. The police just suddenly produced it. They were searching me and there it was. It just . . ."

Donahoo didn't like to prompt. "Came out of the air?"

"Yes."

"Magicians?"

"Sorcerers."

"Which cop?"

"Pardon?"

"Cocos or Marquisa?"

"I don't know. Both of them? When I first saw it, they were passing it back and forth."

"Yes. But who did you first see with it?"

"Marquisa."

"So what you are saying, you were just walking down the street . . ."

"Riding."

Donahoo paused. For some odd reason, the first thing he thought of was a burro. Even in jogging pants, there was a rural look about Juarez. A man of the soil, unsure of himself in the big city, and striving, very hard, not to be a bumpkin.

"My bicycle."

"Yes."

"And they came by in their police car and stopped me."

"And?"

"And found the handkerchief."

Sorcerers, Donahoo thought. He almost smiled. "Where did you learn English?"

"In school. I was going to be an international lawyer."

"You're very good."

"Thank you."

"And why aren't you an international lawyer?"

"There was a more pressing need for taxi drivers."

Donahoo shifted his weight against the bars. He didn't know why he felt so tired. "You didn't get your degree?"

"No. My mother died. I had a younger brother, a sister. So I had to go to work some more."

"Some more?"

"I had a job. But I had to get two jobs."

"Your father?"

"I never had a father."

Donahoo looked at the photographs. *Had* a brother. *Had* a sister. "Where are they now?"

"My brother was killed. My sister . . ." A long pause. ". . . is self-employed."

Donahoo was still looking at the photographs. "What were you doing in the neighborhood? Bicycling in the neighborhood. Why?"

"I was delivering pamphlets."

"Political pamphlets?"

"Yes."

"What did they say?"

"They said the police are pigs."

"Really?" Donahoo wondered why he was trying. He really ought to give it up, he thought. It truly was hopeless. He said, "I hear you're a troublemaker."

"Yes."

"What kind of trouble do you make?"

"The kind that is mostly for myself."

"Because you talk too much?"

"Yes. A great deal."

Donahoo turned. Juarez was staring. "But not now?"

"No," Juarez answered. "Not now."

"And why is that?"

No answer.

"Well," Donahoo said. "You are not protecting yourself by being in here. So why is it I suspect you are protecting someone else?"

A shrug.

"Okay, but think about it, will you, Juarez? I'm going to be here a while. If you change your mind—if you want to talk to me?—get a message to Torres." He pushed off the bars. "Do you think you can do that?"

Juarez smiled. The second time. "I can try."

Donahoo hoped so. He said, "It's true what Torres said: he asked for my assistance, and I was sent down, assigned. The other officer is Marino. Cruz Marino. He's my interpreter. We got here yesterday. We'll probably stay awhile. Torres is showing us the place."

Juarez pushed back onto the bunk. "Do you think you'll solve the case?"

"No," Donahoo said, because he didn't like to lie. He was looking at the photographs. "But I can try." He said, "Who knows? I may get lucky." He started away, stopped. "The next time I come—would you like a blanket for your cot?"

Juarez shook his head. "Thank you, but I have a blanket. It's being washed."

"How about food?"

"Friends bring it."

"That's good," Donahoo told him. He looked around. There was no one rational within earshot. He thought about it for a while. "But not as good as an alibi, Juarez." He thought that he couldn't stand the stench any longer. "Not as good as an alibi."

Five

Torres and Marino were waiting outside in the sunshine. Torres was eating a *carne adobada* he had purchased from a street vendor. Marino was not eating. He looked pale.

"Why do you keep him there?" Donahoo asked Torres, meaning Juarez, meaning the Tijuana Jail. He thought—he couldn't be certain—that across the street he saw Catalina De Lourdes Venezuela. Just a glimpse of her. In haste. Hurrying along.

"Actually, I am not keeping him there. It is the city police," Torres answered. There was a wait while Marino translated. "We have a jurisdictional problem."

Donahoo had lost her. If indeed it *was* her. Swallowed up in the crowd. "I thought he was held as a material witness in the murder?"

"Held, yes. But charged as one, no. Actually, he is charged, by the city police, with theft. That is the only charge."

"The theft of what?"

"The theft of a handkerchief."

Donahoo looked at Torres in disbelief.

"I have no real quarrel with that," Torres said easily, picking at his *adobada*. Sweet, greasy, highly seasoned pork cooked on an open vertical spit and wrapped in a tortilla, it was sold from stalls on almost every block. "The theft charge keeps him—what is the expression?—on ice?"

"You don't really think he murdered Deedee Hernandez?"

"No. But I can't prove he didn't." Torres started to move along the sidewalk. He went in the same direction that Donahoo thought he had seen Catalina go. "That, in his case, is the problem, to prove he is innocent. In the case itself, there is the second problem, which is to find someone else to be guilty. They are

40

really two separate things. Yet you can have one or both. Is that complicated?"

"Yes."

"It always is."

Donahoo swore. "Jesus Christ! This is medieval."

"Not really," Torres said, walking along. "You are just not used to the finer points of the Napoleonic Code. One is guilty until proven innocent; and what that means, usually, is a procedure that examines *how* guilty, not *if* guilty. It is the nature of—what is it?—the beast?" He looked back. "The best thing? The safest? The safest is not to be charged with an offense. So what I think, it is better, for the moment, if Pedro Juarez stayed charged with theft, not murder."

"For the moment?"

"Which is why we must hurry," Torres said, although he was taking his time, eating his *carne adobada*. "If he was charged with nothing, there are people who would be anxious to charge him with something, just to make sure he didn't get away, and they might, in their haste, get over-zealous. It is like I told you. There is a jurisdictional problem. I am not the only one investigating this case. You will see, as you probe deeper, that it is an open sore, covered with flies. This is because of the Presidente's involvement. His close friendship with Jorge Hernandez. These flies would like to find favor with the Presidente."

"By solving the case?"

"Or by appearing to do so."

Donahoo stopped. "Who are these flies?"

Torres stopped too. He waved a hand vaguely. "There are flies. You see them. Do you have to know their names?" he asked. "Does it matter?"

Donahoo decided that it didn't. He thought that he had better concentrate on the case itself, not the politics of it. If he worried about anyone, it should be about Pedro Juarez. He was beginning to figure out how it worked. He couldn't prove Juarez innocent. Only an alibi could do that, and Juarez didn't have one. But Donahoo, if he was lucky, could prove someone else killed Deedee Hernandez.

"Juarez is safer in jail?"

"Yes."

"You're sure?"

"I am positive."

Donahoo wondered. The experience was still fresh in his mind. "I think a lot of things could go wrong in the Tijuana Jail."

"Yes. That's true. But a lot more things can go wrong out here. There is more room for it. More people for it. More people for it." He stopped again. "More ample opportunity." He said, "Well, it seems this would be a good place to leave you, Sargento."

Donahoo wasn't listening to that part. He was still thinking of the wrong being done. "This is unfair," he complained. "It's not right."

"Yes," Torres admitted gladly. "I understand how you feel. I know what you are looking for. And you are starting to learn Spanish. These are for your list of first words." He waited for Marino to catch up. "This is what you ask, 'Where is justice?' " and the way Marino translated it, he was hurrying, the way it came out, the way it sounded to Donahoo, was, "Juarez justice?"

Donahoo stared at them. They were both unaware of what had happened. His first words? They were like an omen, he thought. They spoke of the future and failure, an impossible search, disappointment. It wasn't going to happen. He wasn't going to find justice. Not here, in this kind of place, with this kind of law. Juarez the fucking hope of that?

Torres said again, "It's a good place to leave you, Sargento."

Donahoo hadn't been watching. He had been looking, from time to time, for Catalina, but he hadn't been watching where they were going. They had come about two blocks. They were standing in front of a Chinese restaurant, the Bamboo Terrace, a small, narrow, dingy-looking place squished between a shoe store and hole-in-the-wall farmacia. There was no bamboo and he was pretty sure there would be no terrace. More lies.

Marino was having trouble translating. "I've eaten, and your interpreter here, he doesn't want to, it is because of his experience this morning, so you are on your own. I thought I'd take him on a further tour. To show him—how do you say it?—more of the slimy underbelly?"

Donahoo looked through the restaurant's dirty glass door. Catalina was sitting on a bench near the cash register.

"Here's your chance," Torres said, smiling. "You said you thought she was pretty." He found a slip of paper. "I'll also make arrangements for you to meet these other people. The cops, Cocos and Marquisa. The maid with no name. The good doctor, if that is possible; I'm not sure. We can rendezvous at El Greco. Two o'clock." He smiled some more. "Is that enough time?"

"You are very generous," Donahoo said, and pushed into the restaurant before he could change his mind. He was certain this had been arranged. He thought it must be some kind of trap. Yet in its way it was very close to irresistible. "Good-by." He thought he heard, the door closing, "Good luck!"

Six

Catalina glanced up at him with her dark, slanted eyes. The pouty cocktail-sausage lips parted. And said nothing.

"Well, fancy meeting you here," Donahoo began. He immediately felt like an idiot. "Remember me? Tommy Donahoo? Carlos Torres introduced us. This was yesterday. The Desperate Frog?"

She got out a pair of particularly ugly glasses and put them on. They had thick baby-blue frames with bright red speckles and lenses that could magnify dust. She peered at him. "I don't think so."

"He's a police officer," Donahoo said, flustered. "A captain. Grupo Homicidios." He thought he was as desperate as the frog. To get away. "Policia Judicial."

"Oh, yes, I know Carlos," she said. She took off the glasses and put them away, into a large, briefcaselike, brown leather bag. Today she was dressed like a conservative store clerk. A plain white blouse, a straight, no-nonsense brown skirt, and comfortable-looking, low-heeled brown shoes. Her hair was in a bun again but not as messy as before. "He is my mother's cousin. He worries about me. He thinks I'm going to grow into an old maid. He is always trying to fix me up." Now she smiled, softly. "Actually, I think he just wants to possess me, vicariously. I'm not sure. But I think so. Did he send you?"

Donahoo didn't know what to say. "Yes."

She smiled again. "Yes, of course, I remember you. But I think I liked your partner better. What was his name? Marino? He was cute."

"Yes. Cruz Marino."

"Is he married?"

"No." Donahoo thought that he must escape. But something kept him. The sausage lips? "He is engaged, though. Almost."

"Almost?"

"Just about. Soon."

"Well, then, I guess I will have to settle for you, Sergeant Tommy Donahoo," she said, smiling and offering her hand, and then immediately taking it back. "Unless, of course, you are married?"

"No." Donahoo wondered why he had said that so quickly. He had the awful feeling that he had totally lost control of the situation. "Once. Not at the moment."

She offered her hand again and he took it, having to pull her up, as she had left some, just a little, of her weight for him. Something in the maneuver caused the V of her blouse to part, revealing full, foil-smooth, chocolate breasts cupped in an extremely delicate white lace bra—the flesh somehow a shade lighter than the rest of her.

"Perhaps you would like to have lunch with me," she said. "I'm waiting for some takeout but we can eat it here." She spoke to the cashier in rapid Spanish. "There is enough. What I do, I order for lunch and dinner both, so I won't have to cook when I get home. Do you like fish?"

"Yes."

"Good. That is what you are going to be eating. Fish and rice. It's very good here. It's also very good for you. And you'll also get your vegetables."

She took his arm and directed him to a booth in the back. The place was small and plain. As he had suspected, no terrace. Four booths and a counter against a wall. They were the only ones present so far. "My office is around the corner. I come here all the time. Carlos knows that, so he steers his victims here, rendezvous in the Bamboo Terrace."

"Oh, does he send you a lot?"

"Not many. He knows I am particular."

They sat down across from each other in a booth so small that their heads would knock if they both leaned forward at the same time. She smiled brightly. The dark, slanted eyes crinkled. "So now what?"

Donahoo didn't know.

"What Carlos would want me to say, I think," she said. "Latin lady, professional, still young, attractive, nice body, long hair, considerate, enjoys outdoors, likes to touch and feel, seeks tall man, financially secure. Serious inquiries only." She laughed. "That Carlos. He is such an idiot sometimes. But he means well."

"He left out the lips."

"Oh, you like my lips?" Her eyes crinkled again. "Myself, I think they are my worst feature. They make me look like I am blowing kisses all the time. That can give the wrong impression."

Donahoo thought that there might be laughter in her eyes. Or was it simply amusement?

"There are worse features to have."

"Then I should be happy with them?"

"Yes."

"Well, I'm not."

"Well, I am," Donahoo said, the words out before he had actually thought about them. He hoped he wasn't blushing. His neck felt warm. He said to himself, Oh, boy. Then, to her: "Do people call you Catalina?"

"Yes. That and Cat. Do they call you Tommy?"

"Yes. That and Sergeant. But Carlos calls me Sargento."

"Do you like Sargento?"

"I am starting to like it."

The cashier, who was Mexican, not Chinese, came with the take-out food, still in its boxes, a fat spoon to serve it with, and two plates, and chopsticks. Also two fortune cookies on a small plate. Catalina thanked her and took quick possession of the bill.

Donahoo said, "Let me have it, please."

She looked at him doubtfully. "Are you financially secure?"

"Yes."

"Then you can take me to dinner some night." She put the bill in her big purse, to be paid later. "Frankly, I would rather be taken to dinner than to lunch. Lunch can be so flat, and, usually, you're in a hurry. Dinner though. If you go to the right place, it can be romantic. Soft lights. Music. And you can stay as long as you wish. If it is the right place."

"Do you know such a place?"

"Yes."

"Then I shall take you there."

She looked at him. She was opening the boxes. "Only if I say so."

Donahoo thought that had already been settled. "I thought . . ." he began, and stopped. Well, fuck, he thought. Jesus Christ. He was acting like a kid. And she was . . . what? He wasn't sure. He said—she was serving him with the fat spoon—"What should I call you?"

"Cat." She smiled at him. "I am starting to like it."

He waited while she served the food. It was as plain as her shoes. White fish, broiled. White rice, boiled. A mix of dark green leaf vegetables that he couldn't identify, steamed. It smelled good, though. And he was hungry.

"You visited the Tijuana Jail?" she said then, casually. She was serving the food.

"Yes," he said. "How did you know that? Did Carlos tell you?"

"No. I saw you come out. I was walking past then—coming here."

"I thought you worked around the corner?"

"Yes. I do. But sometimes I have been known to walk down a street."

"I'm sorry."

"You are a suspicious man, Sargento," she said, shoving his plate at him. "But I suppose that is to be expected. You are a policeman, it's probably your nature. What did you think of the Tijuana Jail?"

"I thought it was an abomination."

"Really? Many people think that. I remember a woman from San Diego. Her name was Judith Moore. She visited the jail and then she wrote about it in one of your weekly papers. The *Reader*. She said she had picked up a worm of terror that wiggled up the spine of her fat life."

Donahoo got his chopsticks. "A way with words."

"Yes. I can still quote them. She was talking about her group, they had brought the prisoners food, clothes. She felt that they were doing it, in part, to make themselves feel good, to expunge the guilt of their own good fortune. 'We have fed upon the body of the poor. We are ravens exciting ourselves with their twitches and sores.' Do you think that's overstated?"

Donahoo didn't know. "Overwritten, maybe. Not overstated. Who permits it?"

"Permits what? The jail?"

"Everything."

"Who is responsible? All of us, I suppose. We let it happen. We watch it happen."

"There is always a leader. Someone to blame."

"In a mob?"

"Yes. One runs ahead, screaming."

"Oh, well, if you want to *blame* someone," Catalina said. "Pick one person and say, 'Hey, there is the bastard!' I don't think that is very much of a big secret around here. That would be Salvador Urquidez. He used to be a general and now he is what you would call a crime boss. He controls the criminal element and also has a hold on many civic and state officials. He is very powerful and very brutal. They call him Diablo. The Devil."

"He sounds . . ." Donahoo couldn't think of the word. "Bad?"

"Yes. One bad hombre, huh? Eat your lunch."

Donahoo tasted a bit of his fish. It was, as she had promised, good. He watched her for a moment. He thought that she was beautiful and interesting and that part of the attraction was the mystery she wore like a veil. He wondered if she would be as interesting when the veil was lifted. He said, "What do you do, Miss De Lourdes?"

"I am a lawyer."

"What kind of lawyer?"

"One devoted to fighting injustice."

Oh, Donahoo thought. He suddenly wasn't hungry anymore. He felt betrayed. By Saperstein. By Torres. By Pedro Juarez. By this woman. They had all conspired to bring him here and betray him.

"You know Juarez?" he asked, and when she nodded, he said, "Do you represent him?" and when she shook her head, he said, "Not yet?"

Catalina picked up a fortune cookie. "Perhaps it won't be necessary. That's why you are here, isn't it? To look for the truth?"

Was it? Donahoo wasn't sure anymore. More likely, it was as Torres had said, not truth so much, but justice. He said, sounding, he thought, a little Ms. Moore, "Like you, I look for justice."

"Well, let us see if you are going to find it," she suggested. She snapped the cookie apart and removed the slip of paper. "I can never wait to read these things. It says here, 'You are going to take a long journey.' "

"That's your fortune, not mine."

"No, it's yours. This cookie was closest to you." She pointed. "That cookie is mine." She grabbed it before he could. She put it in her purse. "Eat your lunch."

Donahoo said, "I thought you couldn't wait?"

"To read yours. Not mine."

"I thought you needed glasses?"

"No. They are just a prop. I use them, sometimes, to scare away men who are bothering me. You would be amazed how well such glasses work. Especially if they are shallow men, interested only in my body, not the rest of me, the part that thinks. The glasses work better than Mace. Now, tell me all about yourself, Sargento. You will be surprised to hear this, my being a lawyer. You are my first policeman. Do you have a girlfriend?"

Donahoo thought he was going to have to talk about this sooner or later. He might as well dispose of it now. "No. Not at the moment."

"Oh? Why not?"

"Well—the truth, I guess, I got dumped."

"Really? And why were you dumped?"

"She said I couldn't ring her chimes."

"Oh? And why couldn't you ring her chimes?"

"I couldn't find her doorbell."

Catalina's slanted eyes slanted up. "Did you look?"

"Perhaps not diligently enough," Donahoo admitted.

Seven

Donahoo walked the few short blocks back to El Greco to meet as arranged with Torres and Marino. He was thinking, most of the time, about Catalina De Lourdes Venezuela, aka Cat, and sometimes about Pedro Juarez, and a little—as little as he could—about Salvador Urquidez. He thought that a man would have to be very evil to be called the Devil. One bad hombre. Diablo.

It was after two o'clock, but Torres and Marino hadn't got back yet. The maid was just now making up the room. Donahoo saw that it was going to take her awhile. Instead he got into the Toronado. He rolled the windows down to catch the faint breeze. He was thinking about Catalina and Juarez and also about Salvador Urquidez. He got out his cellular and punched in a call to Lewis.

The captain, Investigations, when he came on, said, "Now what?"

"Another favor."

"No," Lewis said. "You can't have our old squad cars to give away. We auction them to finance the Christmas party." He said, not waiting, "Who do you think pays for those plum puddings?"

"It's a small favor," Donahoo told him, sighing. Like Lewis, he was counting the days. Till the time when Lewis retired his badge and went home to exclusively make his wife miserable. "A name has come up here. Salvador Urquidez." He spelled it. "U, R, Q, U, I, D, E, Z. Yes, Z." He had asked Catalina and she had written it down. He was reading off the card she had provided. "He is supposed to be the crime lord down here. I thought you might know of him. You're so familiar with royalty."

"Salvador Urquidez?"

"Yes. But they also call him Diablo."

"Diablo?"

"Yes. Diablo. The Devil."

50

There was a moment of silence. Then Lewis, complaining, said, "What the hell are you getting yourself into now, Tommy?" and Donahoo, suddenly angry, told him, "I was *sent* here, remember? That boiled prick Saperstein. Have you heard of him? Yes or no?"

"Saperstein?"

Donahoo sighed again. He wondered why he even made the effort with Lewis. There was no winning with the guy. In a few months, weeks, days, he would be gone. Lewis had nothing to lose. The only way he could lose, they could kick him out earlier, and that really wouldn't be losing, it would be winning. He said, "Please?"

"Urquidez," Lewis answered after a while. "Yes, I've heard some things. Seen some intelligence reports." There was a pause. "What are you saying? That he's a suspect in the Deedee Hernandez murder?"

"No."

"Then why are you asking?"

"Out of interest."

"What interest?"

"Jesus," Donahoo said. "I'm a cop. He's a crook. There's a natural interest."

"Not in Tijuana crooks."

"Then why am I here?"

Lewis didn't answer.

"Gotcha there, huh?" Donahoo said. Torres and Marino were arriving. The LeBaron slowed and stopped in the street in front of the motel. "Dig up what you can on him, will you? Let me know. Please."

"Why?"

"Because you owe me."

Donahoo turned for a better view. Marino was getting out of the LeBaron.

"I'll see what I can do."

"Thank you."

The LeBaron was moving away, Torres waving good-by, Marino standing on the sidewalk. Hey, Donahoo thought, clicking off. He scrambled out of the Toronado, but it was too late. Torres was gone.

Marino, smiling, yelled, "I bought a watch!"

□   □   □

The maid was going to take another twenty minutes to clean the room. Donahoo thought that she was pacing herself very well. El Greco had sixteen rooms, and at half an hour each, that completed her day. She could do all the rooms in half a day, but what would that accomplish? They might want to pay her for only half a day. Then she'd have to get another job. So it was important that she pace herself.

"Twenty dollars," Marino said for perhaps the fourth or fifth time, meaning the amount of money that he had paid for his watch, an alleged Rolex. "It's amazing how they can produce an exact knockoff to sell at that price." He held it up for Donahoo. This also was the fourth or fifth time. "You can't tell the difference."

"No." Donahoo had nothing to compare it with and probably couldn't tell the difference if he did. It looked like a Rolex. It had the feel, the weight, of a Rolex. On the face it said, Rolex. "It looks like the real McCoy."

"It looks like a Rolex," Marino said.

They were sitting together in the Toronado. Waiting for the maid to finish the room. The door was open and they were watching her work. Or not work.

"What else did he say?" Donahoo asked, meaning Torres. Marino had already said that there would be no meeting today with the cops, Cocos and Marquisa, or Deedee's husband, Jorge. They had all been scheduled for tomorrow morning, at the Hernandez house, the scene of the crime, and he, Donahoo, could also speak to the maid-with-no-name at that time. Marino had reported on that, briefly. Mostly he had reported on his new phony Rolex. "Did he show you any more of the slimy underbelly?"

"No," Marino said cheerfully. "We mostly went shopping. I didn't have the stomach for any more of the crud. Not after the jail. Could you believe that? It's a fucking vomitory. Enough is enough. So he showed me Revolución. All those stores along it. He knew all the best places, of course. The best prices."

"You told him that?"

"What?"

"No more crud?"

Marino frowned. "Yes, I mentioned it. Why not? There are two sides to this place. You'd think he'd want to show the good side."

"Like bargain watches?"

Marino was still frowning. "Yes. That's part of it, yes."

Donahoo thought that Torres would show Marino whatever it pleased him to show, so the slimy underbelly, the crud, must be reserved for him, Donahoo. He and Marino, they'd been split. They were getting divided attention. "Did he help you bargain?"

"No. But his presence, that helped, I think. They knew him. What he is."

"A cop."

"Yes."

"It wouldn't help in San Diego."

"This isn't San Diego."

No. Donahoo wondered how often Marino would say that before they solved, or abandoned, the Hernandez case. Or how often he, Donahoo, watching the maid pace herself, thought it. He said, "Did he take any bribes?"

Marino looked at him.

"Mordida," Donahoo said. They had previously discussed this too. What, possibly, Torres did when he went into the toilet with Luis at The Desperate Frog, and with Jesus, the bartender at Caramba! The possibility that Torres took money from them, so that they would not be hassled, unnecessarily, by the police. It would be a strange thing for a state officer, a captain of detectives, Grupo Homicidios, to be doing, but this wasn't San Diego. Donahoo also thought that there wouldn't be much opportunity for *mordida* in murder cases, even here. Murders were usually pretty much cut and dried. This one wasn't, but in most, the killer, if not waiting to be arrested, left a trail that a blind man could follow. That was because a lot of murders were crimes of passion of one sort or another. And because a lot of murderers were fools. It was only smart murderers who made life difficult. Well, Donahoo thought. It wasn't only Ms. Moore who would turn a phrase.

Marino finally answered the question. "Yeah, he might have been collecting. It looked like it a couple of times. He'd go in the back with a guy, you know? In and out."

"With no explanation?"

"No. He'd just say, 'Gimme a minute,' or, 'I'll be right back.' "

The maid had finished. She came out of the room and smiled at them. She left the door ajar, put her stuff in a cart. She pushed it around a corner, a dark, pretty girl, maybe sixteen, seventeen, still slim. Stick arms and legs and a flat chest but a good ass. Shiny black hair and flashing white teeth.

Donahoo remembered Torres's story about the American and

the Mexican. He thought that he would rather have a maid than a pet. Especially one who could pace herself so exquisitely. Screw the pet. Preferably, screw the maid. He said, "Here we go. That's all?"

"Yeah."

"What about the case? Did he talk about the case?"

"Listen, I gotta check the dial," Torres said, displaying—this was probably the sixth time—his new phony Rolex. He pushed out of the Toronado. "It is supposed to glow in the dark but I haven't been able to find a place dark enough. I'm gonna try the can. Okay?"

"Sure." Donahoo thought he was probably fortunate. The kid, he'd gotten a deal. If he had been gypped, he'd be talking about it forever. Donahoo had already come to that much of a conclusion about Marino. He felt strongly, *personally*, about things, and he didn't let go easily. He was a short, fat, soft guy, he couldn't do anything much about something, but inside he could obsess. "Of course. Go right ahead. See if it glows."

☐ ☐ ☐

It didn't. Well, maybe it did. It was, apparently, hard to tell. Marino said it didn't glow in the toilet but it did glow, sort of, in the closet. It didn't glow under the blankets. It was a dead loss there. But it glowed, partly, faintly, when he pulled his jacket over his head, made a tight, closed tent for it.

Marino was slowly going crazy. He said, "I dunno. Does it glow or not?" He said, "Maybe it's how you look at it? The angle or something. You wanta try?"

"No."

Donahoo tried not to pay attention. He was thinking about Torres, why he had taken the afternoon off, leaving him, Donahoo, to stew about Pedro Juarez in the Tijuana Jail, and to think, a lot, about Catalina. He was wondering why Torres had not seen fit to mention Salvador Urquidez. Wondering why Catalina had done so, so readily. Why Torres had not. If, as she claimed, Urquidez controlled much of the major crime here, held sway over many of the officials, then it would be . . . what? Only natural to mention him? Especially when the crime in hand touched, however obliquely, upon the highest office in the land?

"How can it glow and not glow?"

Donahoo tried to think most of the time about Catalina. Ordinarily, that would be easy to do. She was a very beautiful woman. She had the face, he thought, of a remarkable person. She had that special grace and elegance and artistry. She projected a somehow definitive image of the ultimate woman, and it made so powerful an impression, it was like looking upon the Mona Lisa. Or (blah, blah, blah, Donahoo thought) an Ingrid Bergman or a Sophia Loren; and let's not forget those sausage lips.

"What makes it glow? Radium. Phosphorus?"

"I haven't got any idea. Maybe bird shit."

"Seriously."

"Okay, cat shit."

Donahoo pushed off the bed and went into the kitchenette. He thought he would start, early, on the Old Crow. He thought he'd get going here. But, like the maid, pace. He had the idea, vague, half-formed, that Catalina might call, suggest dinner or something, and he didn't want to be even slightly shit-faced if she did. He just wanted a couple, three drinks to insulate himself against the day. Tijuana had its good and bad sides, and one of the bad sides was the Tijuana Jail, and another, he knew—because Catalina had told him—was Salvador Urquidez, aka Diablo. He said, "Salvador Urquidez. Did Torres mention him?"

"Who?"

"Urquidez. A crime boss they call Diablo."

"No."

Donahoo was looking at Marino. Marino was looking at his watch.

"Pay attention here."

"What?"

"I mention a crime boss. You're not interested. What fucking kind of cop are you?"

"Oh, sorry," Marino said, flushing. "I thought . . ." He got up out of the room's one easy chair. "What about him?"

"You thought what?"

"That we were through here for the day."

"Why?"

"I dunno." Marino was still flushed. "Torres is gone. There's nothing to do." He took a moment to compose himself. "It's still early. We can beat the rush at the border. I thought we could go home for the night."

Donahoo moved out of the kitchen with his Old Crow.

"There's nothing happening," Marino said. "Let's come back tomorrow. Start over. What are we accomplishing?"

Donahoo said, "Well, you bought yourself a Mexican watch," and Marino, suddenly flaring, told him, "Yeah, and you're buying yourself a Mexican crock."

"You think so?"

"Yes."

Donahoo wanted to hit him. If he wasn't holding the Old Crow, he would have, he thought. He also thought that in the time required to put the glass down, he would have changed his mind, as he was changing it now, because Marino just wanted to be with his girl, Theresa, that's all, and because Marino was right, it was a crock.

"Listen . . ."

"Take the car," Donahoo said. "The keys are on the bureau. I'll see you tomorrow."

Marino found them. He held them up, said, "Thanks."

Donahoo watched as Marino collected his gym bag and toilet kit. Found his Bible. "We've got an early start. Don't be late."

"I won't." Marino went out the door. "Take it easy."

Yeah, Donahoo thought. He went to the door and shoved it shut. Bolted it. He listened to the sounds of Marino leaving. The Toronado's door creaking open and banging shut. The big V-8 coughing and taking hold. The gearshift clunking into reverse.

A crock, huh? he said to himself, sucking on the Old Crow. He knew it was. He'd known that from the start. He just didn't know how big. And now, there was something else he didn't know, and that was how Marino knew. The guy's ass was still wet. He'd only been an investigator six months. This was his first big case. So how could he be so sure? Have the fat nuts to say it?

The clue was Catalina, he decided. He had told Marino a little, a very little, about his lunch with Catalina, and the kid had gotten a wise look, an aw, come-on look, in his Sal Mineo eyes. The kind of look that said, oh, sure, a woman like that, she's interested in you for you, Donahoo, and one size fits all, and the earth is flat, and this watch glows in the dark.

Donahoo fell down on the bed. There were a lot of things he could do, he thought. He could go to the Jai Alai Palace, or maybe the Caliente Book. He could find a nice restaurant, he'd seen a couple, they looked pretty good. He could go to Señor Frog's, switch to beer, drink those little bottles of Corona, they serve 'em stuck in ice in a galvanized pail, they stole the idea from Fud-drucker's, or maybe Fuddrucker's stole it from them. Or he could lie on the bed and wait for Catalina.

He would do that. He knew he would do that. Wait for her not to call. He found the little *diccionario* he had bought while walking back to the motel from the Bamboo Terrace. He had gotten it mainly to check up on Marino and Torres but also for dealing with Catalina. He looked up attraction. *Atracción.* He looked up fatal. *Fatal.*

Eight

Casa de la Mano was a walled estate, more like an office building than a residence, and, in places, more like a zoo. It occupied perhaps an acre atop Lomas de Agua Caliente, one of the most exclusive neighborhoods in Tijuana, a sleek, modern, sharply angled three-story concrete and glass structure set amid extensive manicured grounds and connected, at the rear, to a huge aviary. Inside, a part of the house, forming a whole wall of the drawing room, was a glass cage holding a snow leopard. There was a passage, now closed, that permitted the leopard to enter the aviary, and there were trees, some of them, that looked sturdy enough for the big cat to climb. The aviary's colorful birds— Donahoo thought he might be just imagining this—kept looking over their shoulders.

Donahoo had never seen a snow leopard in the flesh before. Despite being caged, it appeared to be in especially good condition, strong and limber, eyes bright, coat luxurious. It paced back and forth along the glass wall like a restless sentry. Waiting in the vast, antique-furnished drawing room, the cage like a living mural, Donahoo mentioned this to Torres, that he had never seen a snow leopard, and Torres had said, "That is because they are very rare, and also because it is illegal to have one," and Marino had said, apropos of not very much—he was back late from wrestling with the lovely Theresa, and not quite fully with it—he had said, "This is like the Monkey Bar in Pearl Harbor."

They were drinking coffee, very black, very strong, very good, and waiting with the two cops, Cocos and Marquisa, and the maid who in fact did have a name, Maria Contessa. Donahoo had been inclined to start with the cops, or at least with the maid, but Torres had directed that they wait. He'd said they didn't want to start and then have to stop when the doctor arrived, and then start again. It was better, he'd said—if Marino had gotten this right—to do it in a lump.

Donahoo thought it might have something to do with propriety or appearances and also that the cops were something else. Cocos was a brute. Like Torres, almost a giant, but Cro-Magnon. He was standing at the door in the manner of a guard. No, not standing, Donahoo decided. Hulking there. In a black T-shirt that said, PROBLEMS? CALL 1-800-WHO CARES. He wondered what was in the man's mind. Whenever he saw a door, he guarded it? Marquisa, by comparison, was slick as a snake, and he sat coiled like one, enjoying his coffee, holding the fine china cup and saucer correctly. He was tall, dark and handsome, a lady's dream, with brooding teak-brown eyes, greased-back shiny black hair, and a face strong enough to carry a full military-style mustache. Torres had confided that Marquisa, although new to the city and his post, had already acquired what was known as the Avila Condition. He was wearing a sharp blue pinstripe suit and his black cap-toed shoes were shined. His striped tie had a diamond—*maybe* a diamond—stickpin. Cocos in his misshapen castoffs was a rag picker compared to him. Avila had been a cop who dressed well and drove fast cars and lived the good life. Then one day he died in a hail of bullets. It was said to be drug-related.

"The Monkey Bar had a glass wall too, the length of the bar, and a shitload of monkeys behind it," Marino was saying in Spanish, and then, for Donahoo's benefit, in English. "They were flying around."

Donahoo had a momentary vision of a monkey in goggles. Making a kamikaze dive at Marino, who, in his youth, had served in the Navy. This was why he was in Pearl and how he happened to be at the Monkey Bar. Marino had told Donahoo about his stint in the Navy. He had actually joined to see the world. He'd been one of maybe half a million men. He'd been—this is what he had said—treated like a number. He hadn't seen the world. But he had seen Pearl. The Far East.

Marquisa said, in fluent English, "Frankly, I don't see the attraction of a monkey bar."

"It sounds dumb to me," Torres agreed in Spanish, which Marino found necessary to translate.

Donahoo thought that a cage full of monkeys in a bar couldn't be much dumber than having a leopard pacing back and forth in your drawing room, but he said nothing in Marino's defense. He remembered that he was pissed, very pissed, at Marino, who had brought back the Toronado with black scuff marks on the roof liner over the backseat, and who had taken a long time to admit that Theresa, when she parted her legs for him there, had neglected to first take off her shoes. The liner was really scuffed.

Cocos, guarding the door, said nothing. He obviously understood no English. Donahoo thought that he might not understand Spanish either. Marquisa, though—he was really fluent, he had been talking a lot, and seemingly an educated man. It made no sense for him to be a lowly city cop. The pay couldn't be more than a few hundred dollars a month. Donahoo supposed that there was a reason; perhaps Marquisa had been kicked out of other police departments or agencies, for any of a raft of possible indiscretions, and the city cops were the only ones who would have him. Or, being the smartest city cop—and that was possible—might be a great advantage to a young man on the make. He looked to be in his late twenties. He had a long way to go and a lot to make.

"More coffee?" Maria Contessa asked, showing off her English, and they all asked for refills, if only to examine her bosom again. She wore a black polyester uniform with a deep frilly white V. A very short black skirt with apron. A pert black-and-white ribbon cap. High black heels. She looked liked the maids pictured in old issues of *Esquire*.

A car honked, spoiling their anticipation. Donahoo glanced out the big picture windows. A silver-gray Rolls Royce slipped by and disappeared under the porte-cochère. "Pardon me," Maria Contessa said, and left them to their own devices. Donahoo noted that none of them bothered to get more coffee, which was in a big silver pot, readily available, on an ornate, hand-carved oak sidebar. They were going to wait for her return.

Voices in the entry hall. A man, a woman, a child.

"El doctor," Torres confirmed. He stood up, and the rest of them followed his lead, except for Marino, whose chair was better aligned with the port-cochere and who remained transfixed by the doctor's method of arrival. Cocos left his post at the door, responding to, it was barely apparent, a nod from Marquisa. It was as if there was an invisible string between them.

Donahoo looked at his watch. Fifteen minutes late. The appointment, the questioning, the *interview*, had been for ten.

Marino whispered, "That's the first Rolls I've seen in Mexico."

"I'm sure it's not the only one," Donahoo told him. "You just have to go to the right places." He said, "I think you're expected to stand up."

Jorge Hernandez entered the room with studied impatience. He glanced around and found nothing to his satisfaction. He was peeling off black leather driving gloves, and stuffing them, crumpled, into the pockets of a black leather jacket, also designed for driving. He said in Spanish, "What is all this?"

"Sargento Donahoo," Torres told him, pointing, and before Donahoo could offer his hand, Hernandez was looking, askance, at Cocos and Marquisa, and also at Marino. He hadn't expected them and didn't want them.

Donahoo let them sort it out in a rapid exchange of Spanish. Hernandez was much shorter than he had anticipated. Deedee had been of some stature. El Doctor looked like he might have to stand on a box when he operated. He was squat, built like a bull, with big shoulders, a thick chest. His head and neck were like one unit. The graying, balding hair cropped short. The closely shaved jaw a blue sheen. In rough clothes he would be mistaken for a laborer except for the handsome, intelligent face, quick, all-knowing eyes, and a precise, high-velocity manner of speech.

"You arrange one thing and present another."

"Actually, it is one and the same."

"A parade is not an interview." Hernandez went to the glass wall and placed his hand against it. The leopard tried to lick it. "Very well," he said finally, in English, meaning it mainly for Donahoo. "You have permission, but that's the end of it, understand?" Now he was speaking directly to Donahoo. "We can talk privately in the library."

Donahoo said, "Okay, but before we go to the library, I want to see the bedroom."

"The capitán can show it to you later."

"No. I want you to show it to me."

"For what reason?"

Donahoo looked at the woman Hernandez had arrived with. She was waiting in the doorway, a tall, slim, fashion-model beauty, expensively dressed in designer clothes, not as striking as Deedee perhaps, but still very much a winner. Donahoo thought she might be thirty, but she had taken good care of herself, so she didn't look that old. She could have passed for twenty-five if it weren't for the child, a boy, about six, who looked a lot like her, and also somewhat like Hernandez. He was a happy combination of both of them. "My own," Donahoo said, finally answering the question.

A flicker of annoyance crossed Hernandez's dark face. He slammed the heel of his hand against the leopard's cage, the blow so sharp that the whole wall of glass seemed to heave, sending the animal bounding away. Then, with an effort—but also with grace—he said, "This is Pamela Mesa, *mi novia*, my fiancée. This is our son, Philip. Say hello, Philip."

The boy said, "Hello," and Pamela smiled for Donahoo and said to Hernandez, "Are you going to be long?" and, without waiting for an answer, told him, "We'll be in the aviary. Philip wants to feed Fluffy."

Hernandez had Donahoo by the arm now. He steered him past them and the maid, Maria Contessa, who had taken a nearby hovering position. Torres hesitated, then started to follow, leaving Marino behind with Cocos and Marquisa.

"You won't be necessary, Capitán," Hernandez told Torres in Spanish.

Donahoo stopped. He didn't care about Torres. Nor Cocos nor Marquisa. But Maria Contessa ought to be observed under pressure in her employer's presence. "The maid will be necessary."

Hernandez's face darkened again. "This is my house."

"Yes, and it's your maid," Donahoo told him. "But it's my investigation."

Hernandez stared with his all-knowing eyes. Donahoo thought that this was like spitting in the wind. Not going to get far.

There was a bad moment. Hernandez, again with an effort, finally found it possible to exercise restraint. With a hard smile, he tightened his grip at Donahoo's arm, beckoned to Maria Contessa. They went down a wide hallway toward an elevator. When they were out of earshot, Hernandez said matter-of-factly to Donahoo, "Pamela is my mistress. We plan to be married." The elevator door opened, operated by an electric eye. "When the mourning is concluded, of course."

Donahoo didn't know what to say. "Of course," he said.

"We just came from her apartment. I stayed there the night. But we don't actually live together yet. For obvious considerations. After you."

☐ ☐ ☐

Deedee's bedroom, *former* bedroom, was an odd place for a rich man to keep his wife. It was a small, mean, depressing place with a low ceiling, scant natural light. The plaster walls were stained by a leaking roof. The tile floor was cracked.

Donahoo looked around doubtfully. The crime scene photographs had shown none of this dismay. They were all tight shots and Saperstein's crotch shot. The only thing he remembered from the photos was the bed. It was large enough, a queen, and sported silk sheets, a down-filled bedcover.

Hernandez, behind him, said, "She had a choice."

"Your bed or hers?"

"Yes."

Well, Donahoo thought, looking around, she must have hated you very much. He went back to the door. The bolt—the fabled bolt—was a half-inch-thick forged steel bar that pushed back and forth in heavy iron clamps held by lug nuts. The whole apparatus had been ripped away when the door was kicked in. Repairs had not yet been made. It had been put back—perhaps at Torres's request?—only in makeshift fashion. But even stuck in place with the help of patching plaster, it looked formidable.

"She didn't want visitors?"

"No."

Donahoo went to the two high, narrow casement windows across from the foot of the bed. Thick glass set in steel frames. Hinged for vertical outward opening. Locked top and bottom by half-moon steel fasteners. An intruder would have to break the glass to disengage them. There was no suggestion that had happened. The panes all matched and were set in a decaying liner that would crumble away if disturbed.

"These are the only windows?"

"Yes. Except for one in the bath. But you couldn't get your head through it."

Maria Contessa had retreated to a corner.

"When you entered—when the police broke down the door?— were these windows open or closed?" Donahoo asked her.

"Closed."

Donahoo glanced at Hernandez. His expression was blank.

"What did you look at first? The body or the windows?"

"The body."

"When did you look at the windows? Find them locked?"

"Later. I don't know when. Perhaps a minute."

"Did the police point out that they were locked?"

"No. I just noticed . . . when I got over the shock."

"Thank you. That's all for now. But I will need to talk to you later."

Maria Contessa nodded and hurried out of the room. She didn't look at Hernandez. His face was still a mask. Donahoo wondered what he cared about. He said, "We seem to have just the police officers' word."

"Yes."

Donahoo opened a window and glanced about. They were on the third floor, looking down on the curved driveway, the porte-cochère. It would be an easy climb for a cat burglar. The house had a lot angles and protrusions that would afford footings. He could come and go and not leave a mark. Torres's men, at any rate, had not found any.

"What was this before? A maid's room?"

"Yes."

Donahoo left the window open. The place was stuffy and needed the air. He looked around some more, checking the small closet, the tiny bathroom, its miniature window. He wasn't looking for anything in particular. He again was taking Torres's word. A complete and thorough inspection had been made. There was no other entry.

"There are very few clothes here. Personal possessions."

"There wasn't a place for them. So she left them in a storage room."

Donahoo went back to the window. There would be a view west to the sea if it weren't for the smog.

"Are we through here?"

"Yes," Donahoo said, not looking at him. "But I still want to talk to you."

The library was arranged like a public library. It had closely set rows of books, sections with large signs, MEDICINA, ARTE & MUSICA, and LITERATURA & LENGUA, and HISTORIA, BIOGRAFIA & ACTIVIDADES DEL MUNDO. A turn among them revealed CIENCIA & INDUSTRIA and CIENCIA SOCIAL. Then LITERATURA NOVELESCA. The rows were numbered and the books catalogued by the Dewey Decimal System. In the center was a large smooth oak table with some oak chairs around it and a big oval reading light overhead.

Hernandez took Donahoo to the table. He removed his Rolex (it was very much like Marino's Rolex, Donahoo noticed) and put it between them. He said, "We have half an hour."

Donahoo was going to protest—he didn't like deadlines, nor Hernandez's attitude—but he decided to argue, if necessary, on the other end. This might not take half an hour. It could be over very quickly.

"Where shall we start?"

Well, a good place, Donahoo thought, would be Pamela Mesa, and Hernandez's son by her, Philip, who was presently visiting the aviary, feeding Fluffy; but again he opted to pass for the moment. The facts, while perhaps titillating, seemed quite out in the open, and he was looking for information that might be buried along with Deedee.

"Understand, I appreciate your involvement, and if this is what the Presidente wants, fine," Hernandez said, pushing books aside to make more room for himself. "He thinks, because he is Presidente, that he must know everything, but history shows that our presidents, and we have eight decades to prove it, don't even know how to pick a successor." He smiled at his own joke. "Anyway, there is an experience of police cooperation between our two countries, and also . . ." He got the books settled the way he wanted them, looked at Donahoo. "It perhaps would not behoove me to deny assistance from an expert seeking an explanation of my wife's tragic demise."

Donahoo stared at him. He wondered, What the flaming fuck?

Hernandez continued, "Understand, it is not that I doubt your ability, or that I think our own police, the captain included, with all due deference, in any sense approach it. I just feel quite strongly that you are in the wrong territory. I'm a surgeon, I specialize in limbs, particularly hands, and I am very, very skilled, but I would be quite frankly lost operating in the brain. So I think you are in the wrong place. You don't know anything about it. And that it is to your great and lasting detriment."

"You think I'm operating in the brain?"

"I think you're operating in the asshole."

Yes, so do I, Donahoo thought. He waited for whatever remained of Hernandez's orientation speech. He felt it didn't pay to jump in. He wondered what Torres was doing now, a capitán, Grupo Homocidios, assigned to wait in the drawing room, banished along with two low-life city cops, normally he wouldn't share the same toilet with them. Torres must be a very patient man, he thought. Or a wise man. Or maybe just a tired man. It was another tough call.

"Police work, I suspect," Hernandez was saying, "is like acquiring the mumps, it's who you know, and here you don't know anybody. That's a bad start, and I don't see it getting any better, Sergeant. You can't just walk in and, overnight, inherit all the contacts and connections, the informants, that are necessary to properly investigate this matter. It is too much to ask of anyone."

Donahoo couldn't argue that. He didn't try.

"What you need to know about me, the captain can tell you. I've already told him, but I will repeat the major points for you now, since neither of you appear to take notes. Deedee and I were married for ten years. It was not a happy marriage. The situation was exacerbated by the fact that she couldn't bear children. Divorce, of course, was out of the question; we are Catholic. So I began—frankly, I would have done it anyway—a liaison with Pamela, which produced, in due course, Philip. This actually improved the marriage. It removed the thorn of childlessness. Deedee was aware of everything. She had her society party rounds, her charities, activities I gladly funded, because to deny her would reflect on me. I had my work. Pamela, Philip. I had no desire to marry Pamela. Nor to make of Philip more than a bastard child. He is what he is and he knows it. He also knows I love him very much. That is—was—sufficient. To my intention, now, to legalize the union, this is simply what Pamela wants, and there is no good reason to deny her. Her status changes only on paper and in the eyes and ears of gossips. She gains nothing of great value. The prenuptial is a bitch."

Donahoo waited.

"The murder, as you know, took place in my absence, during a trip to, a conference in, Mexico City. I have a hundred witnesses to account for my time. Pamela was with me. I am completely baffled as to why Deedee was killed. She had no enemies I am aware of. No one who would profit by her death. No . . ." He found it necessary to relocate a book. "No lover."

Donahoo thought that he should continue to wait.

"No men friends of consequence," Hernandez went on. "I would have known about them. In our circle, people talk, and they talk all the time. It is the national pastime." He took a moment. There were no books left to fuss with. "Now, as to the locked-room puzzle, the method of murder, the photograph of Elvis in her vagina? This Pedro Juarez and the monogrammed handkerchief? That is your department. It all baffles me. But what I suspect, what I *know*, the cops have got it wrong somewhere, right? You saw that Cocos? He's brain-damaged, a cretin. And Marquisa, slick as shit. The whole thing . . ." Hernandez gave it up, looked at Donahoo, frowned. "Am I boring you?"

"No, no," Donahoo quickly assured him. "I was just wondering when my half hour was going to start?"

Hernandez pushed back from the table. His face was a dark cloud. He grabbed for his watch.

"Understand," Donahoo told him. He also was angry. "I'm here under instructions but I don't have to do anything. I can eat the beans and leave the windows open and just have a good time. Or I can make a real effort, and maybe, just maybe, come to some conclusion. It all depends on you. If . . ."

Hernandez started to speak. Donahoo cut him off. "*If* I have your full cooperation. Which means that, when I ask questions, you will answer them, fully and to the best of your ability, and not just now, but when they occur to me, which could be most any-time as we wade through this cesspool, and also that you dili-gently provide documents, obtain permissions, and smooth the way, as may, in my judgment, be required. If you've got a problem with that, I suggest you see Cocos, take a look at his T-shirt, he's got a number you can call."

"This is . . ." Hernandez began. He was trembling with rage.

"The least that you, as a bereaved husband, ought to do," Dona-hoo said sharply. "*If* you want your wife's killer apprehended. *If* you give a fat shit." He pushed away from the table and stood up. "Don't bother to show me out. I know the way. I turn left at the fucking leopard."

Torres, as they drove away, the LeBaron belching, had trouble adjusting to Donahoo's theory, which was that the Presidente had more to gain than Hernandez.

"How does it help, you make the bastard so angry, he doesn't answer your questions?" Torres demanded.

"I didn't *ask* any questions," Donahoo reminded him.

"Then what have you achieved?"

"Nothing, yet," Donahoo admitted, Marino translating. "Nor will

I, if he continues to dictate to me. So I think I'll wait. For me to learn more about him. Or for him to come around."

"I still don't follow you."

Well, it is a twisted trail, Donahoo thought. His brief, Rolex-monitored confrontation with Hernandez made him think that the doctor had given up all hope of a solution to his wife's slaying, and that the only reason he was cooperating was the Presidente. Yet he wasn't very sure of that even.

"What I would like to know: what is the nature of the friendship, exactly, between the Presidente and Hernandez?" Donahoo said. "When did they become friends, do you think? In childhood? College? Why did the friendship happen? Why does it persist?"

"I don't know."

"Neither do I. But I would like to find out. Who do you think could help us in this?"

Torres thought for a moment. "Catalina?"

Donahoo hadn't expected that. He hadn't thought about her for a while. She hadn't called; and he felt (it was a ridiculous thing to feel) that she had somehow stood him up. "Oh? Why?"

"She has friends in Mexico City. She could ask them."

"Friends who would know?"

"Or could find out."

"They're in the government?"

"No. They're lawyers. Professors."

"She got her degree there?"

"Yes."

Donahoo wondered. And came here to practice? He thought that he ought to ask her about that the next time he saw her. Of course, if she was looking for injustice, she had come to the right place.

"Hernandez, obviously, is rich," Donahoo continued. "What I would like to know, though, is how rich, and how he got to be so rich. Was it inherited? Partly or all? Or, as he thinks, he is the world's greatest surgeon, which would perhaps mean that his services are in demand across the world, his fees enormous, repairing other surgeons, banjo players? Do you know about that?"

"No."

"Who would?"

"Catalina."

"She has friends?"

"Yes."

Where? Donahoo wondered. In doctors' offices? Hospitals? Surgical tents in the far reaches? He glanced back at Cocos and Marquisa, who were following, unsurely, in a battered Tijuana Policia squad car, which was in worse shape than the LeBaron. They were going to get together for lunch, to resume what had not been started—their examination—in a bar that Torres had suggested and which was known, unfavorably, to Donahoo. Club Hemingway, in Pueblo Amigo, near the off-track Caliente Book. Donahoo wondered if Torres had a twofer going here. If he would take both the Hemingway's bartender and the Caliente Book bartender into the toilet.

He said, "Marino, guess what? The bastard was wearing a watch just like yours!"

"A knockoff?"

"No," Donahoo said, smiling. "I don't think so." He found himself thinking about Marino the way he had thought about Hernandez. How about this guy? It interrupted, briefly, his other puzzlement, which was why had Hernandez said, "If this is what the Presidente wants . . . ?"

That was what Hernandez had said: *If*.

Nine

Torres stopped the LeBaron in front of an establishment called Fantasma. It was another bar, a poor place without real windows, just square holes in the adobe walls. "More flowers," he said in apology, and scrambled out, leaving them parked, for once, legally. There was no red curb because there was no curb. Cocos and Marquisa dutifully pulled in behind.

They were in an impoverished slum district south of Lomas de Agua Caliente, and probably still within sight of, if they sought the proper vantage, Jorge Hernandez's Casa de la Mano.

Donahoo thought that perhaps he was misjudging Torres. This bar was so beggared. There could hardly be a *mordida* here. Maybe the guy had a weak bladder?

"Did he take a leak at the house?" he asked Marino.

Marino said—he was looking around, dismayed—"Yes."

Donahoo thought then that maybe he was right about Torres. He visited bars. He took bartenders into toilets. He collected protection money. Whether they were rich or poor. Maybe he did and maybe he didn't. Spit into the wind.

"I don't know about this shithole," Marino complained. "Up on the hill they live in palaces. Down here . . ." He was looking at homes that were pitiful shacks. That were less than shacks. That were scraps of wood and tin and cardboard. He shook his head in disbelief. "This is fucked, man. This is really fucked."

Donahoo wondered if Marino'd had his head up his ass all his life. The guy, he'd been in the Navy, he'd served in the Pacific. Hadn't he seen anything? He said, "It's fucked in a lot of places."

"This fucked?"

Sure, Donahoo thought. This and worse. If you go looking for it, you'll find it. And what else you will discover, there is fuck-all that you can do about it, so stop whining. He thought he should tell

Marino that. He didn't know why he hadn't. Maybe because he wasn't quite one hundred percent sure of it?

"What does *fantasma* mean?"

"Phantom. Ghost, scarecrow." Marino had that let-me-outa-here look. He said, "Uh, can I borrow the Toronado again tonight? I promise to take to care of it."

"Oh, yeah," Donahoo said. "And palmistry is an exact science and you're not losing your hair."

Torres came out of Fantasma. He was shaking his head hopelessly. He motioned to Cocos and Marquisa that they should hurry up and follow.

"Detour," Torres said, pushing into the LeBaron. "I was checking with the station and they got a call. Dios Mediante, it's an orphanage, only a few blocks from here. I said I'd handle it for them."

"What's going on?" Marino asked in Spanish.

"Nothing, probably," Torres told him. "It's the same kid who always makes the call. He claims he's being tortured. He never is, but we've got to check it out. If he keeps making the calls, one day they are gonna torture the little prick."

"What is the kid's idea of torture?" Donahoo asked.

"The same as yours," Torres said.

Marino didn't get it for a moment. The LeBaron lurched away. Here we go, Donahoo thought. There are places more fucked, and now you are going to visit one, Marino. Donahoo thought that he would bet a thousand dollars there hadn't been a phone call. Fantasma wouldn't have a toilet. It wouldn't have a phone. He'd bet that Torres had pissed out back and talked to himself.

They drove into a destitute neighborhood that resembled an old war zone. It looked like it had taken a direct hit and the people had decided to leave it that way. They didn't have the money or strength or will to put it back together, so they had just persisted in their hard, hopeless lives. They were stuck in a bad time.

Marino said, softly, "Jesus," and Torres said something in Spanish that Marino didn't translate, but Donahoo could guess. Jesus, He doesn't come here.

The orphanage was a half-built concrete bunker, rusted rebar sticking up from all the support columns, waiting for a second story that probably would never come either. The rust staining the walls suggested the building had stood this way for years. It flowed like blood across the name, Dios Mediante Orfanato y Refugio.

Torres led the way to the iron gate and rang the bell. After a while an old crone materialized in the shadows. She peered at them from under a long, dirty shawl. Donahoo could grasp only bits of the exchange.

"Police," Torres said in Spanish, showing her his badge; and when she didn't respond, "Open up. There's been a call."

"No. No one called."

"Mother," Marquisa said, very softly. "Don't be afraid. Remember me? I am your friend."

The woman regarded him doubtfully but still opened the gate before fleeing back into the shadows.

They followed her down a hall that was like a tunnel and through a high door that opened onto a concrete courtyard that comprised most of the orphanage. Two dirty, ragged young boys, they'd be about eleven, perhaps twelve years old, were kneeling on the concrete, below a basketball hoop. They looked worn, exhausted.

The woman said, "No one called."

Torres said, "Tell the director we are here."

Marquisa yelled to the boys. "What is it now, bastards? Sucking cocks again?"

The bigger boy looked at him. "I stole some gum."

"Oh? And what did your lover do?"

The smaller boy said, "I told on him."

"Snitch. It serves you right."

Marino was standing close to Donahoo. He was quietly translating all this while they waited for the director. Donahoo thought that Marino, for a man with his head up his ass, was becoming a pretty good translator; he called it as he heard it, without embellishment. He might work out yet.

Torres asked the boys, "How long have you been kneeling here?"

They said, together, "All night."

Marino grimaced as he translated. The boys were looking at them pleadingly. Donahoo wanted to tell them they could get off their knees now. But he thought he should wait, to see how Torres would handle it, and also, more importantly, to see how long it would take for Torres to reprimand Marquisa. The boys had suffered for hours. What were a few more minutes? "Are we going to do something?" Marino asked.

"No," Donahoo said.

"I vote we should."

"Yeah, well, you know what your vote is worth, Marino. Mind your own business."

"But . . ."

"You can't stop it. They'll be kneeling here again tomorrow, and the next day, and the next day. They'll be kneeling here till they crawl across the border and we send them crawling back."

Donahoo turned away, embarrassed. He thought he had come dangerously close to making a speech. He looked around. The building itself was on the street side from which they had entered. There were doors marked Oficina, Cocina, Despensa, Dormitoria, Baño. The rest of the place, three sides, was a high wall, the top imbedded with broken glass. In a far corner, there also was a makeshift structure set on concrete stilts in the fashion of a guard tower, but it looked more like a broken playhouse. A shadowy figure moved behind its cracked glass.

"Capitán!" The director had emerged from a door midway in the building, the storeroom for food, Despensa. He was with the woman, and was holding a small cardboard box. "How can I help you?"

Torres, who had been patiently waiting, told him, "We need to talk. How about your office?"

The director stared uncertainly. He was a large, soft man with thick glasses and a big stomach that hung from him like a basket. He seemed about to object but then shifted the box and beckoned with a fat hand. He said something unheard to the woman and headed for the Oficina. She went the other way.

"What about these boys?" Torres asked.

"Oh, them," the director said, looking. "I forgot about them. Yes, they can go."

The boys were for the time crippled. They rose slowly and painfully. They hobbled away without looking back, headed for a door at the other end of the building: the bathroom, Baño.

"Check around," Torres told Marquisa, motioning to Donahoo. He said to him, "You might as well come with me. You might learn something."

Donahoo said, "Would it have anything to do with the murder of Deedee Hernandez?"

Torres shrugged elaborately. "Indirectly, perhaps. But I will let you make that judgment."

The director moved slowly. He didn't carry his weight well. They caught up easily and went right behind him into his office. He hurried, too late, to clean his desk, which was spread with waffles.

"Breakfast," he explained, putting them in a stack, four of them. The torn frozen-food packaging was in a wastepaper basket. He looked at Donahoo and then at Marino and then to Torres. Marino was quietly translating for Donahoo's benefit. "The gringos donate them. They don't realize we haven't the refrigeration."

"So you have to eat them up?"

The director smiled but didn't say anything. He moved his cardboard box from the desk to a shelf behind him. The printing on the side, in English, said SHRIMP, but it might have contained anything; it had been opened and retaped.

Torres made the introductions, as he had now on several occasions, beginning as he did with Catalina, when she had briefly shown up at The Desperate Frog. Sgt. Tommy Donahoo and Investigator Cruz Marino. Here from San Diego. To assist him in a matter. Then he said, "I'm showing them around."

The director looked at them briefly. He again didn't say anything.

"We had a call," Torres said, looking at the phone, which was on the desk next to a toaster. "From one of the boys. He said he was being tortured."

The director thought for a while. "When?"

"Perhaps ten minutes ago."

"I don't think so." The director was looking at the phone, it was a relic, with dial. Or he might have been looking at the waffles. "I would have seen him. I have been here, close by, in and out."

"But you have been gone?"

"Briefly."

"How many boys are here at the moment?" Torres asked then. He fell easily into a chair without asking permission. "Besides the worshippers."

The director counted on his fingers. "Four; no, five. We have the grippe here. We send them to school and the school sends them back. They are in the dormitory."

"So any one of them could have sneaked in to call?"

"Possibly."

"Let's say he did," Torres said. "Has there been any torturing going on around here?"

"No."

"What about the kneeling all night?"

"We have had this conversation before," the director said. "We have been to the courts for a decision, remember? It is not torture. It is extended prayer." He picked up one of his waffles. "Will there be anything else?"

Donahoo and Marino had been left standing near the door. Marino was continuing with his quiet translation.

Torres said, "Perhaps the Sargento has a question?"

Me? Donahoo thought that he had several. He thought that this was a Catholic country and that he was a Catholic. The idea, for the first time, sickened him, frightened him. He wondered how many Catholics there were in Tijuana. How many were sick at the thought. He said, angry with Torres, but more angry with the director, "Not at this time."

There was a long, uncomfortable silence. It was as if children strange to each other had been put together to play and had not hit it off. That kind of odd, desperate, familiar standoff. Nothing to be gained except a shambles.

"Who's in the tower?" Torres asked finally. "Ramón?"

"Yes."

"Again or still?"

"I'd have to check."

"The tower is the Hole," Torres said, talking to Donahoo and Marino. "They put a boy up there and then take away the ladder. He can't get down unless he jumps. If he jumps, he'll probably break a leg, or maybe his spine. Both have happened."

"Is there anything else?" the director asked again. He half-turned toward the wall behind him. "I have a license."

Torres shook his head. He took the waffle from the director. He put it in the toaster.

"They are bad boys," the director said. He took off his glasses. His eyes were glistening. "They sodomize each other. They shit on the floor. They sneak in radios and listen to non-Christian stations."

Torres was leaving. "Let's go."

"We have to have rules, punishment. You don't know what it is like. They play their stolen radios in the night. They listen to music with drums."

Donahoo and Marino followed Torres out.

"Drums in all their forms are evil. Instruments of voodoo and pagan cult activity. They convey the Satanic beat of Negro religions."

Torres shook his head. He took them briefly to look at the Baño. The toilets were full to the brim. Brown and solid. Donahoo thought the director had been right. The floor was covered with excrement. On a stall wall someone had written a message in it. "Don't wipe your ass with your fingers," Marino said, starting to translate, and then he quit.

In the Dormitoria, the boys who had been sent away from school with the grippe, the flu, were sitting in a circle on two beds that had been pushed together, playing a card game. The two boys who had been in extended prayer were watching. The game's action froze—the same response that passersby on the street might encounter—and then, when there was no objection, quickly resumed. No one looked up.

The room smelled like a gymnasium. The thin blankets were dirty and the pillows and sheets stained.

Cocos had been searching the place. His big hands were full of contraband. A makeshift knife, a zip gun, comic books. A radio.

"Put the radio back," Torres told him.

Cocos started to protest.

"Put it back, *caca!*"

The hulking Tijuana cop reluctantly placed it out of sight on an open beam that ran overhead. He did so by merely rising on his tiptoes. It would take two boys, one on another's shoulder, to accomplish that. The director would have to stand on a chair just to see it.

Torres called over the older of the boys who had been kneeling. He gave him a handful of folded money.

Cocos asked, "You expect him to share?"

Torres nodded. "He's a good boy."

"He's a cocksucker."

"Well, he's a good cocksucker," Torres said amiably. "Why don't you read your comics?"

They found Marquisa in the Cocina, the kitchen, with the crone, beating the edge of a wooden table with a foot-long rubber hose. He was whacking away methodically, with short, measured blows. He was showing her how to use it most effectively.

The table was piled high with bowls used to served breakfast. Scraps of beans and tortillas clung to them.

"The snotty bastards stole her hose," Marquisa said, pounding the table.

"Then whose is that?" Torres wanted to know.

"Mine. I'm giving it to her. A present for my little mother."

Donahoo started to say, "You . . ." Torres had him in an iron grip before he moved an inch. "She'll only get another," Torres said softly, Marino translating. "And another, and another." He said, "Remember?"

On the way out, just starting through the high door that led to the dark hallway and the gate and the street, there was a loud noise, a *twang*, in the Oficina. The toaster popping another waffle.

□ □ □

In the LeBaron, Donahoo thought okay, now he did have a question, and he wanted it answered.

"How the fuck can this happen?" he demanded. "What is wrong with you people? Those are *children* in there!"

"You people," Torres repeated, looking at him. "You people. It sounds like you are starting to look for someone to blame." He was looking right at Donahoo. Donahoo thought that he was somehow looking inside him. "I fear perhaps everyone is to blame."

"Bullshit."

"No. It is true." Torres started up the LeBaron. It moved away. Cocos and Marquisa followed. "What you have seen is just the tip. There are maybe fifty state-licensed orphanages in Baja. Maybe two thousand children in them. Not all are as bad as Dios Mediante, of course, some are quite decent, but others, I'm sorry to say, are worse. You will find dirt floors, terrible poverty, physical and sexual abuse." He was looking in the rearview mirror. He was looking at Donahoo. "But you don't think everybody is to blame?"

"No."

"Well, let's see who we can blame then," Torres said, Marino translating. "Perhaps we should blame you Americans. These orphanages are mostly funded by your donations. But if you didn't fund them, if there were no orphanages, where would the children go? There are already about five thousand abandoned children living on the streets of Tijuana. Did you know that?"

"No."

"We could blame the state. It licenses the orphanages. It is supposed to inspect them. Sometimes it does. But if it closes an orphanage, there usually is no other place for the children to go, so again they are put out on the street, and which is worse? Oh, what I also should say, the children are put out on the street when they are twelve, anyway. This is mostly because the orphanages can't segregate boys and girls. Did you know that?"

"No."

"Myself, I blame mostly the law, the courts," Torres said. "Here, when a child is taken from his parents by the courts, because of family difficulties, legal problems, abandonment, he may be placed in an orphanage for custodial care. Your courts would place him in a foster home." He was again looking in the rearview. "But maybe I should blame the parents. Few of these children are truly orphans. They have mothers, fathers, grandparents, who, for whatever reason, cannot take care of them, but the children are not formally released by them, and thus the children cannot be put up for adoption, and so they have to stay in the orphanage where the parent or parents can visit them, sometimes fairly often, but usually not a lot, especially if they are poor and at a distance. So that is someone else to blame."

Marino was quietly translating. Donahoo wanted to make him stop.

"For a Mexican to give up a child is traumatic," Torres said. "You could say to a mother, 'I am going to guarantee you. Your child will grow up in Beverly Hills. It will attend the best schools money can buy. It will grow up to be a doctor or a lawyer.' The mother would say, 'Well, that is all very grand, but as poor as I am, that child is a part of me, not some inanimate object to be given away. I won't give it up, no matter what you say.' " He looked at Donahoo. "That is what she would say, so I think, yes, the mothers are to blame."

Torres was waiting. Donahoo refused to respond. He felt like the director with his waffles. There was nothing more he wanted to say or hear on the subject.

"But I still prefer to blame everybody," Torres said. "Sometimes, I think, we should blame the fucking Indians. Like you Americans, we should have killed off all the Indians, as many as we could, anyway, because a lot of this problem is caused by the Indians, and now there are too many to kill. The fucking Catholics are to blame too, though. I imagine you are familiar with their stand on birth control? Tijuana, it is eighty-five percent Catholic, did you know that? Only five percent Protestant or Evangelical. The rest are what we call 'Others' or no religion. There are only about a thousand Jews." He was looking at Donahoo. "Maybe they are to blame? It's their fault. There are not enough of them. If there were more Jews, maybe they could do something about this. Yes, we could be onto to something here. I suspect the fucking Jews are to blame, Sargento."

Ten

Donahoo thought that he had become like Marino. He wanted to go home. He hated all of them: Torres. Hernandez. Marquisa and Cocos. The director and the crone. Torres because Torres had brought him here and the others because they were scum. Catalina. He hated her too. She could make this bearable and she hadn't called.

Mostly, he hated Torres, he thought. Mostly because Torres had him on a string, like the invisible string Marquisa used to manipulate Cocos; the slightest yank and he would do his little indignant dance, a cop puppet in a theater of the absurd, hoping for applause from the enlightened. Hoping that, when the curtain went down, everybody would shout, a standing ovation, "Yes, yes. You are right! This is wrong!" and that they would say who was to blame, and how to punish them, and also that they would drown out Torres, who was prompting from the wings, "Everybody!"

Torres, Marquisa, Cocos. Donahoo thought that if he couldn't go home, he could get rid of some of them, not have to suffer their company any longer, and that it would be easy to get rid of Marquisa, because he was a mean prick, and if Marquisa went, Cocos went too, on account of the string.

Prick, you are going, Donahoo decided. Actually, he had decided back at Dios Mediante Orfanato y Refugio. He knew that if he pushed hard enough, Marquisa, with his temper, his pride, his macho maleness, Marquis would go. It would be impossible for him to stay.

Donahoo could sense that—the predictable prick, he thought—sitting in a dark, greasy booth at the back of Club Hemingway, watching Marquisa's smooth moves, listening to his smooth talk. There were just the three of them for the moment. Donahoo with Marquisa and Cocos. Torres had decided that they did not need him for this part, Donahoo's questions about what happened, and perhaps did not happen, at Casa de la Mano. Torres had gone with Marino to the Caliente Book.

Donahoo would have followed except that the Club Hemingway figured obliquely in one of his old cases, which was called, for a reason too lengthy to explain very often, Manila Time. He had come to Tijuana as part of that investigation but it had not been necessary to actually visit here, the scene of a murder, indirectly related. A U.S. Border Patrol officer had been stabbed in the heart with an ice pick, perhaps at this very table, while, under it, a whore named Doxanne, another good cocksucker, was giving him a blow job. Donahoo thought that, being in the neighborhood, he was almost obliged to attend. It was like missing somebody's funeral; the next best thing is to visit the grave.

Club Hemingway's gimmick—actually, it was a bar, not a club—consisted of a huge photo of Papa on the wall and ancient typewriters chained to each table. Patrons were encouraged to tap out some Hemingway and submit it for an annual contest, who could write the best imitation, the prize a trip to Paris. It appeared suspect, though. There were no framed samples of winning entries. No photos of past winners.

"If you want to check up, you'll learn what happened. It's not a secret," Marquisa was saying, talking about his past employment. "But what you need to remember, keep this in perspective, *everybody* in authority is corrupt. Every so often, they have to fire somebody, it looks like they're cleaning house, and it was my turn, that's all. It doesn't mean anything. I am no better or no worse than they are. They just hold higher positions. It just takes longer to get to them. But eventually they too will fall. Everybody is corrupt and everybody falls."

Yes, prick and a liar, Donahoo thought, watching and listening. He been right about the guy. Marquisa had been a federal cop in Guadalajara and an investigator for the attorney general's department in Guerrero. Bounced both places. Tailor-made for Tijuana. He had admitted it with an easy smile. He had been here only a few months. He was entrenched.

Donahoo wondered if that was true. Everybody is corrupt? To blame, perhaps. But not corrupt. It didn't seem possible. But Marquisa—he was corrupt. Marquisa had not been moved by the intolerable conditions at the orphanage. He had fed on them. And he had also steadfastly refused to alter any portion of his and Coco's report as the first police officers on the Deedee Hernandez murder scene. He'd held fast to the basics: Deedee's bedroom door bolted from the inside. Impossible to manipulate from the hall. The bedroom windows firmly secured. Impossible to open from outside.

Marquisa had said, "You asked the maid, she was there, what did she tell you, the door was bolted," and Donahoo had said, "What about the windows?" and Marquis had told him, "It's all in the report."

Donahoo thought he would put more faith in a flying saucer report. In the end, if there was an end, it would turn out that a window was open and that Cocos and Marquis, one or both, locked it upon entering the room, without Maria Contessa's knowledge. Unless, of course, the pretty maid was in cahoots, in which case all bets were off, endless scenarios being possible. He was looking forward to talking to her some more, and also, if he came around, Hernandez. In the meantime, there was the monogrammed handkerchief, DD, and it was enough to keep him busy, and Torres too, if Torres ever came back.

Marquisa had said, "It was in Juarez's pants pocket, jammed there like a snot rag," but Donahoo didn't think that Juarez, if he killed Deedee, would steal just a handkerchief, or, having done so, jam it all up in his pants. He'd more likely keep it folded neatly in a shirt pocket. The handkerchief's real value, Donahoo was sure, was the souvenir value, and he thought it more likely that Marquisa would collect such a souvenir, not Juarez.

Now Donahoo was addressing that likelihood. "If he stole it—I say, *if*—why muck it up? Something that precious, the finest white linen, monogrammed. Isn't that something that you'd give to your mother? Your wife, or your girl? A souvenir hankie, DD. Once owned by Daffy Duck."

Marquisa said, "He had it in his pants."

"Crumpled up?"

"Yes."

Sure, Donahoo thought. "So what you're saying—Juarez stole a dirty handkerchief?"

"No. It wasn't dirty. It was merely crumpled."

"By him?"

"I am assuming."

"Well, I'm not," Donahoo said. "When I steal a handkerchief, I don't wanta have to iron it, you know? I want to keep it neat until

I blow in it. *If* I blow in it." He said, "Somehow, I don't think Juarez intended to blow in it, do you?"

Marquisa looked at him for a while. Then he seemed to shrug, although there was no movement. "I think you are turning a speck into a stone that no one can swallow. Did he intend to blow or did he not intend to blow? What does it matter? And, if it does matter, why don't you ask him?"

"I did ask him," Donahoo said, which wasn't quite true, "and he says you are a liar."

Marquisa was staring. He didn't blink. "I told you he was a troublemaker."

Cocos smiled and signaled for more Coronas.

"How long have you known him to be a bother?"

"A bother?"

"A pain in the ass. We're not talking about big trouble here, are we, Marquisa? We're talking about a guy with some political pamphlets that say cops are pigs. That's not trouble. That's an opinion."

"It's a slander to authority."

Ah, Donahoo thought, happy with that answer; it went to the foundation of the teetery conception he was fashioning. This was going to be something new for him. He had never before made an accusation with absolutely nothing to back it up. It was against his principles. But Marquisa had to go. Otherwise, Torres would continue to drag Marquisa around, and Marquisa would drag Cocos, and the dog-and-pony show in the slimy underbelly would go on and on, and where it stopped he didn't know.

"Marquisa, let me suggest something," he said. "You and Cocos bust into Deedee's bedroom and discover you've got a murder on your hands, not an overdose, and that means it is out of your jurisdiction, you've got to call Grupo Homicidios. This pisses you off. You're brighter than anybody over at Grupo. There's a window open. You close it. Lock it."

Marquisa had been silent through all this. Now he said, "For what purpose?"

"To fuck with their heads."

The Coronas were delivered by a sleepy waiter. His eyes were almost closed. The merest slits.

"Another suggestion," Donahoo said, paying. "The handkerchief. You slip it into your pocket, a small, inconsequential theft.

Later, leaving, you come upon Juarez, and here's the opportunity to fuck some more heads. You plant it on him."

Marquisa got his beer. He scratched at the imprinted label. He said, thoughtfully, "Can you make that stick?"

"No." Donahoo shook his head. He counted his change and gave the waiter a dollar. "Can you make it *un*stick, Marquisa? You had the opportunity. You had the motive."

"Therefore I did it?

"Yes."

"You're making a big mistake," Marquisa said. He took a long pull on his beer. "You have no authority here." He was looking past Donahoo. He seemed relieved. "Take a hike."

It was Torres. Marino trailed far behind. He looked the same as he had looked at the orphanage—like he wanted to go home.

"Your friend thinks *I'm* the troublemaker," Marquisa told Torres, trying hard to be indignant. "He's made accusations. Corrupting a crime scene. Planting evidence."

Torres raised an eyebrow.

"It's true," Donahoo admitted.

Torres considered. He took Marquisa's beer. He drained half of it, returned it. He said, to Donahoo, "Is there any evidence of this?"

"You don't have to prove it. Isn't that what you've been telling me about the Napoleonic Code? It's his problem. Let him do the sweating. Or was that all bullshit too?"

Marquisa started to stand. Torres put a hand on his shoulder. "Normally, we like to have some indication that a law has been broken."

"How about a law of physics? The dead don't lock doors. Nobody can walk through a wall. It didn't happen that way. So your boy here, first on the scene, has a lot to answer for."

Torres looked at his watch. "Perhaps we've been here too long."

Marino was wide-eyed. He translated that slowly.

"It's the calendar you ought to be looking at, and it's not this bar, it's the fucking town," Donahoo responded. "It stinks." He was staring flatly at Marquisa. "Put him in with Juarez. See how he likes it. Maybe he'll tell the truth."

Marquisa removed Torres's hand. He said, "Fuck you, gringo," and stood up, pushing the table into Donahoo, trapping him. "I suggest you go home. The next time I see you—you're not under escort?—we'll see who gets tossed in the Tijuana Jail."

Torres was trying to calm him. "Take it easy."

Marquisa told him, *"Comer mierda,"* meaning eat shit, and stomped away. Cocos quickly followed, drawn by the invisible string.

Torres acted baffled. He watched them go and then turned back to Donahoo. "Jesus Christ. You antagonize Hernandez. Now you make an enemy of Marquisa. Is this how you carry out an investigation? I *need* these people."

Donahoo didn't think so. "Like you need cancer." He pushed the table away painfully. The edge had caught him just under the rib cage. If something wasn't broken, it was badly bruised. He said, "Listen. This is my first advice for you. Stop looking for ghosts. There aren't any. Just asshole cops. Stop looking for ghosts and concentrate on looking for the killer."

Torres said, "The killer came through an unlocked window? That simple?"

"There," Donahoo said. He was trying not to show how much he hurt. "Was that so hard?"

Torres was smiling now. Marino was translating. "Well, you are quite the detective, all right, Sargento. In one fell swoop, you solve half of the Deedee Hernandez Nightmare Murder Case. Now I have a question for you." He was smiling. He was going to laugh. "What took you so fucking long?"

Eleven

Another night in paradise. Donahoo was sprawled across his bed at El Greco, a glass of Old Crow, his third and last (he promised himself) clutched in one hand, the other empty of hope. He again had thought Catalina would call. If only because he had contacted her office and left a message. But she had not done so. He wondered if perhaps he should have said it was business. He also thought he was an idiot for letting Marino have the Toronado again.

The day was like an ambush in his mind. It had surprised him. Hernandez and his mistress, Pamela Mesa, and their bastard son, Philip. Not them so much. But that Hernandez displayed them so blatantly. And so soon after his wife's death.

"It is not so unusual," Torres had said when asked. "Divorce is very difficult here. The Catholic church? So a mistress is the natural alternative. Many men, especially wealthy men, have them, and children by them. Perhaps not so often in the same city. It would be more usual to have a wife, say, in Mexico City, and a mistress in Guadalajara. Cities that it would be normal, for business, to travel back and forth between, or countries."

Marino had said, "Countries?" and Torres had said, "Yes, Rio de Janeiro, I understand, is a very fine place to have a mistress."

Donahoo thought no doubt. Or London or Paris. There was a side to Mexico, the wealthy side, that he was just beginning to comprehend, because he had frankly never gotten far past raucous Calle Revolución and the putrid slums that hung on the canyons fronting the Ensenada *libre* road. He had known, vaguely, that the wealth was there (yes, Marino, there are Rolls Royces), but he hadn't given much thought to its form and fabric. He had not expected it to be so . . . what? Brazen and uncaring? Defiant?

Questions plagued him. How does a man with a Rolex walk

86

among emaciated beggars and keep his last meal down? How does he keep his hand attached to his arm? Answers mocked him. Hernandez, he was a hand surgeon, he could sew it back on.

Torres had surprised him more, though. He could see Torres smiling, saying, "What took you so fucking long?" Torres laughing.

Donahoo wondered. In reversed circumstances, Torres in San Diego, assisting with a similar case, how long would it take for Torres to suggest that a couple of San Diego cops smelled fishy? Not as long? Or longer?

Probably not as long, Donahoo decided. For a devious guy, Torres was very straightforward. He would say what he thought, fairly soon, pretty quickly. He would say, "These cops stink, Sargento."

Yeah, Donahoo thought. But who is to blame? He also thought—he knew this now—that Torres was testing him. To see how softly he walked, how carefully. To see where he was willing to go. And how far.

The cellular rang.

Catalina? Donahoo answered right away, without sitting up, without setting his glass aside. "Hello?"

"Our Man Under the Border," Lewis said, meaning him, Donahoo. "Don't use my name. Understand?"

"Why?"

"I dunno. I have that information you requested. It makes me very uncomfortable. I don't want to be known as the one who passed it along."

Donahoo pushed up, suddenly alert. Lewis didn't sound like himself. He sounded sarcastic, which did sound like him, but he also sounded a bit worried, and maybe even a bit afraid. "What the hell are you talking about?"

"I dunno. Eavesdroppers? It's easy to pick up on a cellular phone."

"Yeah, but . . ." Who would want to? Donahoo was going to say that, but then he changed his mind, because this was information, obviously, about Salvador Urquidez. "What are you saying? You need a secure line?"

"That would be nice. Or you could come up here. Look at this shit personally. That would be another way."

Donahoo tried to think. Marino had the Toronado. But he could catch a cab to the border. Take the Tram into San Diego. Or maybe a black and white could drive it down?

He said, "Do you deliver?"

"No. This is shredder stuff. It's not going anywhere."

"Come on."

"I don't make the rules. You wanta look at it or not?"

Donahoo put his glass aside and searched for his shoes. He said, "I'm gonna go for a walk, find a secure phone . . ."

"Across the border."

". . . and call you back."

"When?"

"Half an hour. Where are you?"

"In my office. Hurry up, I wanta go home."

Yeah, you and Marino, Donahoo thought. He clicked off. He thought it would take a lot to scare Lewis.

Catalina called as he was going out the door. First she laughed, then she said, "Hello, my new friend, how are you today?"

"Hi." That was all he could think of. She had caught him by surprise. He had thought it was Lewis again.

"You know what? I think I would like to say so now, that you can take me to dinner, Sargento. Can you meet me? Half an hour? How does that sound?"

Donahoo thought it sounded wonderful. But he would be across the border then.

"Banana Verde. Every taxi driver knows it. It is on Revolución. Near the Jai Alai Palace."

Jesus, he thought. She sounded so warm, so good.

"I'll have a rose in my sausage lips. Is it a date?"

"Yes."

"Wonderful."

She hung up laughing.

Donahoo stared at the phone. When they laugh, they really laugh, he thought. Torres had laughed that way. Filled with pleasure, knowingly. He thought he ought to call Lewis. Tell him that he would call him tomorrow for the information. Or, tomorrow, before Marino drove back, have Marino go in to see Lewis.

He knew that wouldn't work. He'd have to call tonight. Well, what the fuck, he thought. A pay phone was a pay phone. There weren't all tapped. He'd stop on the way over to The Banana Verde.

□ □ □

Marquisa followed him. The Tijuana cop didn't care that he was seen. When Donahoo left his motel room, Marquisa was standing on the corner, drinking from a paper-wrapped bottle and smoking a cigarette. When Donahoo left El Greco's Oficina, to take the cab he had called, Marquisa was parked up the street, waiting in an old Ford Fairlane. He followed about a block behind. The cab had a big billboard on top, DANZA, advertising some nightclub, so it would be easy to keep in sight.

Donahoo wondered if perhaps he had been mistaken about Marquisa. Maybe the guy wasn't as smart as he thought. Maybe he was going to do something stupid? He felt uneasy—and not so smart himself—until they reached Revolución. The crowded sidewalks, busy stores and bright lights made him feel safe.

He saw a pay phone. It was right on the street. This is not yet a police state, he thought. They can't all be bugged. "Can you park somewhere?"

The driver shook his head. *"Imposible."*

"Well, circle then," Donahoo said, handing him a ten-dollar bill. "I'll be at that phone. Keep going around until I'm finished. Okay?"

The taxi stopped at the corner for a red light. Donahoo got out and looked back. The Fairlane was a block away. He went to the phone and used a credit card to call Lewis.

"That was fast," Lewis said when he was switched through. "Where are you?"

"The border."

"It sounds Mexican."

"It's a Mexican border," Donahoo said. Marquisa was driving by. He was alone, staring straight ahead, drinking from his paper-wrapped bottle. "What have you got for me?"

"Poison. I am reading from an interagency dossier. It would make a hippo throw up. Diablo is a combination political boss/ crime boss. Above the law. How do you say that in Spanish?"

"I don't know."

"You may not wish to find out."

Donahoo looked up the street. Marquisa's Fairlane had disappeared. "I'm more interested in the dossier."

"This guy is a scorpion. He used to be one of the most powerful men in the military. Misused his authority to amass an enormous fortune cooperating with drug cartels. Discharged, finally, by the previous regime, for, quote, unspecified irregularities. Now, to all intents and purposes, he runs Tijuana. What people are afraid of—the good guys?—pretty soon it's gonna be the 'old' Tijuana. He's turning back the clock. Anything goes. They've been making some progress there and he's shit-canning it."

"One guy?"

"With the help of some old army buddies and drug cartel partners. They showed up a few years ago and took advantage of the confusion and unrest that followed the Colosio assassination. Got a lock on some key state and civic officials. The usual shit. Payoffs, kickbacks. Now nothing happens politically unless he says so. He's also like the Godfather. There was a power struggle and some crime kingpins knocked each other off and he moved into the vacuum. Listen to this. Drugs, his big meal ticket, but also alien smuggling, white slavery, kidnaping for ransom, murder. Not to mention roadshow perversions. Are you familiar with a donkey fuck?"

Donahoo thought that seemed like a lot of activity in one piss pot, but the guy, if he had the drug trade, he could take the rest. Tijuana was the major thoroughfare for drugs coming into the U.S. The profits were enormous. The money to buy anything.

"I thought alien smuggling was mostly freelance."

"Not any more. He's got it organized and he takes a cut from everyone. Immigration agents. The cops."

"Like he'd make payoffs to move drugs?"

"Yeah. Customs agents. The cops."

"What about the white slavery?"

"He's working with *yakuza*, the Japanese mafia, and they're scooping 'em up like bottom feeders. Would you believe more than three thousand young women sold into sexual servitude?"

"How the hell do they get away with that?"

"Protection. *Yakuza* runs Mexican employment offices staffed by Japanese nationals. Diablo makes sure they're not hassled. The women are lured by big money. Ten times more than they ever heard of. They think they're gonna be entertainers and hostesses. They get to Japan, they're sold to bars and adult-entertainment joints, then forced to have sex with the customers, no charge."

"Jesus Christ. What's a sex slave cost these days?"

"Depends on the girl. Three, four thousand. Up to ten."

"And Diablo collects a grand or so for making it possible?"

"I guess." Lewis's sigh was a rumble. "This looks like a guy with no conscience. He rules by sheer terror, torture. He's got his hand in everybody's pocket. And the other hand around their throats. You don't want to go near him. Understand?"

"I won't," Donahoo said. He was looking for his cab. The big sign, DANZA. It ought to be coming around. "I promise."

"I don't know what's wrong with you, Tommy," Lewis complained. "The San Diego PD has been cooperating with the Baja cops for years. We've put five, six guys down there, big cases. But nobody ever went down and got mixed up in the politics of the place."

"I'm not mixed up in the politics."

"This whole dossier is politics. Every page, it's who he knows, who he's making rich, whose arms he's breaking. Oh, no, not you, Tommy. You're not mixed up. You're down there two fucking days and you need a profile on the worst sonofabitch political power in the country. You're outa your fucking crock."

"I was just asking."

"Stay away from him. You're supposed to solve a murder. Not fix the world."

"Okay."

"You goddamn dipstick."

Lewis slammed his phone down. Donahoo hung up and looked for his cab. It should have come around by now. He thought maybe he was getting old. Had he just given a Tijuana cab driver ten dollars and told him to drive around the block? The guy, he was probably at the beach by now.

He started walking. The Jai Alai Palace was a few more blocks up Revolución. He had plenty of time. He thought about Salvador Urquidez, aka Diablo. It sounded like he operated in the open. How was that possible? Above the law?

He got about half a block and the cab caught up to him. The billboard on the roof, DANZA. It pulled into a bus stop space. Honked.

Donahoo was going to wave it away, and then he thought, hell, no, he had five bucks coming back. He pushed through the crowd and got in the backseat.

The driver turned to face him. It was Marquisa. He still had the paper bag. There was a gun in it. He said, "Why don't you ride up front, amigo?"

Donahoo did as instructed. He didn't have any other choice. The paper bag, the gun, followed him as he moved around, got in the front seat. The sidewalk was crowded with people. No one was paying any attention.

Marquisa patted him down. Took the cellular that Donahoo had not used because it might not be secure. "Are you armed?"

"No," Donahoo said. "It's in the trunk of my car. I hadn't planned to get into a gun battle down here." He was looking into the bore. "I thought the local cops would protect me."

Marquisa smiled and eased the cab away from the curb. He drove with one hand. The other kept the bag pointed at Donahoo.

"I thought we ought to have a little talk," he said. "Just you and me. No gallery. No grandstanding."

Donahoo thought, Jesus Christ. Marquisa smelled of liquor. He was slurring his words.

"I didn't like what you did to me today. You accused me of being a rogue cop. You made me look like a fool in front of Torres."

Donahoo wondered if he should take a chance and grab for the gun. He slid back but also turned so that he was in a better position for it. "I suppose it's too late to say I'm sorry?"

Marquisa looked at him. "Don't make jokes. This is serious."

"Yeah. But is it something we can work out?"

"I don't know. I'm not sure yet. It depends."

They were going by the Jai Alai Palace. They were going by Banana Verde. Donahoo thought, at a sidewalk table, under a market umbrella, he could see Catalina. He wasn't sure. The sidewalk was crowded. He'd caught just a glimpse. Maybe Catalina.

"You're gonna have to do some major ass-kissing here," Marquisa said.

They stopped in a dark empty field at a distance from any buildings in a district that Donahoo thought would be Zona del Rio. On the way, he had seen the Caliente Book, Señor Frog's. Both were near Club Hemingway, which was in Pueblo Amigo, and he knew that, for sure, to be in Zona del Rio. They hadn't gone much farther before turning into the field.

"Get out," Marquisa ordered.

Donahoo got out of the cab. The field was dark. The light from the streetlamps didn't reach here. The cab's overhead provided the only illumination.

"Do you like to get drunk?"

"Sometimes," Donahoo said. He thought of the three Old Crows. He wished he hadn't had them. "Maybe not tonight though."

Marquisa got out of the cab. He had two six-packs of Corona. The gun was out of the bag. He put it down, on the hood, where he could easily grab it, and then, watching Donahoo, he opened the twelve bottles of beer, setting them in a row on the hood.

He was grinning foolishly. He motioned to Donahoo. "Okay, amigo. Let's see you get drunk."

Donahoo came around the front of the cab. He'd been a little afraid and now he was very afraid. He got a bottle of beer and drank it.

Marquisa had the gun on him. "Continue."

Donahoo drank another bottle of beer. He wondered if maybe he could throw the empty bottle at Marquisa. He thought no, if he was going to do that, he'd throw a full one, but he didn't think he was going to do that either; the gun was pointed at his heart.

"Continue."

Donahoo drank another. He looked around. The field drifted into the night in all directions. He wondered if anyone in the distant buildings could see the cab's overhead. If they did, what would they think? Probably nothing.

"Continue."

Donahoo got his fourth beer. He thought he should start spilling some of it. But Marquisa and the gun were very close.

"Uh, listen," Donahoo said. The gun was scaring him. "I think, about now, I'd really like to apologize to you, Marquisa. My heartfelt apologies."

Marquisa, grinning, said, "Do you like to get naked?"

Donahoo looked at him. Oh, whoa, he thought. This was going to go all the way. He was going to get drunk, and he was going to get naked, and, maybe, he was going to get killed.

"Take 'em off."

Donahoo undressed. His coat, his shirt, his pants. The shoes came off with them.

"All of it."

Donahoo took off his socks and shorts. He was naked.

"Have another beer."

Donahoo got it.

"Do you like to dance?"

Donahoo looked at Marquisa. He thought the guy was going too far. He didn't think he should be asked to dance. He was too big to dance. His whole life, he'd been too big, he'd never danced. He had shuffled around a bit when a lady absolutely demanded it. But he had never actually danced.

"Why don't you get the fucking thing over with?" he asked. "I don't want to dance. Why don't you just fucking kill me?"

"Dance."

Donahoo looked deep into Marquisa's eyes. He drank the beer and got another one. He started to dance, small steps at first, slow, tentative, but he got into the spirit of it after a while. He danced in the dark field for Marquisa.

"Continue."

Dancing. Dancing.

"It's too bad about Juarez. The wrong guy. The wrong guy at the wrong place at the wrong moment in history."

Donahoo wondered if he was hearing things. He sure heard that line a lot.

"Continue."

Dancing. Dancing.

Twelve

"Twenty dollars?"

"Yes. Pay the man."

"Jesus," Marino said—he was saving up to get married. "I don't think I've got that much cash. Can I write a check?"

The beggar said, "I don't want a check."

"How much money have you got?" Torres asked.

Marino counted. "Twelve bucks."

"I can loan you ten."

"Then it's settled," Donahoo said. "Now can we get the fuck outa here?"

Marino collected the ten, all in singles, and put it together with his two fives, and counted it out to the beggar, who watched with bright, bloodshot yellow eyes.

"I don't believe this," Marino said, counting.

Donahoo thought that he didn't believe it either, but when he woke up naked in the dead of night, practically freezing to death on the floor of the drunk tank in the Tijuana Jail, it had seemed like a fair price for a stinking dirty blanket, and besides, the guy had trusted him. He'd gotten it on good faith.

"It's a ripoff."

"Maybe you had to be there."

They were clustered on the walkway in front of the first cell on Tier A. Donahoo and Marino and Torres and the beggar and a guard the beggar had enlisted to make sure the money was paid and who was now collecting his five-dollar fee. Donahoo was putting on the clothes that Torres had brought, which were his, Torres's, clothes, not Donahoo's. Everything was too big. The pants, the jacket, the shoes. Especially the shoes. The guard, who spoke a little English, had pre-empted Marino, and was doing the translating.

"Tell him," Torres said, smiling and shaking his head, "next time he parties, I wish he'd invite me, designated babysitter. Twelve beers. That's a lot. But if you have a friend, there's less chance, when you pass out, you'll have your clothes stolen. Tell him I know a couple better places than a cow pasture."

The guard translated. Donahoo swished around in Torres's shoes. He thought it would have been nice if Torres had been generous enough to bring socks. He was going to say something but he already knew the logic of it. He was only going as far as El Greco. Why get all this lovely excrement on anything more than necessary?

"What's the matter? Cat got your tongue?"

The guard translated.

"Tell him," Donahoo said, swishing around, "to crawl up his leg and hide in his ass. Tell him to eat shit there."

The guard was probably smarter than he looked. He said, "Tell him yourself, Inspector Naked."

☐ ☐ ☐

They were out on the sidewalk before Donahoo remembered that he wanted to talk to Pedro Juarez. He apologized to Torres. It was a long way back and a steep climb to Tier C. But he'd be the one getting the blisters.

"Juarez?" Torres said, Marino translating now. "He's not here anymore."

Oh? Donahoo was getting cranky. "Where is he?"

"La Mesa Jail. The Baja State Penitentiary. I arranged for his transfer yesterday. It's such a pisshole here and he's got a cousin in La Mesa. The cousin's got a condo. He can stay with him there. It's going to be much nicer for him."

"A condo?"

"Yes. A *carraca*, which in Spanish means a hulk, but which here means a condo."

"In the penitentiary?"

"Yes."

Donahoo thought, fuck. He wondered if he should go into it a little deeper. Maybe something had been lost in the translation. Maybe they were talking about two different things. Maybe in Spanish a condo was a snake or something.

"A condo? Like a two-bedroom condo?"

"Yes."

"Uh," Donahoo said. He had a headache. He looked around.

Torres's LeBaron was parked at the curb illegally. The Toronado was across the street. It looked like it might be parked illegally too. Marino must have been in a hurry. He usually was pretty careful about things like that. "Can we see him?"

"Juarez? Anytime."

Donahoo made a motion. The keys. Marino handed them over.

"Uh, where do you think I could find Marquisa?" Donahoo asked then, casually, indicating that Marino should translate. "Would he be on patrol today?"

"No," Torres said when the question was posed. "That's a funny thing. I was going to tell you. Marquisa went on vacation today. He had some time coming, so he took it. He went to Guadalajara. I think he has family there."

Donahoo closed his eyes. He had a bad headache. It wasn't from the beer. It felt more like the aftereffects of some sort of drug. He also had a memory loss. Between the time that he was dancing, dancing, and the time he woke up in the drunk tank, no clothes, no badge, no wallet, no watch, no cellular. There was a blank there.

Marino was staring. Donahoo thought it must be the way he looked. Like a clown in Torres's big jacket and pants. In his big shoes.

"How long will he be away?"

"I think two weeks."

"How far is Guadalajara?"

"If you're driving, two days. You're flying, a few hours."

Torres said that and Marino translated and then Torres had an awakening. "Oh," he said. "Oh."

"Yeah," Donahoo said. He thought he'd need some help locating Marquisa. "What are you going to do about it?"

"Me?" Torres looked puzzled now. "I don't think I'm going to do anything. Whatever was done, it was done to you, Sargento. It wasn't done to me."

Donahoo stared at him. He couldn't believe it.

"Frankly, I think he let you off pretty lightly," Torres said. "No bullet holes. No bones broken." He got out his own car keys. "Mexicans are a very proud people. It doesn't pay to insult them." He tipped his cowboy hat and got into the LeBaron. "I've got a few errands. Why don't you get cleaned up? I'll see you at El Greco. Half an hour? We'll have breakfast at La Mesa."

"The pen?"

"Yes. They've got some pretty good restaurants there. I would recommend Chango's. They do a very nice *huevos rancheros*. But it might be too crowded. This is Thursday? It's Family Day."

The LeBaron sputtered away.

"What the fuck is going on?" Marino asked.

Donahoo sighed. He said, "The education of Sargento."

Thirteen

They arrived at La Mesa in time to witness a part of *El Grito*, The Cry, during which new prisoners walk down a narrow alley formed by guards, the prisoners calling out their names and their crimes. They yelled, "Enrique Salinas Valdez, *asesinato*," murder, and "Ricardo Arce, *violación y robo*," rape and robbery. Marino translated the crimes for Donahoo. Torres said the new prisoners would be required to do this several times until they were introduced to all the guards. In this way the guards would know who they were up against and why.

Donahoo hadn't seen anything like it. The huge crowd waiting outside the main gate, about a thousand men, women and children, was starting to pour in for Family Day. They were being processed haphazardly in a small holding pen with only a cursory check for drugs or weapons.

"Yes, it's a little like a world unto itself," Torres said. "They don't really care so much who or what gets in. They just want to be sure that the wrong guys don't get out."

He held up his badge and maneuvered them through the pen and another gate and into the main prison yard.

"It may be the most crowded penitentiary in Mexico. It was built to hold seven hundred, and, last count, it had about twenty-five hundred. They're also going to pack in about fifteen hundred visitors today. They open it up three times a week. Tuesday is Ladies' Day, for conjugal visits, and Thursday and Sunday are Family Days, which include conjugal visits, so what we've got here, a lot of the time, is a real fuck factory. It is jumping."

Donahoo looked around. It was like a little town had been hidden behind the towering prison walls. Two blocks of ramshackle restaurants, grocery stores, butcher shops and other businesses crowded around a two-acre dirt square with a small park and kiosk in the middle. Small shacks, fashioned from everything imaginable, most notably packing crates, perched atop the commercial enterprises, a second story. Donahoo thought that he had discovered the "condos." Some of them.

"Welcome to La Mesa," Torres said, Marino translating. "A thriving place. There are about sixty businesses here, mostly restaurants, because the prison food is so very, very bad."

Donahoo asked it like a setup. "How bad is it?"

"It's slop. Some of the prisoners who have to eat it get sick. You want to hear the menu? Breakfast is a watery soup, with potatoes, vegetables, some kind of old meat, sometimes rice or beans, a couple of tortillas. Lunch is the same but they get three tortillas. In the late afternoon, they are fed atole, a powdered cornmeal with sugar and milk, and a bolillo, a roll of bread. There's only one meal on Sunday."

"So the answer is to eat out? Or cook your own food?"

"Yes. The merchants here are all prisoners. They pay the prison maybe several hundred dollars a month to rent space. Friends and relatives on the outside act as jobbers. So it is quite a cauldron of free enterprise."

Donahoo said, "Where I come from, the general theory is, if you have convicts as bosses, the convicts will end up running the jail," and Torres, winking at Marino, told him, "Where I come from, I think maybe it is better if the convicts run the jails."

Visitors were pushing into the yard now. Prisoners were coming out of their tanks and shacks to meet them. It was a kind of bedlam. Already, a mariachi band was playing—it sounded like a request from someone far from home—"Guadalajara." Donahoo was reminded of Marquisa. He hadn't quite decided what to do about him yet. The only thing for sure, it was going to be something drastic, he thought. He also thought (the music was very romantic) of Catalina. He had called her office from El Greco. She wasn't in. The recorded message had said, in Spanish, "You have missed Catalina De Lourdes Venezuela. Please try again." Marino had done that and had translated it for him.

Torres took them to Las Tumbas, The Tombs, which was in one of the *tanques*, or tanks, flanking the yard. He explained that the new prisoners were housed there before being assigned to one of the main tanks. The Tombs door was open and most of its cells were empty. Torres asked a few of the remaining prisoners if they knew Pedro Juarez. None of them did.

"Well," Torres said. "He's new here. He wouldn't have a cell yet.

He'd still be sleeping here, in the corridor—they call it the free-way—so maybe he's not that well acquainted, moving from spot to spot."

Donahoo was suspending disbelief again. "Where does he keep his stuff?"

"With him. All you get is a blanket and a two-inch foam mattress."

They left to look for Juarez's cousin, Tribuno Rosetto Obeso, whose condo was in Tanque Z. Torres pointed out Chango's, where he hoped they could have breakfast, and also a second choice, The Godfather Steak House.

"Chango's is my first choice, though," he said, Marino translating. "Chango no longer owns it. He was released several years ago. But I must say the quality has kept up. Chango wanted the new owner to change the name but he refused, he said it was too famous, and after a while Chango decided not to press the matter, because the quality was kept up. You will like the new owner. Jesus Chowking Saville. How's that for a name? He's in here for an ax murder."

Marino asked, "Uh, he's the cook?"

"Yes, and your smiling waiter."

Juarez's cousin, Rosetto, was still asleep in his condo, which was a five-by-ten packing crate on an outside row, with ventilation, a hole in the building's wall, in Tanque Z. He came to the door sleepy and out of sorts.

He said to Torres, "He's not here," and then to Donahoo, more amiably, "Let me guess. Inspector Naked."

Donahoo got the drift. He couldn't believe the story had made the rounds so quickly. Only a few hours had passed and already it had reached the depths of La Mesa Jail. He wondered if perhaps it was in the morning paper. Catalina, had she read it? He said, "Actually, I'm only a *sargento.*"

Torres interceded. "Don't take offense. Please understand, we're still watching 'Streets of San Francisco,' so every gringo cop is an inspector, or else one with a very large nose."

Donahoo gave up. "In that case . . ."

Torres invited himself in. The place was small, but there was room for all of them, because it was sparsely furnished, a rug, a cot, a hot plate, a refrigerator, a television set, some boxes containing dishes and cooking utensils. Rosetto had retreated to the cot. Torres sat down on the floor. Donahoo and Marino followed his example.

"He's not in The Tombs?" Rosetto said then in Spanish, meaning Juarez. "He didn't go back after *El Grito?*"

Torres shook his head.

"What did they say there?"

"They don't know him."

Rosetto considered. He was a small man, very thin, very dark, with black marbles for eyes and snow-white hair. He looked like he might be pure Indian, no Spanish, but the chances of that were as slim as he was, and anyway the name belied it. Some *conquistador* had fucked somebody down the line. His age, like Torres's age, was open. He might be sixty. But then he might be eighty. Years in the sun had permanently tanned him. His skin was leather.

"Sargento here," Torres began, and then corrected himself. "The inspector here needs to see him. He has some questions."

"Oh, yeah?" Rosetto was watching Marino light a Pacifico. Marino, translating for Donahoo, passed Rosetto the package, which he kept. "He is going to have a time of it today."

"Maybe we should get a shouter?"

"Yes. I think he should do that."

"Do you know a good shouter here?"

"Yes. Domino. He's in the animal farm condo. The one with all the cartoons painted on it. Three doors down. But he is going to charge him a dollar."

"The price has gone up?"

"Yes."

Torres told Marino, holding out his hand, "You have all my money," and then, "I can remember when you could get a shouter for a penny. A nickel, a dime."

Marino gave Torres a dollar. Torres excused himself and went to look for Domino.

"What is a shouter?" Marino asked.

"Someone who shouts," Rosetto said. "Domino will go around shouting Juarez's name in the crowd, and when Juarez identifies himself, Domino will give him Torres's message, that the Naked Inspector wants to see him here in my condo, Tanque Z."

Donahoo was going to say something but then he remembered that he had given up. Instead, he said, just making conversation, he wanted to get to know the guy before he made any serious inquiries, "So, Juarez is going to be living with you?"

"Yes, he thinks so, but no, I don't think so," Rosetto answered. "He's got friends with money. He can rent his own condo. One like this? It's only two hundred dollars a month. There are others that are cheaper. If you just want to curl up in a hole like a dog, maybe twenty dollars."

Donahoo thought about that for a while. He said, "Friends with money. They're rich?"

"You can also buy a condo," Rosetto said, ignoring the question. "They have some very fancy places in here. Hot and cold running water. The works. They can cost thirty thousand dollars."

"Really? Who would buy them?"

"Drug traffickers, mostly. They have the money. It's not much different for them here. They can have their wives and children live with them. They can keep pets."

"Their children?"

"Yes. Until it's time to go to school."

Marino was translating as best he could. Rosseto was talking quickly and not answering directly. There was no way to expect what he might say.

"Juarez, you know, I have talked to him, and he struck me as a poor man," Donahoo said. "I'm surprised to hear he has rich friends." He waited for an answer. "Should I be?"

"Surprised? I don't know. I suppose that depends on how easily you are surprised."

Donahoo decided that he would wait for Torres. He leaned back against the packing crate wall and breathed the secondhand smoke of the two fiercely burning Pacificos. He thought that before this was over, he'd probably start smoking again, or maybe, the way it was going, he might try drugs for a change. He thought he might get on heroin.

"What are you in for?" Marino asked. He too was making conversation.

"Twenty years," Rosetto told him. "I'm going to serve my full term. If you work, they give you a day off for every two days you work, so it's too bad I'm retired. It's a good place to work too. They pay you by the piece. You earn more here than you can earn in Tijuana. My wife says it's quite a deal when you think about it. But it's only a good deal when she thinks about it. Who needs to work when they're retired?"

Torres came back after a while. He was smiling, and he had a six-pack of Tecate, which he passed around, then put the last two in the fridge.

"I'm sorry, they didn't have your brand," he said, looking at Donahoo, and then, "Well, we have our shouter, gentlemen. Domino is out there. Working the crowd."

Donahoo imagined that he could hear him. Juarez Juarez?

"I was just telling them, how the condo business works, nobody wants to be stuck in a cell with a bunch of *malendres*, bad guys, murderers, drug addicts, rapists, robbers, society's misfits," Rosetto said, sampling his beer. "I appreciate Juarez's problem. But I'm an old man. I need my privacy. He's going to have to rent his own."

Donahoo thought he would try once more. "He's got rich friends. Maybe he could buy one?" Marino translated.

"I don't think that's necessary," Torres began in Spanish.

"Yes, I know a good one coming up," Rosetto said, as if he hadn't heard Torres. "Small but nice. Free and clear. The paperwork is fouled up, there has to be a title search, but they'll get it straightened out all right. It's over in Tanque F. That's a quiet building. Two thousand dollars."

Torres looked at Donahoo. "Not necessary, right?"

Donahoo still had his headache. He said, "You know, you're fucking up my line of questioning, Carlos. I'm inquiring about rich friends, which is of consequence, and you are predicting early liberty, which, at best, is inconsequential, at least at the moment. You're not being much help."

Marino said, "How much of that do you want me to tell him?"

Donahoo thought about it. "None, I suppose." He wondered where Torres had got the Tecate. He wondered if he could get more. "There is an advantage sometimes to a language barrier."

"*Qué?*" Torres asked.

"See?" Donahoo said. He'd learned another word. What?

☐ ☐ ☐

It turned out that there was an ample supply and Torres's chit sufficient payment. Eating was out of the question. The lineup at Chango's was too long. The same everywhere. It was Family Day and a festive spirit prevailed. Donahoo, on the grounds of a hard night, gladly went along, forgetting most of his problems. He thought less of Marquisa and what Marquisa had said about Juarez and also less about Juarez. He thought hardly at all about Salvador Urquidez, aka Diablo. It got to where he was merely obsessing about how to explain/apologize to Catalina.

The four of them spent several hours drinking beer and discussing the pros and cons of the Mexican penitentiary system.

"How I see it," Donahoo said at last, he was becoming ponderous and couldn't help it, he had gotten rid of his headache. "There is an upside and a downside. The upside is you can get laid three times a week, which, frankly, is a lot more than I'm getting laid now. The downside is you can get killed."

"That's true," Torres said. "What I know, this is something that we could immediately substantiate if they were to bring in the army again, make a search, the prisoners are better armed than the guards in La Mesa. Right now, even without the army, I know where there's a prisoner, he's got an Uzi."

Marino asked, "The army comes in?"

"Sometimes. It can get out of hand here. Last year, sixteen prisoners died violently, felled by drug overdoses, shootings, and a couple of suicides."

"That's a lot."

"Now multiply it by all the jails in Mexico."

Rosetto was becoming patriotic. "You don't think California jails are as bad?"

Marino didn't know. He shrugged.

"I'm pretty sure you don't get laid as much," Donahoo said.

Rosetto nodded wisely. "You'd think that would be a deterrent. You'd think, in California, all the jails would be empty, wouldn't you? What kind of men are these in California?"

"Listen," Marino said, he had a spark of patriotism too. "The prison population in California is mostly Hispanic." He looked around. "After blacks, of course."

Donahoo thought it was starting to unravel. Rosseto had smoked all of Marino's Pacificos. There could be trouble.

Domino came in then. He was an earnest youngster, perhaps sixteen, anxious, tired, sweaty. He reported to Rosetto. "Listen, man, I've been all over twice, the fucker isn't here, man."

Torres said, "He's got to be here."

"Then why doesn't he answer?"

Yes, unravel, Donahoo thought. He got the last Tecate. He had a premonition. Somebody else would take it if he didn't. Also, that Juarez wasn't just missing, he was gone.

"I'm keeping the dollar, man," Domino said.

They sat staring at each other for a while. Finally Torres pushed up. He didn't say anything. He left, taking Domino.

"Juarez, he's got some bad ideas, but he's a good man," Rosetto said. He started to clean up. "I don't think . . ." He stopped, plainly worried. "Maybe I'm changing my mind. Maybe he should stay here until he gets his own place."

"What kind of bad ideas?" Donahoo asked.

"He thinks he can fix things."

"Where? In Tijuana?"

"In Mexico."

Donahoo finished the Tecate. He crumpled the can. "What do you think?"

"I think things fix themselves." Rosetto took the crumpled can. He was cleaning up. "Eventually."

Donahoo thought that eventually was a long time. "You said rich friends. Can you give me the name of a rich friend? One?"

"You know," Rosetto said, as if he hadn't heard. "It used to be that there were twelve ruling families in Mexico. Now I am told that there are thirty ruling families. So you see how well we are progressing? In a million years we'll be a democracy."

Torres came back. He looked shaken. He had his cowboy hat off. He was holding it like he was in church.

Donahoo used the word he had learned. *"Qué?"*

"I'm not sure," Torres said solemnly, Marino translating. He sat down on the cot. He put the hat on his knees. "At the morning *lista*—when the prisoners are required to be accounted for?—the guards couldn't find Juarez. They weren't too worried. That sometimes happens in The Tombs. It is so crowded. But now they have found a whore slaughtered in The Labyrinth. The pile of tiny *carracas* in Tanque B? The killer stole all her clothes."

They waited for him to finish.

"There is speculation that Juarez murdered her. It is also speculated that he has escaped disguised as a *prostituta.*"

Now there was silence.

Rosetto was next to Donahoo. He whispered in his ear. "You wanted a name? One rich friend? Her name was Deedee Hernandez."

Torres said, a lament, "Why would Juarez do anything so stupid?"

Now Donahoo was getting his headache back. He took hold of Marino. "Tell him he asks too much of the Naked Inspector."

Fourteen

Catalina was sitting under a market umbrella in the sidewalk café part, which was the main part, of Banana Verde. The other part was a small bar, in the manner of an oyster bar, customers could sit there and annoy the chef/bartender, who was very busy. Donahoo thought that it must have been Catalina, sitting at the same table, under the same umbrella, when he passed the night before, as Marquisa's prisoner. He thought it must be her favorite table. Or perhaps her favorite umbrella.

He crossed Revolución with trepidation. She didn't look very happy. Nor had she sounded pleased on the phone. "Actually," she had said, "I have other plans, a dashing playboy has invited me to the opera, then we're going to spend the evening on his yacht, but seeing how it is you, I will, of course, disappoint him."

Donahoo thought that he would try to explain things to her as best he could. If she accepted his story, it was because, impossibly, she was interested in him. Or, less impossibly, because she was a part, as he had suspected from the start, of Carlos Torres's hidden agenda. Either way he couldn't lose. Because either way he would be with her for a while. So why the trepidation? Well, for one thing, he was in Tijuana, and he was crossing—*trying* to cross—a street.

He was also trying to think of something to say for openers. You are very beautiful tonight. He had thought of saying that. The street sparkles with a thousand passing taillights. Look closer—and they become stars in your eyes.

He said, "There you are."

She looked at him. "Yes."

Donahoo joined her at a small metal table halfway out on the sidewalk. She was in a trifle more disarray than he was used to. Her rose silk pleated dress, which buttoned all the way up the front, was buttoned crooked, so that the collar didn't match at the top. One end was higher than other, and it was turned up, while the other was not. Her messy bun was all over the place. It looked like a manic spider fern.

"Thank you for coming."

"I had to eat anyway."

He wondered if the dress, and the bun too, were more props, like the thick glasses with the baby-blue, red-speckled frames. Perhaps it was prop time? He thought he should have brought her flowers. He had wanted to, but there weren't any flower shops, the whole walk from El Greco. He would have bought her a present but he hadn't seen anything suitable. There were a thousand things to buy but nothing worked. It was too early for jewelry. Too uncertain for a chess set. Too late for perfume? The way she was looking at him, he must smell pretty bad.

"I can explain," he said. He wondered how often she had heard that. But maybe she hadn't heard the next part very often. Although, again, this was Tijuana. "I was kidnaped."

"I know."

"You *know*?"

"Yes. Carlos told me. Also, it's in the paper, Inspector Naked. The whole story. It takes up half a gossip column. Marquisa, I fear, must have phoned it in, before going on vacation."

Donahoo stared at her. "Well, Jesus Christ, if you know, why are you angry?"

"Because you let him."

"Marquisa? I *let* him? The sonofabitch had a gun, okay? He got the drop on me."

She appeared to relent somewhat. "Oh? What is the drop?"

"The advantage."

"So you did let him?"

"What?"

"Get the drop."

"Yes."

"Yes."

"Yes," Donahoo admitted, because it was true, and because, apparently, she wasn't going to have it any other way. He got a guacamole-smeared menu. He thought fuck. If she was so devastated by his unmanly behavior, why, for God's sake, had she come? Why not just kiss him off on the phone? Why bring him here and rub his nose in it? "It was stupid of me to let my guard down that way. I thought, inasmuch as he is a fellow police officer, I could, to some small degree, relax in his presence. But no, stupidly, carelessly, and to my everlasting regret, I let him get the drop. Now, are you satisfied?"

"No."

No? "Well," Donahoo said, angry. "There are several things that can happen now. One, I can leave. Two, I can stay. Three, I can kick your bony ass. Which is it that you want?"

"I beg your pardon?"

"You heard me."

"It's not bony."

"No. It isn't."

"Then why did you say it?"

"It's an expression."

"Like the drop?"

"God. Yes, like the drop."

"You know," she said, getting her purse. "We have an expression in Spanish. *'Lo siento. Necesito salir.'* "

"Which when translated means?"

"You were nicer when you wanted something."

Donahoo put his menu aside. He was pretty sure that wasn't what she had said. He began, "That wasn't . . ." but she cut him off.

"No," she admitted. "It was just something that occurred to me. I would like to go home now." She stood up. "If you will excuse me."

"No."

"No?"

"Sit down," Donahoo said, he was still angry. He had quite a long speech forming in his mind. Let's talk about what you want. If there is something you have to say, say it. Is it something Carlos Torres told you to say or do? If so, say or do it. This is your last chance to do so. I won't be as receptive later. He thought he could say that and a lot more. He said, "Please."

She was staring at him blankly.

"Your dress is buttoned crooked."

She flushed and returned to her chair. "I know. I dressed in a hurry." She brought a hand up to her collar. "I couldn't make up my mind what to wear and then the taxi came and started honking. It's not something you can rectify driving along and having somebody look at you in the rearview mirror. You know exactly what they're thinking. I was going to fix it in the washroom here . . ." She finally met his gaze. ". . . and of course it is hammered up tighter than a nun's diary."

"Did you get them all wrong?"

"What?"

"The buttons."

"Yes. Right from the bottom."

"How many are there?"

"I don't know. A lot."

"I used to do that with cardigan sweaters," Donahoo told her. He got the menu again. "It's funny, I used to do it with cardigans, but not with shirts."

"Yes. I know what you mean. It's really odd, actually. I never do it with blouses."

"Do you do it with cardigans?"

"I never had a cardigan."

"Good. You'd probably muck it up. What do you want to eat?"

"How rich are you tonight? Could you buy me a lobster?"

He'd already seen it on the menu. It was from Puerto Nuevo. Ten dollars. "Yes. I'll use your flower money."

"You were going to buy me flowers?"

"Was," Donahoo said.

"Are we friends again?"

"I hope so."

□   □   □

He walked her home. It was a pleasant evening and still early and therefore safe. Revolución and its side streets were crowded. Most of the shops were open.

She lived on Avenida Mutualismo, several blocks west, still in Zona Central, so that it was also well lit, and with a lot of foot traffic. Donahoo thought that he would be uncomfortable on a dark street with no one around. The previous night's encounter with Marquisa had left him edgy and unnerved. He had thought for a while that he was going to be killed. That was worse—but not much worse?—than being made a fool of.

"I have a list," he said, getting it out of his pocket. They were walking along. "Perhaps we could discuss it now?" He had been going to discuss it at dinner but had been distracted. She had asked a lot of questions and he had answered them at greater length and with more honesty than he normally preferred. She had asked, specifically, if he and his former wife, Monica, found time to talk together a lot, and he had disclosed that the thing they said most often to each other was, 'Call him.' Monica had a miniature daschund, Beemer, or BMW, for Black Mucky Worm, and it was always bothering one or the other of them, and so they were always saying, 'Call him.' Monica still had Beemer. He had the cat, Oscar.

"Yes. Please. The list."

"Okay." It was in code. Nobody would ever figure it out. VBG. That was at the top. Salvador Urquidez, aka Diablo. A very bad guy. "I checked up on Diablo. You were right. He's a sonofabitch."

"Snot, and a maggot wouldn't eat him?"

"Yes."

"Why would you check up on him?"

"I don't know. Because you mentioned him, I guess."

Her pace had increased slightly. She was about a half step ahead. "Maybe that's not something you should do."

"Why not?"

She was moving away. "I don't know. It's not your business."

Donahoo remembered Torres saying exactly the same thing. Word for word. Partly word for word. In La Mesa Jail after too many Tecate. 'Fuck, piss, shit, Diablo is not your business, Sargento. He is our business.' He took her arm. "Wait up."

She pulled free and stopped and looked him. "Don't you know how to stay out of trouble?"

Donahoo went back to his list. If he persisted, they'd get back to Marquisa, and Marquisa hadn't been resolved, he was like a sharp pointed stick between them. If they got too close the stick would puncture him and his new hopes. She hadn't put it there. He had done it to himself. He had stupidly stuck it there and he stupidly wouldn't let her take it away. It was going to stay until Marquisa got resolved.

FRENZ. That was the second entry. "Torres suggested I raise this question with you. He said you might have friends in Mexico City who would know. Perhaps he has talked to you about it?"

"About what?"

"Jorge Hernandez's friendship with the Presidente. Torres says it is deep and close but he doesn't have any details. Do you know someone who might know how long they've been friends? Whether it's social or business or . . . ."

"Political?"

He looked at her. "Yes. What I thought, why the Presidente is so interested in this murder—the reason he wants it solved so badly?—why is that? Maybe he has something in mind for Hernandez but first he must be sure about who killed Deedee? It wouldn't look very good if it were to come out later? He's in cahoots with a killer."

"It never does."

"So do you suppose you could help with that?"

"Maybe."

"Fine." Donahoo checked his list. $. "How rich is Hernandez? What is the source?"

"I know someone who might know."

"Good." The next entry was JJ. Someone might guess that. Juarez Juarez? "The first time we talked. I suggested that you might, at some point, represent Juarez, and you didn't deny it, so what I was wondering, are you acquainted with him?"

"In a small way. He is a friend of a friend of a friend. I met him a few times. We talked briefly. That sort of thing."

"Politics?"

"Are there other topics?"

Donahoo laughed. "With Juarez, you mean?"

"Yes. He's PAN. I'm PAN. We talked politics."

"Do you know any reason why he would break out of La Mesa Jail?"

"Other than to escape?"

"Torres wondered how he could be so stupid. But maybe he's not. It's possible that Juarez did kill Deedee Hernandez. And that he was afraid he was going to be found out." He looked at her. He waited for her to look at him. "I am going to say this for you, so you won't have to say it. Now that I'm on the case."

"You were always this modest?"

"No. It came to me. At the urgings of others. Why do you think he wanted to escape? He's guilty. Forget that. What other reason comes to mind?"

"You mean is it political?"

"Maybe."

"I don't know," she said thoughtfully. "This is something that hadn't occurred to me. Not that he is guilty. But that there might be a political connection. I would still say that he is innocent. Why would he do it? He is not that type of person. He is a malcontent, perhaps. Perhaps with reason. But not a rapist and a killer. Nor did he kill the prostitute. It isn't in his nature."

"But you don't know him."

"No. I am with speaking with my heart."

"Which you trust more?"

"Sometimes."

They had come to Avenida Mutualismo. It was more residential here. Fewer shops. But still offices.

Donahoo asked it out of the blue. "Do you think Juarez might have been a friend of Deedee Hernandez?"

The idea obviously amused her. She smiled. "I don't think so. Wrong circle. But you never know, I suppose. Have you asked Carlos?"

"Torres? He laughed."

"Then you have your answer. Carlos is the society expert. He finds it fascinating."

Donahoo wished that he did. Have the answer, that is. He wondered about Juarez's cousin, Tribuno Rosetto Obeso, retired in La Mesa Jail. The old man's motive. Why would Rosetto tell him, Donahoo, that Juarez was a friend of Deedee Hernandez, and not tell Torres? Donahoo could only think of one reason. That Rosetto was afraid to share with Torres. Yet he felt it important enough to share with him. So he had to respect the old man's confidence. He had to protect his source. "How about Juarez's political friends?"

Catalina grew serious again. "Do you know what it is like in the PAN? It is like it is in any political party. Everybody is your friend and nobody is. It changes all the time. The power shifts, the agenda turns, the loyalty adjusts."

"I would like to talk to some."

"Of his political friends? Why?"

"I have a theory."

"Oh? What is it?"

Donahoo wondered. Should he tell her? He couldn't think what harm it would do. If she was the enemy, then Torres was the enemy, and if Torres was, then he should go home now and come back later to fix Marquisa. "I was wondering why he was circulating pamphlets that morning in Lomas de Agua Caliente."

"He always circulated pamphlets."

"Yes. But why there and why then? It didn't occur to me to ask when I saw him in the Tijuana Jail. Now, I've been wondering, what if somebody else was supposed to do it, and, you know, for some reason, he took their place?"

She was looking at him. He was thinking of what Marquisa had said when he was dancing. He shrugged. "The wrong place. The wrong time."

"Marquisa framed the wrong guy?" She stopped, considered. "Well. You've certainly brought me full circle, haven't you?"

"Oh? You live here?"

"Yes, as a matter of fact," she said, smiling. "I'm sorry. Did I spoil your joke?" She pointed across the street, to an ornate concrete building with shops on the street level and, above, with bay windows, what looked like a mix of apartments and offices, there were names painted on some of the windows and curtains at others. "Tomorrow I will ask someone in the PAN. What you want are the names of Juarez's two or three closest political friends. Those whom he might trade back and forth with distributing pamphlets."

"Yes."

"Very well. Thank you for a nice evening. I did not think it was going to be so pleasant but I enjoyed it very much. I enjoyed you and I enjoyed the lobster."

He wondered if he should ask if he could see her again.

"If you are going to kiss me, you should kiss me here, I think," she said, waiting. "My father watches like a *halcón*. That's a hawk."

He looked at her. He had in no way expected the invitation.

She raised on tiptoe to kiss him. Then turned and ran.

He watched her hurry across the street to the concrete building. It had a name. It was set, carved deeply, over the entrance, PEREGRINAR. Oddly, he knew what it meant. He had been thumbing through his new *diccionario*. Looking for words that he could drop casually and raise an eyebrow. He had come across *peregrinar* and had been surprised at the length of the meaning in English. To travel as a pilgrim. To journey through life.

He shouted after her. He had another question. "That gossip column. Did it mention that I danced?"

"Yes. The Highland fling."

"Have you really got a father?"

"Honest. And he's almost as old as you!"

He turned and started for El Greco. It was only a few blocks but he felt drained and he wished he had the Toronado. Marino had it again in San Diego, courting the lovely Theresa, he'd brought it back, this morning, without additional scuff marks, and therefore could be trusted.

Old, huh? He wondered if he was too old. That had never bothered him before. What bothered him, normally, was how he looked, which was something like Cocos, a guy who ought to be carrying a rock. He was a bit big for a lady and he had a busted nose and his mouth was too hard and he needed a shave after he shaved and he always needed a haircut. He had been kind of good-looking at one time. But that was before the nose. Before the nose and before he became a cop.

Fifteen

The next morning they went looking for Juarez. Torres said it was a priority for him. It was on his authority that Juarez had been transfered to La Mesa from the Tijuana Jail. And, of course, he, Torres, was in La Mesa when Juarez escaped, so that appeared a bit fishy. The bright side was that another escaped prisoner was also suspected in the murder of the *prostituta*. Juarez didn't necessarily kill her to win his freedom.

Donahoo figured they weren't looking for Juarez so much as looking for informants who might know where they should look. He gathered that without much help from Marino. His interpreter, again, was going to take awhile to recover, he was always a little benumbed after a session with Theresa.

Before, Donahoo would have been jealous, Marino dragging in at two in the morning, smiling like a rock cod. Awakened, Donahoo would have stayed awake, trying to imagine, while Marino slept, the kind of passion that would not permit a young lady time to kick off her shoes. "Perhaps they were laced?"

"What?" Marino asked.

"Nothing," Donahoo said quickly, embarrassed. He had been daydreaming. Before, he would have been jealous, but last night he had kissed Catalina, or, more correctly, she had kissed him, and the Toronado's roof liner could be in fucking shreds for all he cared, it was a new ball game.

They had been to Rick's in Zona Norte's "Little Saigon," to a careful selection of bars along Revolución, El Tigre, Bol Corona, Tia Juana Tilly's and Tequila Circo, all hangouts for the locals. To as many restaurants, Alcazar de Rio, Bocacio's, La Lena and Pedrin's. To what was, Torres said, if not the best, the most expensive hotel, Fiesta Americana. They had been again to the Caliente Book and the Jai Alai Palace. Now, a favorite place for pickpockets, they were in the plaza at the Omnimax Theater.

117

Everywhere Torres had met people he knew. Some of them
were other cops. Some of them were crooks. Often there were
cops and crooks together. Torres, when this happened, would say
hello to the cops, but not to the crooks. He would only say hello
to crooks when they were not with cops. Donahoo decided that
Torres didn't want to validate cops with crooks. Yet, apparently,
he still collected *mordida*. He had taken an obvious thug into the
toilet at the Caliente Book. And, at the Jai Alai, where the bets
were made from the stands, by stuffing money into cut tennis
balls, then tossing them to the bookies down front, and winnings
were paid by the same method, Torres had caught, and kept, a
purposely wayward ball, to no one's surprise or protest. He had
calmly pocketed it.

"I don't know how he could be so stupid," Torres kept saying,
meaning Juarez. "To run away is an admission of guilt. It is like
signing a confession."

"That he stole a handkerchief?"

Torres gave him a dirty look.

"Hey, that is the charge," Donahoo reminded him, Marino translating. "The only formal accusation."

"Not for long," Torres grumbled. "What would you like to bet?
The District Attorney files a murder charge today? Juarez ran.
Therefore he is guilty. How much?"

Donahoo backed down. If, as Torres claimed, the whole Baja
justice system, such as it was, was trying to kiss the Presidente's
ass, then that could be a way to go, all right.

"We've got to find him first," Torres said, looking around, as if
Juarez might be hiding, like a rabbit, under a bush. "He might
have some other explanation. It might be something we could
work with."

Donahoo got a slip of paper from his pocket. Another list, but
not a long one, just two names. He had been waiting for a good
time to introduce them. Now, Torres at the end of his string,
seemed like a good time.

"I talked, as you suggested, to Catalina," Donahoo began. "She
is going to speak to her friends in Mexico City."

Torres was looking at him impatiently.

"I also asked her for the names of some of Juarez's political
friends. She called this morning with two of them." Donahoo read
them from the slip of paper. "Jose Verdugo Melgoza. Keno Ortiz
Gonzales."

There was no reaction.

"I realize," Donahoo said, "you didn't talk to them before, because you believed Juarez innocent, but now that you are not so sure, maybe you would want to talk to them."

"They're his friends. You think they'll say where he is hiding?"

Donahoo shrugged. "I don't know. But that's what you want to talk to them about. I want to talk to them about something else."

"Really? What is that?"

"Trading places. A thought prompted by Marquisa. He said something to me, a worn bit of philosophy. That people, through no real fault of their own, arrive in the wrong place at the wrong time."

Torres mulled that for a while. Donahoo thought that one of Torres's more pleasing traits was that he was almost always pretty amenable.

"Well, it can't do any harm, I suppose," Torres said finally. He took the piece of paper. "These places? It's where they work?"

"Yes."

"Then let's go."

He moved away without waiting for an answer.

"What I also thought," Donahoo said, he'd again been waiting for the right time. "Is there any chance of my getting a look at . . ."

Marino's translation ended there. Torres stopped, waited, turned.

"Salvador Urquidez," Donahoo said directly to him, because the name was the same in any language. "Diablo."

Torres stared at him. He seemed more distressed than puzzled.

"Not to speak to, of course. Not to approach. I just want to look at him."

"What the fuck for?"

Marino, translating, had the same sort of uncertain expression, anxious and bewildered.

Donahoo didn't know what the fuck for. It had become, for some unknown reason, without rational explanation, a *need*. It had been growing in him ever since Catalina had mentioned Urquidez in the Bamboo Terrace. 'Very powerful and very brutal.' It had spurted up again last night. 'Snot, and a maggot wouldn't eat him.' "I want to see him. I want to see what he looks like."

"Jesus Christ," Torres said. "You want to *look*?"

"Yes."

Marino said, "Lewis said stay away."

"God*damn* you!" Donahoo told him. "Do your job. And keep your mouth shut."

"Hey," Torres said. "Hey." He was suddenly between them. "Let's not get into a fistfight. Cruz, tell him, this is my decision, not Lewis's, okay? We're not going to 'look' at Diablo. There is no value in doing that. Permission denied." He said to Donahoo, "So, you talked to Catalina?"

"Is that your final answer?"

"Yes."

"Oh? And I was just thinking. How you are usually amenable."

"This is different. You look for him, I wonder why. You look *at* him, *he* wonders why. Trust me in this instance, Sargento. He is best left alone. You don't want Diablo wondering why."

Donahoo weighed how strongly he should argue and when. He thought that it was a relatively simple request. If, as everyone claimed, Urquidez operated openly, surely he could be seen? Was everyone so afraid of this snot that they could not even look upon him?

Torres, moving away again, said, "She's a pretty girl," and Donahoo, briefly deflated, thought yes, but sometimes she wears glasses and she's got a father. He made a promise to himself. Fuck Lewis, and fuck Torres too. Before this was over, he was going to fix Marquisa, and he was going to look at Urquidez. He was going to do both of those things, and, if he got really lucky, he was going to solve the Hernandez murder case. If he got luckier still—this is what he was starting to think—he was going to *peregrinar*, journey through life, with Catalina De Lourdes Venezuela. He thought that he was a lucky cop, and that when you are lucky, anything is possible.

☐ ☐ ☐

José Verdugo Melgoza owned an auto upholstery shop on Calle Segunda Avenida Benito Juarez in Zona Central. Not a shop, actually. It was more like a roadside stand. Some sticks and corrugated iron patched together to form a shelter. Enough room to work on two cars at a time.

Today there was just the one car. It was an old Monte Carlo, maybe a '73, a '74. The top had been sawn off to make a convertible that didn't convert. The top was off, permanently. Verdugo was applying an upholstered trim, a kind of puff cushion, atop the jagged metal.

Dressed in overalls, no shirt, a Chargers cap, jailhouse tattoos rippling, Verdugo was working on it industriously as he talked to Torres. He was a short, stocky man with a machinist's face, his eyes close together for close work. The tools of his trade were piled on a small bench. An old industrial sewing machine. Bolts of cloth and Naugahyde. Padding. Fasteners. Glue.

Donahoo thought the Monte was going to look pretty good when it was finished. Marino thought that only an idiot would saw the top off a car.

"Yeah, well, there's no roof liner to muck up, is there?" Donahoo pointed out, he had to get that in, he was still pissed at Marino for mentioning Lewis. He was starting to imagine Theresa kicking around strenuously in the wild blue yonder. "A girl could really go at it."

Marino flushed red.

"Hey, you two," Torres complained. "Can we do this together? I don't know what you want to ask this guy."

Torres had already asked Verdugo what he wanted to ask. Question, did he know where Juarez was? Answer, no. Could he think where he might go? No.

"Okay," Donahoo said, it was his turn. "Did you cut that top off yourself? Or did somebody bring it to you that way?"

Marino translated and Vergudo answered at length in Spanish.

"He says some idiot gringo asshole did it," Marino reported. "He says it spoils the car."

"Hey," Verdugo complained. He was a little guy but he had a temper. "That's bullshit." He looked at Donahoo. "Where the fuck did you find this mallie? He can't translate squat."

Marino flushed again.

"So where did you learn English?" Donahoo asked, he was trying to be angry, but actually he thought it was funny. "Maybe I'll hire you. Get rid of this devious sack of shit."

Verdugo stopped working. He grinned. "San Diego. I lived there fifteen years. My family is still there. Lots of relatives. But I don't know. This is my country. My heart is here. Besides, in San Diego, try as you might, you can't start a business on the side of the road. They're over-regulated up there."

"What about the Monte? Who's the genius?"

"I wish it was mine. I already could have sold it six times."

"So go into the business."

"Maybe. But it takes capital, huh? And there are not that many cherry Monte Carlos around. And when they are cherry, the guy usually wants an arm and a leg. So I don't know. Maybe, maybe not. I know I could sell 'em but I don't know about the rest of it."

Torres said, "Pardon me?"

"You've got a question?" Donahoo asked.

"I thought this was a police matter?"

"Well, you know, you could do it with a different car," Donahoo told Verdugo. "Maybe—let me think here—maybe a Chevelle?"

Verdugo shook his head. "Same problem. If it's cherry . . ." He pointed like he thought there might a cherry moon in the sky today. Very unlikely. "No way, José."

"It's gotta be cherry?"

"If it's a convertible?"

"You're right." Donahoo considered. Torres was looking at him. "Listen, did you ever think Peugeot, Verdugo? Those little buggers . . ." He caught himself. "No. Forget it. I think they're all four-door. They'd look like fucking Nazi staff cars."

"They might be cute."

"Maybe. You couldn't be sure till you saw one."

"It would be a gamble."

"What if you drew it first?"

Torres said, "Jesus Christ."

"Okay," Donahoo said, frowning. He thought that he had been patient with Torres. All those long hikes back to all those toilets. "Verdugo. Help me here. I need to know something about Juarez. The day he was arrested—the morning Deedee Hernandez was found murdered?—Juarez was circulating political pamphlets in Lomas de Agua Caliente. What I wondered, you're a friend of his, this is something you might know—did he happen to be doing that for somebody . . ."

Donahoo stopped. He knew he had something. He could see it in Verdugo's eyes.

". . . else?" Donahoo said. "Maybe he took their place for some reason?"

"Yeah. He subbed for me."

"You?"

"Uh huh. Something came up. A funeral, actually. My uncle's. So I asked Juarez to do it for me and he said sure."

Donahoo could see his theory falling apart. If framing Juarez didn't make any sense, then framing Verdugo made less sense. Blame a taxi driver. Blame an auto upholster. Except for having a patsy, nothing else was gained. Juarez, Verdugo. It didn't matter. Anybody would do when picking on no-account small-fry. They were readily interchangeable.

Marino had been translating for Torres, who said, "There goes that."

"Yes."

"The funny thing," Verdugo said, returning to his work. "I wasn't assigned there. Playa always does Lomas de Agua Caliente. He likes to stick it to the crème de la crème. In his mind, he's not circulating pamphlets, you know? He's littering their fucking streets. Anyway, he had a cold, he asked me to do it for him, I said okay. Then my uncle dies and the funeral is the next day." Verdugo laid down a strip of precut padding. "They bury 'em fast here. Dead today, gone tomorrow. It's what they say." He grinned. "It's what they do."

"Playa?"

"Playa Pampano. That's all anybody calls him. I don't know his real first name. They call him Playa, the beach, because he says he's the common man, he owns it. That's all the common man owns in Mexico. The sun and the moon, the stars. The wind and the rain. The beach."

Donahoo looked at Torres. "Playa Pampano. Do you know him?"

"Yes, I do," Torres told him, Marino translating. "He's got a criminal record. Organizing a demonstration with intent to commit a crime. Defying state authority. Damaging property. Striking a police officer. Resisting arrest. He's a shit-disturber. He's never happy. He used to be a political power and now he is nothing and he cannot accept that and so he just makes trouble. You can ask Catalina. Within the PAN, when the party turns right, Playa turns left. When it goes forward, he hangs back. He is a real pain in the ass."

"*Used* to be a power. What does that mean?"

"He headed Grupo Tijuana. That was a bunch of squatters who seized some disputed vacant land that is now Colonia Third of December. At one time Playa could deliver ten thousand colonia votes in return for the state's non-retaliation. But then the state got smart and bought the land from its rightful owner and sold lots to the peasants for a very cheap price and they weren't there illegally any more. That undercut Playa and he lost all his power. The illegality of the colonia was the reason for Playa's existence."

"But he'd still have enemies?"

"Does the tide come in?"

"In both camps?"

"Does it go out?"

"Torres," Donahoo said. An idea was forming. It made him happy and sad at the same time. "Try not to speak to me in questions, I have enough of my own. Do you know what Playa looks like?"

"I don't know," Torres said, Marino translating. "What he looks like? Jesus Christ. He looks like a fucking Mexican."

Verdugo was pulling a photo off the makeshift wall behind his workbench. "This is him."

Donahoo took it. He knew before he inspected it. Playa Pampano, shit-disturber, real pain in the ass, marching in a protest parade with Verdugo, holding a banner on high, YANQUIS GO HOME. Donahoo thought that Playa looked like a Mexican, all right, and that there was a resemblance, quite a marked resemblance, to Pedro Juarez. He thought that a crooked cop who was new to town and had only a description could make a mistake. He could mistake Juarez for Playa. He could arrest him. He could put in motion a frameup for murder. And he could take it to the point where there was no turning back. After all, there was only one handkerchief, and it had been found on Pedro Juarez, not Playa Pampano.

"What do you think?" Donahoo asked, passing the photo to Torres, and Torres, not waiting for the translation, said, "That fucking Marquisa," and Donahoo knew, in his heart of hearts, that he might look forever and never find the prick. He was gone.

☐ ☐ ☐

They went looking for Playa. He wasn't at work at the Alborozar, a restaurant in Independencia, where he was a waiter. They hadn't seen him there since what? The day before yesterday? The owner was thinking of firing him. It was the same story where he lived, in a shared room in a crowded house in Jardines de la Mesa. The landlady and other lodgers had no idea where he was. He had disappeared. The day before yesterday.

"I'd bet," Donahoo said, he was becoming a betting man, "I'd bet, when we find Playa, we find Juarez."

Torres nodded. He looked very unhappy. Donahoo wondered if, like him, Torres was thinking more about finding Marquisa. Finally Torres said, sounding defeated, "Shit. Where would they go?"

"Maybe the beach?" Marino suggested. He also said it in Spanish. *"Quizá la playa?"*

Torres got into the LeBaron. They fitted in after him. Donahoo in the backseat, as usual, because that was how it worked best, for translating.

Donahoo said, "Maybe we could put out an APB," and Marino said, "Do they have an All Points Bulletin down here?" and Donahoo said, "Actually, I was thinking of an All Playas Bulletin." He was still pissed at Marino for mentioning Lewis.

Marino said, "When are you gonna get off my back?" and Donahoo said, "Not anytime soon."

Torres didn't say anything. Yeah, Donahoo decided. He's thinking about finding Marquisa. He leaned back into the pleasure of that idea. He closed his eyes. He drifted away with his thoughts. Catalina running across the street to PEREGRINAR. She had looked awfully good. The Monte had also looked pretty good. He wondered about the Toronado. That clunker with its top off. Naw, he thought.

Sixteen

They were at the Agua Caliente Galgódromo, the dog track, which, when the ponies were running, was the Agua Caliente Hipódromo. Donahoo, Torres and Marino, who, this evening, was staying in Tijuana, not off cavorting with the lovely Theresa. They were drinking lots of Dos XXs and losing lots of money and thinking very little about Marquisa and only a bit about Playa and Juarez. Marquisa was too far and long gone for them to worry about right now. He was in Guadalajara, or, which was equally possible, maybe Puerto Vallarta. A man can have relatives anywhere, so perhaps even Mexico City. If he was smart, and he was smart, he was long gone. Not smart enough, in the heat of the moment, to distinguish between Playa Pompano and Pedro Juarez, but smart enough, Donahoo thought—he'd had quite a bit of Dos XXs to drink—smart enough to get his smart ass out of Tijuana. There was an APB, an All Pricks Bulletin, out for him, and, maybe, they were going to find him somewhere, in which case there would be a reckoning, but in the meantime, tonight at the galgódromo, he, Donahoo, could stop looking over his shoulder.

Big mistake.

Donahoo wasn't quite certain when that realization started to take hold. It might have been in the toilet, when a man who looked like a thug told another man who also looked like a thug, *"Ese hombre,"* that man. Donahoo knew this from his *diccionario*. He had been looking up "That woman" and it was a natural bonus. Or, another possibility, when the realization started to take hold, it might have been when the two men who looked like thugs were joined, in the grandstand, by another man who looked like a thug and they all looked at him, Donahoo, as if to say, *Sí, ese hombre*. Donahoo thought that he would remember the last man. His face had a certain stolid acceptance. It would make a good kickplate.

"You know, you were right, Sargento," Torres was saying, Marino translating. They hadn't been talking about the case but now they were. Torres's choice. "I am sure of it now. It all revolves around the pamphlets and the trading of places. I have my own theory, gradually arrived at, but I don't wish to take anything away from you, so it is my pleasure to hear your theory first."

Really? Donahoo thought that was either unexpectedly nice of him or inordinately cautious. He almost declined—he could fall on his face here—but it proved too much to resist. He was pretty sure he had it figured out.

"This is just speculation," he began slowly. He'd have to think about Marquisa now. He'd have to talk about him. He hadn't been doing that for a while. So this was going to be like a dam bursting. A torrent released? He said, "The key—and this could be self-serving—the key, I think, is Marquisa. The twisted prick got me going in the wrong direction. You already know what I think about Deedee's bedroom window. Marquisa locked it on a shitty impulse just to fuck with your head. And that made me think his taking the handkerchief was another impulse. And that framing Juarez was yet another impluse. He was just a bad bastard doing all the mindless harm he could do."

"Yes."

"But now I think stealing the handkerchief and framing Juarez were calculated acts in a frameup. Try this: Someone, for whatever reason, decides to murder Deedee Hernandez, and, again for whatever reason, they decide to put the blame on Playa Pampano, using Marquisa. They expect Playa to be distributing his pamphlets that morning in Lomas de Agua Caliente. Not Juarez. Playa."

"Yes."

"Okay, then, if we accept Playa's frameup, we must have Deedee's premeditated murder, not the random act of a prowler or rapist. One can't exist without the other. They're inexorably tied."

There was a wait this time. Then, "One would think so."

"So the next question is, which takes precedence? Is Deedee murdered so Playa can be framed? Hardly. He can be more easily, more readily, framed in a thousand different, better ways. So Deedee's murder is the most important thing that has happened here. Playa's connection, his *proposed connection*, is secondary.

It is more along the lines of—how do you say it in Spanish?—two birds with one stone?"

Another, longer wait. "Possibly."

"Let's assume. Say that's what happened. Still, we've gotta ask, Why him? Why her and him together? Why not one at a time and at different times? And, finally, if one is in the killing business, why not kill Playa? Why just . . ." Donahoo paused. He again was searching for a word. "Why, with such a flimsy charge, why choose to issue a warning?"

"A warning?"

"Yes."

Torres frowned. "That is your theory? The intent was to strike fear?"

"Yes. It's such an easy choice here. Why not just shoot him and dump his body? Why go to all the trouble of a doubtful murder rap that he's probably going to beat?"

"That's your theory? That he would be put under suspicion? That he would eventually be proven innocent?"

"Yes."

"How did you arrive at this theory?"

"Well," Donahoo said. He was certain now he was on the right track. Torres's expression told him that and more. "You take a man who controls ten thousand votes. He can't deliver them when he's dead. But he can if he's alive. Especially if he wants to stay alive."

Torrres took a moment. "Playa is history. He hasn't got ten thousand votes."

"How do you know?" Donahoo asked. "Do you know that for sure?" He said, "Playa was a power. He could become a power again. And that could happen without your knowledge. It can be a gradual, hardly noticed process. Do you know what they say about the Nazi party? It started with two members."

Torres shook his head. Donahoo wasn't sure about what.

"Anyway," Donahoo told him, "that's my theory." He waited for Torres to volunteer his theory. He thought they might be the same. Pretty close. He said, "I think that when we find Playa, we will find that he is a power, or a potential power. What do you think?" Then, after a while, "Take your time." He looked around for the men. Especially the one with the kickplate face.

It would have been a good time to mention them to Torres, he thought, all the men together in the grandstand, the new man and the two from the toilet. But, trying to recoup his losses, he'd had a twenty-dollar bet on a mutt named Faust Eddie, and it had just left the starting box like a Tomahawk missile, which had proved too much of a distraction, although, on the far turn, Faust Eddie apparently suffered a heart attack, or perhaps had been shot by a disgruntled bettor—there was a loud report at the time—and when Donahoo looked back into the grandstand, the men were gone.

No other opportunity had presented itself. Torres was a relentless bettor and expected equal enthusiasm from his guests. He claimed to be an expert and talked like one. He knew that greyhounds were as old as recorded history and that in tenth century England the price of a greyhound and a hawk was the same as that of a man. He knew the bloodlines of his favorites and the best kennels. Donahoo would have preferred that he knew how to win the Perfecta or the Daily Double, but he didn't mention this, because, as it happened, Torres suffered very badly when he lost; he didn't need carping.

The other thing, Torres seemed to know almost everyone, cops and crooks alike, in the other places they had visited, and he had been very alert to them, so it was unlikely for him not to have noticed the men on his own. If he, Donahoo, was aware of them, then Torres should be too. Torres had a radar going at the other places, at the hangout bars and restaurants, and at the Jai Alai Palace and the Caliente Book, and on the narrow back streets of Zona Norte's "Little Saigon."

"Ask him what his theory is, Cruz."

"I think he wants to think about his theory."

Yes, I suppose, Donahoo thought. He relaxed and let himself get caught up again in what Lewis would term the magic of the momentum. The bright lights and the call of the race and the roar of the crowd and the lunging dogs and the hurtling mechanical stuffed rabbit. The rush to see the posted photo-finish. The gasp when a long shot's payoff went up.

"What some people say, the dog races are the only honest thing in Mexico," Torres said now, sounding happy to be able to make the claim. He was educating Marino and Marino was passing some of it along. "It's too hard to cheat. The dogs are tested for drugs and stimulants, the same as horses, and a ringer would be spotted right away, because the toenails are unique, the same as fingerprints. The other thing is it's not worth the trouble. The purses are too small and so is the betting. To fix a race would cost you more than you could hope to win. So it is a very honest thing. Maybe the only honest thing in Mexico."

Donahoo wasn't convinced. Faust Eddie had hit an invisible wall. He'd gone down like an El Cajón whore.

"The banks," Marino said. "Surely the banks are honest?"

"Maybe. But not as honest as the dog races."

Bang. They were watching the tenth race now. They had purposely stayed for it. By mutual agreement, they'd all bet on Poker Joe, Torres's definite sure thing for the evening, to place first. Twenty dollars each at five-to-one. To recoup.

Poker Joe had come out of the box very strong. He was in the lead pack. Donahoo had the numbers memorized, 3, 5 and 8. Bing Bang, Mabel X and Poker Joe. He didn't have to trust the announcer.

Torres swore, and when Donahoo asked what was said, Marino told him, "Well, fuck this," and Donahoo wondered why, Poker Joe was in the lead pack, and Marino finally got an explanation from Torres, "He's supposed to be *six lengths* ahead."

They watched in silence and Socker Mac took it with Bing Bang second and Poker Joe third.

"Well, fuck this," Torres said once more, tearing up his slip. Marino was grudgingly translating. "Let's get out of here." He found his wallet and looked into it. "We could check out the cockfights."

Donahoo thought he'd pass. He'd already lost about a hundred dollars. And he really didn't relish watching some roosters debone each other just so he could lose another hundred. He said, "No."

"You're sure?"

"Yes, very." Donahoo looked around. The men were gone. There was no sign of any of them. He thought he should mention them and then he thought he'd sound like a wimp loser. "You go ahead. It's been a long, unprosperous day. I'm ready to quit." Now he was looking at Marino. "Don't let me stop you though, Cruz."

Torres said, "Yeah, come on, Cruz, we'll leave the old man," and Marino said, meaning a cock fight, "I saw one in the Philippines, I think I'll pass."

"Okay. You mind taking a taxi back? I'm going in the opposite direction. We'll get to work tomorrow, looking for Playa and Juarez. They are mice hiding in holes. Maybe the same hole. I'll come by in the morning. Eight o'clock. We'll have breakfast."

"Bueno," Marino said, answering for them, and Donahoo, having got just a little of that, the old man part, and the Philippines part, said, *"Adiós, jugador."* It was another word he had learned. Gambler.

Torres grinned and tipped his cowboy hat and pushed into the crowd and was gone.

"How much did you lose?" Marino asked.

"A hundred or so. How about you?"

"I won fifty."

"You won?"

"Yeah, well, a couple of times I changed my bet," Marino said sheepishly. "You remember we were all gonna go with Ground Hound? I went with Big Whizzer. And I didn't go with Country Hick. I had Gurley's Girl."

"But you went with Poker Joe?"

"Yeah. But just for two bucks."

Donahoo couldn't believe it. "We all agreed on Poker Joe."

"Hey," Marino said, doing the arithmetic in his head, "but I coulda put it all on Socker Mac, in which case, chinga, chinga, chinga, sixty dollars."

Yeah, Donahoo thought, and they could have quit three hours ago, they could be home in bed. He thought that he wasn't much of a *jugador.* He much preferred sure things. The sun in the morning, pouting sausage lips, and a Monte Carlo convertible. Well, two were sure anyway. Pretty sure.

"Are we outa here?"

Donahoo looked around. No sign of any of the men. But he had the feeling they must be somewhere close. He thought he should put them on his pretty sure list. They'd had that stick-around, wait-for-the-moment look. The patience of a railroad crossing.

Seventeen

It happened at the traffic signal at Boulevard Agua Caliente and Avenida Cuauhtemoc. They were in a taxi, headed north away from the track, to downtown Tijuana and El Greco, and it seemed perfectly safe, Boulevard Agua Caliente was jammed with traffic. They were stopped for the signal. An old nondescript car in front. A large van with dark-tinted windows behind. Donahoo was wondering what happened to old greyhounds when their racing days were through. The good ones, they'd be put to sire, he thought. But the also-rans? He worried about them. You didn't see a lot of greyhounds around. Maybe they had some home for them in Florida?

When the light changed, the car in front didn't move, it looked like it was stalled out, the man at the wheel was waving for them to go around, but when their cab driver tried to back up, the van moved forward and boxed them in.

"Here it comes," Donahoo said, and Marino, completely off guard, said, "What?"

Donahoo turned around. The driver of the van was already out on the street. He was wearing a black ski mask and pointing a sawed-off over/under shotgun. "Do what they say."

"What?"

"Cruz," Donahoo said. He was glad he didn't have the Colt Python. He might have been tempted to use it, reflex action, and then he probably wouldn't have any head, the shotgun would take most of it. "Do what you're told here. No sudden moves."

Marino looked back. "Jesus Christ."

"Take it easy."

"You in the cab," someone said on a loudspeaker, in English. "The passengers get out. Hands up." The driver was ordered to stay. *"Chofer, quedese en el carro."*

Donahoo got out with his arms raised. The van driver had been

132

joined by another masked man. He also had a sawed-off shotgun. He was covering Marino.

The loudspeaker continued. "Put your fingers together. Put your hands on top of your head. Put your head against the van. Spread your legs. Do it now."

Donahoo did as instructed. The shotgun was shoved into the small of his back. He was patted down expertly in a quick search for a weapon. Marino, next to him, was handled in the same swift, expert way.

"Okay. Get in the van. The back of the van. Do it now."

Donahoo went around to the rear of the van. The doors were wide open, waiting. The cargo space was empty, bare metal. A blackout curtain was drawn across it about midway.

The van driver motioned with his weapon. He said softly, "Pronto."

Donahoo saw that the shotgun was a Woodward-Purdey. He couldn't believe anyone would saw it off. He got into the van. Marino clambered in after him. The door slammed shut behind them. It was pitch black.

A man spoke from the darkness. Rough but good English. "So . . . you have been asking about Diablo?"

Donahoo didn't answer. He tried the door. It was locked.

"We can do this any way you want."

The curtain rattled as it was pulled aside. The cargo hold remained in total darkness. The man couldn't be seen. The van started up, swerved out of its lane, then moved away at high speed. It turned right, tires squealing.

"I'm a police officer," Donahoo said, reaching out blindly for Marino. He found a shoulder and laid his hand on it for a moment. "A detective sergeant from San Diego. I'm here at the request of your state police."

"We know who you are. And that you're not here to investigate Diablo."

"That's true. And I'm not investigating him."

"Then why did you request information on him?"

Donahoo hesitated. He thought about his telephone conversations with Lewis. It was possible that someone eavesdropped on one or more of them.

"A final reminder," the man said, menace in his voice now. "We can do this your way."

"Yes, I did check on Diablo," Donahoo admitted. "But it was

merely out of curiosity. I have no intention of taking it any farther. I'm down here . . ."

"We know why you're here, Detective."

". . . by invitation . . ."

"We know. The Hernandez murder."

"Yes."

"So why would you ask for a dossier on Salvador Urquidez?"

"I told you. Out of curiosity."

"Really? What made you curious?"

Donahoo wished he could see the man. The cargo space was inky black. Nothing showed.

"Do you consider him a suspect in the murder?"

"No."

"Then why the dossier?"

"I'm a police officer."

"But in a foreign country?"

"Yes."

"With no authority?"

"Yes."

"And no business . . . ?"

"Yes," Donahoo said finally. Now he wished he had the Python. "None whatsoever." He thought for a moment. Marino was breathing heavily beside him. "Perhaps I owe Señor Urquidez an apology."

"Perhaps?"

"My error. I do owe him one."

"Yes, that's true, but we're not interested in apologies," the man said. "There is only one thing that would satisfy us, and that is if you were to leave here and not come back, Detective. Leave Mexico and return to the United States and not under any circumstances come back."

The van left the paved street. It bumped along a rough road. Donahoo held on and stared into the darkness. There was nothing. Just the voice.

"Do you think you can do that?"

"Yes."

"Good," the man said, "because if you can't, if we find you here again, we will be obliged to kill you, and because you will have angered us, it will be a slow, painful death. I have been speaking on behalf of myself and now I am speaking on behalf of Diablo.

Your death will take a long, long time, Detective, and every moment you will wish that you had kept your word. You will wish
with every fiber in your body that you had stayed in the United
States and had not come back to Mexico. What I am saying you
must believe. Because it is true."

"Okay," Donahoo said. He was holding on. The road was very
rough. "My partner here? He's just my interpreter. He didn't know
about my inquiries."

"Your interpreter?"

"Yes."

"Then he can intrepret this. *Te voy a ensartar tu verga por el
culo.*"

Donahoo waited. "What did he say?"

Marino answered in a strangled voice. "He says he's gonna pull
my dick off. Through my asshole."

"Yeah, well," Donahoo said, holding on. "That won't be necessary. He won't be coming back either."

"If you say so," the man said. "But I hope you're wrong. I hope
you are so stupid as to not heed my warning. Because it would
give me a great deal of pleasure if you did come back. Something
you can be certain of—in my anticipation of that pleasure and
entertainment?—my men and I will be watching for you."

The van stopped. There was a brief wait and then the rear cargo
door was unlocked and pulled open.

"Adiós, curious detective and his plump interpreter."

Donahoo got out. They were on a dirt road in an undeveloped
area. The nearest buildings were several blocks away. Black
lumps against the night sky. No lights. Beyond, several miles
away, there was a bowl of blue light, and a jetliner was rising out
of it. Tijuana's international airport.

The driver was standing back with his shotgun. He motioned
with it. Get going.

Donahoo started down the road. He expected a shotgun blast in
his back at any moment. He didn't think they would let them go.
Marino caught up.

The cargo door banged shut. The van got underway. Soon it
was gone.

Marino let out a whooshing sound.

"Hey," Donahoo said. He had never been more relieved in his
life. "Don't pay any attention to that guy, Cruz. You know you're

not plump." He said, "That was sure black in there. It was a good place to test your watch."

Marino said, "Are you trying to tell me you weren't scared?"

Donahoo grinned. Yeah, trying, he thought.

Eighteen

Donahoo got his Python. He thought he ought to go home. Half an hour and he would be home in bed. Safe, relatively safe, in the big Murphy bed in his studio apartment at The Arlington, looking through the bamboo slat blinds at a fat yellow moon hanging low over the eucalyptus canopy covering Balboa Park. The TV working. Captain Mike with the weather. National Geographic on Ten Things You Didn't Know About the Barn Swallow.

He checked the Python's load and looked around. The street was empty. The last beggar had gone to bed. The last hooker had turned her last trick. El Greco, doubtful haven, was battened down for the night, the neon sign off and the rooms dark except for the one he shared with Marino. The door there was open, casting a widening, diminishing path of light across the parking slots. He put the gun in his waistband and slammed the trunk of the Toronado. He ought to go home, he thought.

A Woodward-Purdey. Who would saw off a Woodward-Purdey?

He remembered the pay phone outside the liquor store on the corner. He went there to call Lewis. He didn't care if it was bugged or not. He thought that he wanted it to be bugged.

Lewis said, coming out of his sleep, "Do you know what time it is?"

"No," Donahoo lied. He looked at his new watch. Marino had sold him his Rolex knockoff for ten dollars. It had failed its final test. It hadn't glowed in the hijack van. "All the clocks here are busted." He could have waited until the morning but Lewis would be really pissy in the morning. Now he would be more sleepy and less pissy. It would be a lot easier now. "Listen . . ."

"It's after midnight."

"Listen," Donahoo repeated. "My apologies. But this is important. I've got something going here, I don't want it blowing up in my face, okay? I've got to get it sorted out and I've got to do it now."

"The fucking Midnight Marauder. Jesus Christ."

"Lewis. Listen. That dossier on Diablo. Who all knows you told me about it?"

"Huh?"

"Who knows I asked?"

There was a moment. Lewis becoming less comatose. He said, "Saperstein. Murdoch. What's going on?"

"That's all?"

"Yes. What's going on?"

Donahoo tried to think. Murdoch headed Organized Crime. He was mainly a liaison with the FBI. He made sure that the FBI knew what the SDPD knew and he tried to make sure that the SDPD knew what the FBI knew. He had one of those thankless jobs that never got done. Most things, you kill the head, the body dies. But in Organized Crime, you kill the head, it grows two more and they fight with each other. Sometimes it was best to let the head be. The head you know.

"I told you to forget about that goddamn Diablo," Lewis complained. "Now what have you done?"

"I did forget about him."

"Then what's going on?"

"Nothing."

"Bullshit."

"Lewis. Listen. Nothing you need to worry about. I'm sorry to have disturbed you."

"Then why did you?"

Donahoo had been trying to think of an answer for that. "Some cops down here seemed to know that I'd inquired, and it kinda threw me, that's all. So I thought, you know, that maybe you had talked to someone in the Baja AG's office, or the DA's."

"I talked to Murdoch. Period."

"Then it's just my imagination. I must be getting spooked."

"That fucking Diablo. I told you . . ."

"Please."

"Okay. And that reminds me. Come and get that voodoo shit you needed to be a hero."

"Huh?"

"The identification kit you wanted to donate? I've got it and a pile of other voodoo shit waiting for you. It's gonna make you look really good down there."

"Thanks."

"You wanta look good down here, don't you?"

"Yeah."

"Yeah, well, you wouldn't look good on a fucking cross, Tommy. What you need is a fucking stake in your fucking heart. Calling at fucking midnight."

"I said I was sorry."

"Don't ever talk to me again about Diablo." Pause. "Martha. Go back to sleep. It's just Tommy. He's chasing his dick in Tijuana."

Donahoo laughed and hung up. He got his little black book and found Murdoch's number. Murdoch would be awake. In Organized Crime, you went to bed at four, slept till noon. You kept the same hours as the bad guys. You sat outside all the fancy restaurants. You hung out in fast bars and slow bowling alleys.

Murdoch answered on a cellular. Behind the static it sounded like he might be having a good time. A live band, maybe a live band, was playing "I Wanta Be Loved By You." He said, "This is Murdoch."

"It's Tommy," Donahoo told him. "I was just talking to the grumpy old man."

"Lewis?"

"He says he got a Salvador Urquidez dossier from you."

"So?"

"So who knows he did?"

"Nobody."

"You're sure about that?"

"Does the Pope pull his pud?"

Yeah, Donahoo thought, and does the tide come in, and does it go out?

"What's going on?"

"Nothing."

"Tommy. Don't k-kid a k-k-kidder."

Donahoo said, "Thanks," and hung up.

☐ ☐ ☐

Marino was standing in the open doorway of their room when Donahoo got back to El Greco. He was wearing his holster. Putting his .38 Special in it. Kicking his suitcase out ahead of him. He said, "Are we outa here?"

Donahoo thought about it some more. He'd already had a lot of time to think, on the walk out of the wasteland where they had been dumped, and on the ride back downtown in the cab they had hailed on Camino de Regreso del Aeropuerto. His head was sore from thinking about it.

"You are," he said finally. He still had the car keys in his hand. He went around and put them on the hood. He didn't want to get too close to Marino. He wanted to keep the space between them. It was easier with space. "Take the car. Bring it back tomorrow. Leave it in a border parking lot. The $5 E-Z Park? The keys under the mat." He waited for some response. "Get it back by noon, okay? I'll pick it up. You can take the trolley back. Or somebody can drive you." He said, "Take the car."

Marino kicked his suitcase back into the room and closed the door.

Donahoo stared. Now what? He picked up the keys. He thought his head really was sore. He had been dealing with large issues. Personal worth, true values, pride, fear. Maybe fatal attraction, because, a lot of the time, he had been thinking about Catalina. He thought just a while longer—his limit for the night, he thought—and went inside.

Marino was stretched out on his bed. His Bible was beside him. Like maybe he planned to consult it but had been distracted by the wavy lines on the TV.

"I want you to go," Donahoo said, leaving the door open. He put the keys on the bureau. "Come on, get outa here. Take the car."

Marino said, "No, you're not doing that to me, man. If you're staying, I'm staying."

"That's an order," Donahoo told him tiredly. "I'm your superior officer and I'm ordering you to leave. Get outa here. That's an order. Now."

"Fuck you."

Donahoo thought for a while. He had promised himself he wasn't going to do that anymore but he did it anyway. He said, "I can throw you out."

"You can try."

"Yeah, well, you know I can," Donahoo said, becoming angry. Marino's right hand was on his chest. It seemed just a little closer than necessary to his gun. Donahoo didn't remember Marino putting it there. It just seemed to have happened. "Don't make this difficult, Cruz. You're wrong and you can't make it right. So do what you're told."

"Fuck you."

"What about Theresa?"

"She's not involved here."

"Okay. Let's just talk about unnecessary risks."

"There's nothing to talk about."

Donahoo wondered. What was he supposed to do? Kill the crazy bastard?

"It's not your decision," Marino told him, staring at the wavy lines. "You've decided for yourself, sure, that's okay, but you can't make the call for me, not on something like this, it's personal."

"Goddamn . . ."

"I don't know your motive or reasoning," Marino continued. "You're not scared? You're a living legend who can't stand to be tarnished? You've got a job to do and you plan to see it through because you're that kind of guy? Whatever. It doesn't matter to me. I couldn't care less. The thing is, left to my own devices, I'd be the fuck outa here in a nanosecond, but if you're staying, I'm staying. You're not gonna look good while I look like a piece of shit. That's not gonna happen."

"That's what this is about?"

"You're goddamn right. It's about me and who I am."

Donahoo found himself thinking again. You never know, he thought. You never, ever know. He closed the door, bolted it. Hung the chain. He put the Python on his night table. He started undressing. He said, "You've got the first watch."

That was about it. Donahoo could feel himself going to sleep almost immediately. He had a window—a time when he could fall asleep easily, readily—and if it closed he had a terrible time. He'd lie awake for hours. Sometimes until dawn.

He was glad now for the window. He could feel it open for him and he surrendered himself to it. He thought, a familiar refrain, that he wasn't a good leader of men, he was a lot more productive, and succesful, when he worked by himself. He didn't want or need all the horseshit that command involved. He wanted to be free to focus on the problem and find the solution. That was a part of it. He liked to think that was the biggest part. The other part was that he didn't make a very good leader. He didn't have the patience and he couldn't spare the time. He couldn't work out the proper levels of subservience and obedience. His men were either fighting him or kissing his ass. He could never establish that warm, but not-too-warm, middle level.

Also, he was falling asleep now, the window shutting behind him, he never got to know them properly. Sometimes he thought he knew them but then it would turn out that he didn't. Not even close. Of all the men on his squad, the only one he knew, that he really knew, was Cominsky. Palmer, he had thought he knew Palmer, just another tough guy looking for a fight, a bright little rat terrier who wouldn't let go, but Palmer was a lot more complex and complicated than that. He wanted to lose the fight. Because if you could beat him, that made you special. And, until you met him, Palmer, maybe you didn't know you were special, so that was his gift to you. He was a very giving guy, if you could take it. Gomez? The Spick of the celebrated union of Spick and Spook? Now there was another improbable. You'd think, watching him, all Gomez ever wanted, it was just to stop being a Mexican and start being an American, that simple. But again it wasn't. Actually, Gomez wanted to be the Supreme Mexican, and it really didn't matter where he accomplished that, it could be in Lemon Valley, Pittsburgh, or Schwabisch Gmund, that was of no consequence, just as long as it wasn't in Mexico. Montrose, aka Spook. Maybe the hardest of all to figure coming off the blocks. You'd think a guy that good-looking couldn't possibly be that smart but Montrose was the smartest guy on the squad and maybe the smartest guy in the department, with the exception, of course, of Saperstein. Probably as smart as Lewis. Nobody was as smart as Saperstein. Montrose came close though. You'd think he wasn't. The matinee idol profile. The GQ body. That high black ass. They all combined to throw you off. Then he'd do something really sharp and wise. So, yeah, of all of them, the only one he really knew was the geek, Cominsky, and that wasn't exactly a landmark accomplishment. You put anybody in a locked room with Cominsky. Half an hour, and they'd come out knowing him. They might not want to know him, but they'd know him. Of them all, the one he missed the most, it was Cominsky, Donahoo thought. They had a love-hate relationship. Cominsky loved him. And he hated the guy. Well, not really, but there were times, you know? There were times, a few times, maybe more than a few, when he hated Cominsky.

Donahoo could feel himself slipping away. From the day's cares and woes and from Cruz Marino. Here was another guy he didn't know. Not one of his men. Not precisely one of them. But, for the moment, assigned to him, and therefore temporarily—not putting too fine a point on a stretch?—a member, ex officio, of Squad 5, aka SCUMB.

Fuck you? God, in a million years, he never would have expected to hear those words from Marino's lips, Donahoo thought. Never would have thunk it. Never. And shit, the guy, you know, he's gonna get his ass whipped, and suddenly the .38 Special is handier than before. Donahoo went to sleep thinking that he didn't know Marino from a Liberian sitcom but he was glad that Marino was staying.

Nineteen

They weren't the only ones taken off the street that night. Donahoo found himself listening to what someone called fragmented and unconfirmed reports. A kidnaping in Tijuana. Bodies found at Rosarita Beach. One survivor. The victim was asked, *"Quién te lo hizo?"*—who did this to you?—and he said, *"La policia."* He said the cops picked them up and took them away and executed them.

"We hope to talk soon to Captain Carlos Torres . . . Grupo Homocidios . . . Baja California State Police . . . who, as we speak, is on the scene."

Donahoo heard it in the same kind of disjointed way. He thought he was dreaming. "Now we are here with . . . Sargento?"

Yes, that's me, Donahoo thought. Maybe it was Torres asking for him. Torres asking him to stay in Tijuana, so that, together, they could solve the Deedee Hernandez Nightmare Murder Case. Torres saying don't be afraid. Those guys were kidding. They never cut off dicks. That's not their style. Their style is . . .

Actually, it was a news anchor, talking to a reporter who was talking to a cop, and nobody knew very much of anything, because the anchor was in San Diego and the reporter and the cop were in Tijuana and the bodies were in Rosarito with Captain Carlos Torres.

Donahoo slowly came fully awake. San Diego's KNXT on the TV. Marino must have fixed it. Or maybe it fixed itself. He looked at Marino on the other bed. The "first watch" was asleep, snoring faintly, still in his clothes, he hadn't even removed his bookkeeper shoes.

"Hola?"

Zzzzz.

Donahoo liked to think that he wasn't a coward, yet he was still acutely aware of the previous night's choreographed terror. He spent a moment trying to figure Marino. He thought that he must be very brave or very stupid or very unreliable. He was at least one of those and possibly all three of them.

Marino hadn't stirred. Donahoo got up and went to the door in his shorts. He took the Python with him, just in case. He peered through the crack allowed by the chain. It looked safe enough. He unchained the door and pulled it open. Still clear. He went out and looked around. There wasn't much activity. The maid with her cart. A gardener. Nothing suspicious.

"What's going on?" Marino asked.

"I dunno," Donahoo told him. He headed for the bathroom. He kept the Python. "Torres is in Rosarita Beach. The TV says they've found some bodies there."

"Playa and Juarez?"

"Possibly. That's all it said. Bodies."

Marino rolled off the bed. "We going?"

"Yes. Make some coffee, willya?" Donahoo left the bathroom door open a crack. They could talk while he shaved. He thought he ought to mention the dereliction of duty. "You stand a hell of a watch."

"Sorry. I guess I drifted off."

"Is that something you learned in the Navy?"

"Huh?"

Drifting off, Donahoo thought, but he let it go, it was early, he'd dazzle him later. He decided not to shave. He stepped out of his shorts and into the shower. Who did this to you? "La policia." He thought he'd never get himself clean down here.

Donahoo took the *libre*, or free, road to Rosarita, not just to save the few dollars in tolls, but also because it was the original road and it ran closer to the beach, sometimes at the water's edge, and the news report said the bodies had been found on the beach. It was only a fifteen-minute drive, so the police should still be on the scene, a small cluster of vehicles pulled off the road a bit, or perhaps not that far off, because they were, after all, cops, and cops could do what they wanted. Torres should still be around too. This wasn't something he would wish to mop up in a hurry, Donahoo thought. He'd want to spend some quality time. Be very careful.

Marino sat silent for most of the drive, lost in his dark thoughts, smoking his Pacificos. Once he said, "Cops did it? Fuck!" and later, "I don't know about this country," but mostly he brooded and smoked.

Donahoo had his own thoughts too. He was struck, as always, by the beauty of the countryside, the green hills falling into the sea, and by the awful contrast between wealth and poverty, the luxurious hi-rise condos within sight of pitiful shacks.

There was a lot of that in Mexico, he thought. The extremes. Palace or outhouse. Steak and lobster or beans and tortillas. Fate decreed it and most people couldn't do anything about it. It was written in the sand, Kismet. You will live the good life on the hill. Or you will beg on the street and die in the gutter.

Donahoo wondered, with those kind of stark choices imposed, if that's what made the other, lesser choices so easy to accept. If that was why the poor and the oppressed didn't rise up en masse and tear the whole stinking thing down and start over. The other choices were always there. You could drive the *cuarto*, the money, or toll, road, or you could drive the *libre* road. They went to the same place and they took almost the same path. One got you there a little faster, a little more comfortably, sometimes a lot more comfortably, that's all. It was the same with a lot of things. You could pay two bucks for Marlboros or thirty cents for Pacificos and they both got you early to the cancer ward. There were no old cowboys in the Marlboro ads. They just looked old.

"What gets me," Marino said. "This is just an observation, okay? I'm not trying to start an argument. What gets me, this is a great country, it's got all kinds of natural resources, arable land, a marvelous climate and incredible scenery, okay?"

"Okay."

"Most of the people, you're not gonna find any better. They're good people who work hard and want the best for their children."

"Agreed."

"They started out—this is not an argument—they started out at the same time as us, in the States, *before us*, actually, with everything we had in the way of resources, possibly more. They had a better shot. So how come they're so far behind?"

"Well," Donahoo said. He didn't know. It wouldn't make any difference if he did know. "They're not behind. It's just that we're ahead." He thought for a moment. "Because we killed the Indians."

"Jesus Christ. There's no talking to you."

"There's no arguing."

Donahoo briefly wondered about himself and Marino. He was driving the *libre* road. Marino was smoking Pacificos. What did that say about them? Were they too willing to accept lesser choices? Did they know in their hearts that they'd never rise up?

□   □   □

They drove through town, down the long, lots-of-construction commercial strip, past the old Rosarita Beach Hotel, and almost to Puerto Nuevo before they came upon the cop cars pulled not quite off the road. Two patrol cars and an unmarked car and an ambulance and Torres's LeBaron. Fifty yards farther a television station's news van.

Donahoo slowed and was waved on by a uniformed officer. He showed his badge and was still instructed to keep going. He pulled off anyway.

"No!" the cop yelled, starting for them, and then Torres, coming up from the beach, shouted, *"Está bien!"*

Donahoo got out with Marino. The tide was coming in. The water was surging close to three tarp-covered lumps scattered across the sand. A man in a dark business suit, his shoes and socks off, his pantlegs rolled up, was looking under one of the tarps. Several other men, also wearing suits, were standing off a short distance, safe from the water.

Torres made the road. He said, breathing hard, *"Qué onda?"*

"He wants to know what we're doing here."

Donahoo was looking at the three lumps. "It's not Juarez and Playa?"

"No," Torres said tiredly, Marino translating. "It's some punk kids. Four of 'em." He gestured toward the beach. "The three there and a survivor in Santa Lucia Hospital. I don't know how the hell he made it. Shot in the back of the head at close range and he lives to tell about it."

Donahoo waited. His first reaction was that he was glad it wasn't Juarez and Playa. But now this sounded like it might be something more obscene. There might have been at least some rationale for killing Juarez and Playa. But some punk kids?

"Car thieves," Torres said. "This is what the survivor says. The cops were pissed at them for stealing cars. So they grabbed them and stuffed them in a van and drove them down here. They walked them out on the beach and shot them. One each."

"Four cops?"

"Yeah."

"You believe that?"

Torres looked toward the beach. "I don't know." He turned back to Donahoo. His face was creased with defeat. "Yeah, I suppose so. The kid says it was state cops. We've got the rep for that kind of shit. Torture. Executions. It was really bad for a while and then we got it cleaned up and now it's started again. There is so much crime. Not enough police. No room in the jails." Now he looked away once more. "I didn't say it was an excuse. I said it was a reason."

Donahoo didn't know how to answer him. He'd heard it so many times before. We're cleaning it up down here. No more corruption. They'd say that and it would sound like they meant it. They'd fire a few hundred of the worst cops and begin anew. They'd raise salaries. Improve training methods. Make all the right noises. But the good intentions never lasted very long. Pretty soon they were back rolling sailors and demanding *mordidas* from hapless motorists. They were back collecting bribes from the smugglers taking drugs and undocumented aliens across the border. They were back killing punk kids without benefit of arrest or trial.

"You're here," Torres said. "You wanta take a look?"

Donahoo shook his head.

"That's the medical examiner with them now. We'll be moving them soon."

"I'd like to," Marino said in Spanish. Then, to Donahoo, "You mind?"

Donahoo again shook his head. They went down to the beach and he went back to the Toronado. The brutal executions had given him pause. He wondered if he was doing the right thing by keeping Lewis in the dark about the threats made by Diablo's men. But if he revealed any of it, Lewis would tell Saperstein, and Saperstein would probably cancel the assignment, and he, Donahoo, didn't want to go home, he wanted to stay. Torres also would want him to stay (he'd almost dreamed about it, hadn't he?). Donahoo was sure of that. The guy needed all the help he could get. So Torres would say, Hey, don't worry, you're a grown gringo, you don't have to be afraid. We'll work this out. It's okay.

Torres and Marino were at the tarps. Donahoo thought that until now he had been kind of flat about Marino, he could take him or leave him, probably leave him. He was flat because he thought the guy was flat. That sure was what he had thought at first anyway. He said, this to himself, softly, "There was no varoom."

Marino had left his Pacificos. Donahoo tried one while he waited. He thought that he should have told Torres right away about the previous night's encounter but he wanted to test Marino. He wanted to see if he was just a stubborn, foolhardy rookie, or if maybe he really knew what he was doing. If Marino knew what he was doing, he wouldn't breathe boo to Torres.

When they came back, he said to Marino, "What did you tell him?" and Marino, who looked very pale, said, "I told him you'd tell him."

"Me estoy muriendo de nervios," Torres said. He got in the Toronado, up front with Donahoo.

Donahoo looked at Marino. Who after a moment glanced at him and managed a faint smile. "The suspense is killing him."

"We've got our own problems," Donahoo began, thinking that Marino did know something after all, a little anyway, about rank and privilege, it was his, Donahoo's, duty and pleasure to recount the encounter. He snapped away the Pacifico, which wasn't bad, it was better, in his recollection, than a Marlboro. "Some goons picked us up after we left you at the racetrack. They were upset about my interest in Diablo. They told us to leave and not come back. Or else they'd kill us."

Marino was in the back seat now. He was translating. Torres stared blankly. "Kill you . . . ?"

Donahoo nodded. He told the story, briefly but with sufficient detail, not omitting anything vital except the one thing that Marino didn't know, or apparently didn't, because he hadn't mentioned it. The driver's sawed-off over/under was a Woodward-Purdey. There probably was just that one mutilation in the whole world.

Torres sat silently through it all. Then he said, very quickly, Marino translating, "Well, this is an outrage, I am of course shocked and shaken, nothing like this, to my knowledge, has ever happened here before, and you have my profound apologies, Sargento. You and Cruz both. I regret you didn't point out the men you saw at the racetrack. Frankly, I wasn't paying attention, my interest was the dogs, which are my affliction, one of them, as you know. I will ensure that you have safe conduct to the border. I don't know what else to say. I'm deeply sorry."

Donahoo listened in disbelief. He thought that he was really losing his touch. He had figured Marino all wrong and now he had figured Torres all wrong. He said, "Tell him thank you. Tell him we're not going."

Marino translated.

"That's not . . ." Torres started to say something and then changed his mind. He began again. "That's out of the question. There is no way to protect you. So you have no choice but to leave."

"Tell him we're staying."

"I can't guarantee your safety. Let me remind you. A badge is no protection here. The police chief, the prison warden, a special federal prosecutor—the first Colosio prosecutor?—that's how high the assassins are reaching here. You think they can't bend to reach you?"

"Tell him we don't care. We're staying."

Torres turned to face Donahoo. His face was grim. "Maybe I too will have to order you to leave?"

"Maybe," Donahoo said. He was getting confused. He'd thought that Torres really wanted him. Really needed him. "But I'll sure as fuck challenge it. And, if you make it stick, I'll only come back. You can't stop me."

Torres studied him as Marino translated. His face darkened. Then, without saying anything, he got out of the car, slamming the door so hard that the window dropped. He turned abruptly and went crashing back towards the beach.

"You think he'll come back?" Marino asked.

"Yes."

"Why?"

"He hasn't thanked us."

"You think he will?"

"I think he must."

Torres was already back. He went around the front of the car so he could speak directly to Donahoo. *"Mil disculpas. Quiero agradecerles a todos su ayuda."*

Marino said only, "Okay."

"He thanked us?"

"Yes."

"Okay," Donahoo said. He started the car. "Maybe we'll see you in Tijuana."

Torres pulled the door open with one hand and grabbed Donahoo with the other. *"Un momento."*

"No." Donahoo started away. "There's nothing more to talk about."

Torres yanked and pulled Donahoo out. The Toronado, in first gear, kept going. Marino went over the seat to stop it.

Donahoo managed to keep his feet. He and Torres had hold of each other in an uneasy draw. They slowly released but remained squared off.

Marino got the Toronado stopped. He scrambled out. "Jesus Christ. Settle down, huh?"

"Yeah, well, get this guy outa my face."

"I don't think I can do that."

Donahoo measured Torres. He didn't think he could do it either.

Torres methodically folded his arms, tucking his big hands out of sight, as if he was putting them away somewhere, so that they couldn't cause harm. He said, *"Porqué?"*

Donahoo had heard that often enough. He didn't need a translation. Torres wanted to know why. As in why were they staying? "There's a long reason and a short reason. The short reason is I don't want to leave until I'm ready to leave. Marino might have another reason. You'll have to ask him."

Torres listened to the translation and then looked to Marino. *"Tu?"*

"Vine con él," Marino said. "I came with him."

Torres relaxed. He let his arms fall to his sides. If he had been angry, he wasn't now. If anything, he was resigned. Donahoo was happy with himself again. He might have misread Marino, he thought. But he had figured Torres pretty close. The guy just had to do it his way.

"Well," Torres said. "There's no longer any question about you carrying your weapons. You must of course by all means do that now. But what I would ask—this is a special favor?—I wonder if you might return to San Diego temporarily. For just a day or so. To give me some breathing space. So I can clear up this matter here. And also ask around about the men who threatened you. So that I will have a better idea of what we're up against. Okay?"

Torres translated it all. Donahoo didn't see how he could object. It made sense.

"I'll also see to it that you have discreet bodyguards upon your return." Torres raised spread fingers to restrain any objection. "Please. I insist. And, if it assuages your honor any, what you can be sure of, they won't be very competent."

"In that case," Donahoo replied, thinking that he really ought to go home, "we accept."

Twenty

Donahoo went to say good-by to Catalina. He wanted to do it in person rather than call her. It was possible that she might hear something about the threats by Diablo's men. From Torres or some other source. He didn't want to risk her being misinformed. He wanted to personally assure her that he was coming back, within a day or so, and that he wanted to see her then, very much, and that—yes, this was part of it—he wasn't afraid. Not, at any rate, too much afraid. Just prudently alert, as it were. He felt like a schoolboy who had lost a fight to a bully. He wanted to tell her he wasn't quitting. He'd be back, okay?

Her office was above a *carniceria*, a butcher shop, on Calle Quinta, a few doors down from Avenida Mayo. She had given him the address when he walked her home. She had invited him to stop by if he was in the neighborhood. Until now, although tempted, he had been busy. The Hernandez murder case and other diversions.

Marino, designated chauffeur, parked the Toronado illegally, a practice that he had acquired from observing Torres. He got out his Pacificos. He didn't say anything. He'd been quiet on the drive back from Rosarito Beach. Subdued while they packed and checked out of El Greco. He hadn't said so, but it was a mistake, probably, for him to have looked at the bodies.

"This won't take long."

"No hurry."

Donahoo went through a glass street door marked ABOGADO, and up a steep, narrow, dingy staircase that smelled of raw meat and disenfectant. The stairs turned twice before he reached the top. There was a heavy wooden door there. Her name was on it. CATALINA DE LOURDES VENEZUELA. Below that, ENTRADA. He went into a small waiting room furnished with a sagging sofa and two mismatched easy chairs. There also was a wobbly coffee table with old magazines fanned across it. A coffeemaker, with not quite a cup of coffee in it, was on a stand in a corner, surrounded by styrofoam cups and packs of sweetener and creamer. The windows, facing Calle Quinta, or so the street noise would indicate, had been whitewashed with a pale green that was also on the walls. No one was present. The door to the inner office was closed. It had a hand-printed sign taped to it. PRIVADO.

"Hola?" Donahoo said. He was practicing his Spanish.

"Tommy? Is that you?"

"Sí."

"A surprise!"

"Uh huh. If it's convenient."

"Yes, of course." The door was pulled open after a moment. "I'm just finishing with a client here." She came out, slightly flushed, and crossed to gently embrace him, offering her cheek so quickly that he had no chance to respond. He did have time though to notice her clinging rose silk pleated dress and the new in-a-swirl way she had her hair up and the fact it smelled of lilacs. "Come in. You can meet him."

Someone made a correction. *"Her."*

"I'm sorry," Catalina said. "Her."

Donahoo let himself be led into the tiny office. A stunning brunette in a fluffy pink blouse and blue skirt with a high slit was perched on the edge of a chair, rearranging things in her purse. She had been crying. Her eyes were smudged.

"I'd like you to meet Lois. But you are duly warned that she is really Louis."

Lois smiled tentatively. "How are you?"

"Uh, fine," Donahoo said. He couldn't help staring. He was certain it was a woman. "Listen, I, uh . . ." He looked to Catalina. "I don't want to interrupt."

"That's okay," Lois said. She snapped her purse shut. "We have no secrets around here. I'm under intense gender dysphoric pressure and need to share." She rose gracefully. "Is this the policeman friend you were telling me about? From San Diego?"

"Yes. Sergeant Donahoo. He pokes around in the entrails up there. So he may be able to help you."

Lois smiled again and offered her hand. It was heavy with cheap jewelery. "That would be nice."

"Uh," Donahoo said again. He was baffled. "I'll certainly do my best."

"Thank you. And come to the club sometime. I'm presently dancing at the Sans Souci."

"Sure."

Catalina escorted Lois out. Donahoo, feeling a little shell-shocked, took the vacated chair, using the moment to survey the office. It was painfully simple. Spartan, almost. A second set of greenwashed windows. A small desk fronting a steno's chair. An early word processor with built-in printer. A copier of similar vintage. Some abused bookcases filled with tattered law books. Several scratched and dented filing cabinets. A phone. A recording machine. A gooseneck lamp and in- and out-baskets. The only decoration was a diploma in a cheap black frame.

"So," Catalina said, returning. "What did you think of Louis/Lois?"

"She looks like he'd be a kick."

"Yes." Catalina smiled and went around the desk and fitted onto her steno's chair. "A hoot. But also kind of pitiful." The smile faded and she pulled off an earring. "Were you with Carlos this morning? I heard about it on the radio. It's hard to believe. Is it true?"

Donahoo was uncomfortable with the question. He had the feeling that it was her country. It was her town. He didn't want to condemn it. "I just know what you know. What the surviving kid said. It was cops."

"What did Carlos say?"

"Not much."

She took the other earring off. She placed them together on her desk. Two small silver balls. "When is it going to stop?"

"I don't know."

She looked at him as if he should know. Pain on her face and hurt in her eyes. For a brief moment she wasn't beautiful anymore. She was old and tired and disgusted with herself and her life. For that moment she couldn't help it. The anguish showed.

"Well." She found the will to return. "I'm glad you came by. You were asking me about the Presidente and Jorge Hernandez. What I've found out so far—this is from a confidant in Mexico City—but not mine, actually, it's Carlos's. It is that the Presidente has big plans for Jorge. He wants him in his cabinet as the new minister of health and welfare and to head up a special program against poverty. The appointment is a priority but he can't act while a cloud is over Jorge's head. In the present atmosphere, there can't be any suspicion, he must be cleared. So that is the reason for the urgency."

"The reason that I'm here?"

"To save the day for Jorge."

Donahoo wondered. If that was true, why wasn't Hernandez more cooperative, and, this would be nice, perhaps a little more grateful? He said, "Thank you. That, uh . . ."

"Helps, I trust?"

"Yes." He wished it helped more and didn't raise other questions. He was thinking, on something so important, the Presidente might have personally called Saperstein, offered every assistance, and good luck. But then perhaps he did. Maybe Saperstein sat on that part. Maybe Saperstein wanted Donahoo working for him, Saperstein, not the Presidente.

"Good. I'll keep asking about the other things. What else is going on?"

Donahoo thought that he would like to know that himself. There was an urgency and yet there wasn't an urgency. Jorge Hernandez didn't seem to know about the urgency. How come no one had told him? He thought he should change the subject but his mind was blank. Then he thought about Louis/Lois. "Tell me more about your client. You said I might be able to help."

"Yes. He's right in the middle of transsexing and now they do this to him. It's not fair."

"The middle?"

"Uh huh. Changing his name was simple. All he had to do was drop the *u*. But you have no idea how complicated it gets. The breast implants. The hormones. The poor thing is taking six or seven of them. Perlutal. Lutoral. Nordet. Estinil. I don't know. It goes on and on."

Donahoo didn't respond. He didn't know what to say. Boys will be girls? He had just come in to say good-by, he thought. Marino was waiting.

"And working in those damn clubs? He doesn't get paid. It's just a way of advertising himself. He makes his living as a prostitute. Always getting beat up. The police shaking him down."

"You're not getting involved with that?"

"No. This is about his sex reassignment surgery. It was going to be performed here by a San Diego surgeon associated with a Tijuana doctor. Louis saved up for two years. The doctors wanted the money in advance. They wouldn't operate otherwise. Five thousand dollars. Which Louis paid. Only now the Tijuana doctor says the San Diego surgeon refuses to perform the operation."

"And the San Diego surgeon's got the money?"

"Most of it. Four thousand."

"Jesus." He wondered why she would take such a case. He was going to ask and decided it would offend her. She fought injustice. She was a champion of the downtrodden. She couldn't pick and choose. That wasn't how it worked. In the downtrodden business, you were like the Salvation Army, accepting everything that came along. "That's, uh, a shame."

"It's outrageous. Louis has already been to a lot of expense in psychological counseling. I'm going to take the local doctor to court. But I can't find a lawyer in San Diego who wants to chase the surgeon. The problem is, there's no receipt. The local doctor signed for the money. Not the surgeon."

"And you want me to sniff around?"

"Will you?"

No, Donahoo thought. Not in a million fucking light-years. "What's the surgeon's name?"

"Dr. Sheldon Denke. D-E-N-K-E. Like it sounds. The funny thing. He's supposed to be good."

Donahoo paused, suggesting, he hoped, that he had committed Denke to memory. "Qualified?"

"Yes. They don't just cut it off, you know. The genitourinary system is very complex. You've got to know what you're doing."

"If they knew what they were doing, they wouldn't do it."

"That's so like a man."

Donahoo laughed. He was never sure about her, he thought. She always had him just a little off course.

"So. You're going to ply me with lobster again?"

"No. I've got to go. Marino's waiting. We're going back to San Diego for a day or two." He was glad to see the disappointment on her face. "I just came to say good-by."

"Oh."

"Reluctantly."

"I hope so."

He pushed up slowly. It struck him that now he had a different reason for telling her about Diablo's men. He had been worried about his reputation and now he was worried about her safety. She poked around in the entrails herself. Down and dirty with the downtrodden and therefore perhaps high profile. There were a lot of people who wanted to keep the downtrodden down. He wondered if her association with him might bring her harm.

"When do you think you'll be back?"

"It depends. I'll let you know." He started away. He stopped and looked at her. "Hypothetical question. If Diablo wanted me out of town, he wouldn't pick on you, would he?"

She seemed to have been waiting for the question. She shook her head. "No. He'd pick on you."

"You're sure?"

"Positive. To hurt me, for such a reason, would ruin his image, and image is very important to that kind of person. He may be a monster but he must also appear to be a man."

"Okay." He felt better. "The other thing. I wanted you to know that I'm not afraid . . ." Correction. He felt better and foolish. "Of your father."

"The hawk?"

"Sí." He was practicing his Spanish. *"El halcón."*

Marino's mood had undergone a magical transformation. He got out of the Toronado like an eager chauffeur and hurried around to open the passenger door. He did so with a bow and a flourish.

Donahoo looked at him. What the hell?

"It's a good thing I'm almost engaged," Marino confided. "A woman came by a while ago, she was all over me, man. Flies on a cow pie. She was hot."

"She took an interest, huh?"

"More than an interest. A desire."

Marino smiled and went back and got behind the wheel. He looked like he was going to pop some buttons.

"Uh," Donahoo said. "Puffy pink blouse. Blue skirt, slit?"

"Yeah. You saw her?"

"Yes."

"Hot, right?"

Donahoo indicated that they should leave.

"Boy," Marino said, starting away. "The lady in pink. Now she was something. I'd crawl a mile to lick her smile." He was full of himself. "What do you think?"

Donahoo thought that must be Navy talk. He also thought that things weren't always what they seemed.

"Let's go."

"We're going."

Now take Catalina, for instance. She wasn't worried for herself and that was good. But she didn't seem worried about him either. Donahoo didn't know whether that was good or not. Probably not, he decided. It made him suspicious again. It filled his head with unresolved doubts and concerns about hidden agendas. He wished he hadn't gone up to say good-by. He was a little off course again. Not sure where he was going. Or if he'd get there.

"You didn't think she was hot?"

Donahoo smiled for yes. About the only thing he knew for sure was that Marino belonged back in San Diego. What he, Donahoo, was going to do, he was going to get him back there, and he was going to make him stay there. The guy talked a good game but he really was an innocent. He was a fucking babe in the woods. He wanted to look at dead bodies and then he didn't want to talk about them. He thought Louis was Lois. He didn't know marmalade from mustard gas.

Twenty-one

Donahoo spent the morning confirming that he had another life in another land. After putting Marino on the trolley for El Cajón, he went home to The Arlington in Uptown, to the one-room box where he lived, in a wary truce, with his cat, Oscar, and his Old Crow and his memories and his hopes and not much else. There wasn't room for much else.

He had rented the tiny studio during a financial crunch, when he was paying alimony to his ex-wife, Monica, and helping support his elderly father, Charlie, a blackballed, destitute priest. It had been about the most he could afford then if he was going to patronize restaurants and drink with the boys and play cards and have the odd—that was the correct word—odd date.

Now Monica was off the dole and Charlie had gone to his reward and Donahoo could indulge himself in something larger but he was reluctant to make the change. He was good friends with some of the other tenants, Cody, a boozy ex-Navy fighter pilot and his ever-vigilant, Prohibitionist wife, Vera, and the building's rooftop gardener, a spinster bookkeeper, Barney. Cody talked endlessly about man's ingenuity to man. Barney hung radishes on his doorknob in a plastic bag. Hard stuff to give up.

The thing though, and he was reminded of this as he unlocked the door and pushed inside, lugging his two-suiter and attaché and record player, plus the precious 'I Wonder Who's Kissing Her Now' record, he was reminded that restricted space had its rewards. For one thing, you knew where everything was. It was within ten feet. And you knew you couldn't/shouldn't acquire anything else because there was no place to put it. Unless you made room for it. And so, in time, if you were careful about it, paid attention, you ended up with only those things that were truly important to you. There was no excess.

"With the exception, of course, of a certain cat," Donahoo an-

160

nounced, but Oscar didn't appear to greet him. He tried again. "Hello?"

Nothing.

Donahoo shrugged, telling himself, as he had many times before, that it was nothing personal and one shouldn't concern oneself with a stupid cat's studied indifference. He dumped the two-suiter and put the attaché on a chair and the record player in its slot in the entertainment center that was fitted between the bar kitchen and the door to the shower-only bathroom that together took up one wall. The Murphy bed took another and a fireplace and some bookcases a third, filled mostly with volumes acquired at Friends of the Library book sales. Masked now by the bamboo slats blind, the fourth wall was glass, sliding doors overlooking a canyon, State Highway 163 winding at the bottom, and, on the other side, the semitropical forest of Balboa Park.

"Oscar?"

Nothing.

The red light was flashing on the answering machine. He pushed the button and checked the fridge.

"Amigo," Gomez said. "What is this I hear? You're on a secret mission? Be kind to my people."

Some secret, Donahoo thought. He checked the expiration date on some doubtful low-fat ham. A couple days past.

"Sarge," Cominsky began, faltering. "I'm sorry to bother you." Sound of something dropping. Long delay. "I need some help here. Call me, huh? It's . . ." Another long delay. "I dunno. Thursday?"

Donahoo put the ham out and found a note in the sink. It was from Barney. WHY DIDN'T YOU TELL ME HE WON'T EAT TUNA?

Cominsky was back. "It's about the O'Flanagan case."

Donahoo read Barney's note again. Oscar, he does so eat tuna, he thought. It's one of his favorites. Maybe he was just off his chow? Upset, you know, it could happen, by his master's absence?

"Tommy," Lewis was saying. "Where the hell are you? I've got all this crime lab voodoo shit in my office. If you don't come and get it I'm throwing it away."

He located a stale end of a French loaf and snapped it in half and made a pocket. He stuffed the ham in the hole. He looked for some mustard.

"It's me," a woman complained. "Millie. Remember? Bully's?

You didn't call so I thought I should. Maybe you lost my number, ha, ha. I'm leaving it up to you, okay? If you want to call, call. Frankly, I thought we had something going. Maybe it was just me." She gave her number. "It's up to you."

No mustard. Donahoo felt like a shit. He should have called, he thought. You meet somebody at Bully's and you chat her up and exchange telephone numbers and promise to call and you don't, is that a shit? He thought about it. Yeah, that's a shit. She was a nice lady and she'd probably been looking forward. It sounded like it. He'd been looking forward himself, as a matter of fact. He'd just kind of forgot all about her in the wild rush of events. Millie at Bully's. Big blonde girl. Nice smile. Nice personality. Great ass.

Torres on the machine now. *"Bueno* news, Sargento. *Teléfono, por favor."*

He got the phone and moved around the place as he dialed. Looking under things. Behind things.

"Captain Torres."

"It's Donahoo."

"Bueno. Está Lewis allá?"

"No."

"Habla con Herradura."

The phone was passed. "Sergeant?"

"Yes."

"He says he has checked into that matter and what he thinks, it is an empty threat, not to be taken seriously, so he would like you to return now, please."

"That was fast."

"Yes. So when will you return? Today?"

Donahoo hesitated. Tonight was The Dinner. "No. Tomorrow."

"He says nevertheless there will be discreet bodyguards."

"His concern is appreciated."

"He wonders if you want your room back at El Greco."

"Oh, yeah. That's a must. Is that all?"

"Yes. He says he'll see you tomorrow. He says good-by."

"Adiós."

Donahoo hung up and made another call. That was fast, he thought again. Really fast. He wondered how it could have been checked out so quickly. He also wondered how Diablo's people had gotten onto him, but if they had a large criminal organization, controlling things so lucrative and competitive as the drug trade, they would have better intelligence than the police. So maybe they knew he was essentially harmless and were just having some fun with him? Now he felt vaguely annoyed. He could have stayed in Tijuana if it was going to be cleared up so fast. Then he wouldn't have to go to The Dinner.

"Yeah," Lewis grumbled.

"It's me," Donahoo said. He checked with his new watch and remembered that he had to get a new cellular. He put it on a mental list of things-to-do today. He kept thinking that was fast. Too fast? The annoyance faded and he was apprehensive again. Maybe the danger was still there and Torres for whatever reason was bullshitting him? That was a definite possibility, he thought. There were a lot of turns on a crooked road. "Can I take you to lunch somewhere? That all-you-can-eat Chinese place you like? The Mandarin Szechuan?"

"You can come and get this voodoo shit."

"I'm gonna do that. Three o'clock. I'm meeting Marino at the station at three o'clock. We're gonna load it then. But first I want to take you to lunch. How about Kung Food? You remember how you liked Kung Food so much?"

"You only take me to lunch when you want something."

"That's not true."

"So what do you want? Tell me now."

"Can't I tell you when I take you to lunch?"

"No. I want to know now. Then I'll know whether or not I want to go to lunch with you."

Donahoo looked behind the TV. Oscar was a big cat but he could fit into very small places. He once fit into a half-gallon milk carton.

"Tell me now or forget it."

"Okay," Donahoo said. "I've had a bellyful of Marino. I want him off the case. I don't need an interpreter. He's just in the way."

"That's what you want?"

"Yeah. Say good-by, Marino."

"You think you know enough Spanish?"

"No. I think Torres knows enough English."

Lewis was silent for a moment.

"Please," Donahoo said. "It's a waste of resources. Put the kid to work doing something useful. He could work on the Gangs Unit. Or liaison with the Border Patrol."

"When did you care about wasting resources?"

"I've always cared about wasting resources."

"You're lying and when you're lying there's something fishy."

"There's nothing fishy."

"Bullshit, and the answer is no, and I don't want to go to lunch, and come and get this voodoo shit."

Donahoo hung up. Goddamn, he thought. There had to be a way. He was wrestling with a major parade-size premonition. He didn't want to be responsible for Marino when the crossfire broke out in Tijuana.

He flipped through his Rolodex for FBI Special Agent William Galloway. He punched in the number. He tried to think. What would work?

"Galloway," Galloway said.

"It's your choice. Dancers, Dirty Dan's, or Déjà Vu. My treat. Including a supply of dollar bills to stick in their pantyhose."

"You must want something."

"Oh, yeah."

Oscar came sauntering in off the balcony. He went by and into the kitchen. He didn't meow and he didn't purr.

Donahoo followed him. He bet he knew what was wrong. Barney, she forgot to put pickles in the tuna.

"Oscar," he said. "How can you ever forgive me?"

□   □   □

Marino was waiting, sitting outside Lewis's office, reading a large-print *Reader's Digest*, when Donahoo showed up to collect the crime lab equipment they were going to donate to Grupo Homicidios. He put the magazine aside reluctantly, as if there was something he wanted to finish.

"Does he know we're here?" Donahoo asked, looking through the glass partition at Lewis, who was busy with a file.

"He knows I'm here."

Donahoo got the *Reader's Digest*. He looked at the contents. "I Survived the Ice Age." The amazing cockroach. "Why Grown Men Don't Cry." It all starts in the crib. "The Third World." Who's to blame?

"Studying up on the cockroach?"

"No. The Third World."

"Oh? So who's to blame?"

"We are."

"In the *Reader's Digest?* Bullshit. In the *Reader's Digest* the Third World is to blame."

"Maybe they've had a change of heart."

Lewis was still busy with his file.

Donahoo tapped on the glass. When Lewis looked, he did a couple of giant eagles, jumping up with his legs spread, his arms stretched out.

Lewis shook his head and went back to his file. He closed it and opened another.

"We're here," Donahoo said, but not very loudly. He sat down next to Marino. He opened the *Reader's Digest* and turned to "Life's Like That." He said, "You talk to him?"

"We said hello."

"That's all?"

"Yeah."

"He, uh, didn't ask how things were going or anything?"

"No."

"Whether you liked it?"

"No."

Donahoo read "Life's Like That" and started on "Humor in Uniform." He thought he might find a Navy joke.

Lewis came out then. He said, "Tommy, it's not gonna happen, okay?" He tucked in his shirttail and headed for the Coke machine. He said, "Get that voodoo shit outa there. I want it gone by the time I get back."

There were two Dirty Dan's Pure Platinums, one on Kearny Mesa Road, near Montgomery Field, and the other downtown on Pacific Highway, at the back end, which on foggy days was the front end, of Lindbergh Field. The locations were probably arrived at by coincidence but the fact was that in both places the roar of a takeoff sometimes accompanied a takeoff.

Donahoo knew the Pacific Highway Dirty Dan's. The Waterfront, a bar where he watched *Monday Night Football,* was up the hill a couple of blocks, and he drove past when he took I-5 home to Uptown. If he happened to be giving somebody a ride (or if somebody happened to be giving him a ride) he could be talked into looking at the girls for a while. It was only a five-dollar cover and the drink prices weren't too stiff and there was an unwritten rule that a dollar tip stuck in the waistband of the sheer see-through pantyhose was quite acceptable. You could get out of there okay if you didn't have the food. The food was terrible.

Marino said, "What do you mean, terrible?"

Donahoo sighed. He was doing this all wrong. Why had he mentioned the food? He should be talking about the girls. The buck in the pantyhose. Not the food.

"You mean it's inedible?"

"No. Not inedible."

"You've tried it?"

"I've seen it."

"What are you saying? It *looks* terrible?"

Donahoo didn't answer. He was doing this all wrong, he thought again. Trying to lure Marino into a strip joint was like trying to teach Einstein arithmetic. The guy knew it already. He'd been to the Philippines, remember? Darkest Honolulu. San Pedro. He was a sailor.

"What did you see?"

"A sandwich."

Donahoo threw away the game plan. The game plan was for him to drive by, ever so casually, and say hey, what do you say, let's have a drink at Dirty Dan's? and Marino, still fondling memories of Louis/Lois in Tijuana, was supposed to say sure. Instead they'd gotten into a discussion of the food that was totally unnecessary because they weren't going to eat. They were just going to have a drink. Later they were going to The Dinner. Marino had invited him to meet Theresa and her parents, the Battistonis, Dominic and Gina, and he had accepted. The idea here, they were just going in for a drink, that's all. Spur-of-the-moment thing. Impulse purchase. An easy, natural decision. Arrived at mutually. But now they were drifting by. It was too late.

"We're going in for a drink," Donahoo said, starting around the block, or actually several blocks, he had AmTrak to contend with, the tracks ran parallel to Pacific Highway. He was going in. No discussion. "Fuck you."

☐ ☐ ☐

Galloway was at a table by himself. A pretty little black girl was dancing on the table just for him. He was wearing a light-green suit old enough to have been tailored in Sherwood Forest and he was like a fat frog watching a buzzing fly. Pretty soon the bug eyes were going to blink and a long red tongue would snap out.

Donahoo gave him a look as he went by with Marino. He'd agreed to pay the whole shot and that solo wasn't going to be a dollar tip. It would be at least a five. Probably a ten. He said, "Wild Bill. How the hell are you?"

"Uh, Tommy," Galloway said. He hardly looked. He was staring at the girl. He had his hand over whatever he was drinking. "We don't see you anymore."

"I've been busy."

"Yeah."

Donahoo took Marino to one of the big square stages with stools on three sides. There was a thin crowd that time of the afternoon. A couple noisy Marines, a salesman type, a guy in a RotoRooter smock and the usual pervert. Donahoo chose an open section where he could unobtrusively save a stool for Galloway. There might be a sudden rush of tourists or something. They got settled in and ordered Coronas from a waitress who looked like she was a dancer. She had long dancer's legs and a tight dancer's ass. A pretty flat dancer's chest.

"So who's that?" Marino asked, meaning Galloway.

"FBI," Donahoo told him. He tried to see what was going on backstage. There was something going on there. "William Galloway. He's a Special Agent in the San Diego office."

"Where do you know him from?"

"Police work."

"Yeah, I thought you might have worked a case together or something."

"No. We just exchange information once in a while. He can be a fat puke sometimes but he knows what's going on. Some of those guys, they watch too much *X-Files*, but Galloway, he's a down-to-earth guy, very reliable."

"You gonna introduce me?"

"No."

"Why not?"

"Because he's not gonna wanta meet you."

"How do you know?"

"Because he didn't come here to meet you. He came here to have a girl dance on his table."

Donahoo got out his wallet. The waitress/dancer was coming with the Coronas.

"I thought of going FBI," Marino said, looking at Galloway. "But, you know, there's no telling where they'll send you, and Theresa, she's happy here."

"A California girl?"

"San Diego. Both her parents were born here. They've never been anyplace else. She's the same kind of a stick-in-the-mud. She lives with them, as a matter of fact."

Oh? Donahoo hadn't known that. It hadn't come up. It explained, in part, perhaps fully, the scuff marks on the roof liner. It made them easier to forgive.

Galloway drifted over with the waitress/dancer and paid for the Coronas. He was nursing what looked like a Scotch. He didn't order another. He said, "Who's this?"

Donahoo shoved over the stool he'd been quietly saving. "Cruz Marino. New to the investigative ranks. He's working on something with me."

"I'm . . ." Galloway started to say, and Donahoo interrupted, saying, "I already told him," and then, "Cruz, he was gonna go FBI, but he's got a girlfriend."

"That'll do it."

"I guess."

Galloway got on the stool, which put Marino in the middle, and which reminded Donahoo of when they were in The Desperate Frog, Marino in the middle then too, between him and Torres, and that was the start of it with Catalina.

"Cruz. You're a Latino, huh?"

"No. Italian. The Cruz is a nickname."

Galloway's bug eyes moved over him. "Oh. I thought, you know, Cruz, he's gotta be a beaner, I'm sorry. Italian, huh?"

The next dancer was being introduced on the sound system. "We have a first for you this afternoon, gentlemen. We are introducing Marlene. This will be the first time that Marlene has danced in the nude in public. So let's get her off to a good start. Let's have a warm Pure Platinum welcome for Marlene."

They applauded roundly. Galloway said, to Donahoo, "What are you guys working on?", and Donahoo leaned across and whispered, "We're on a secret mission. Tijuana."

"Oh, yeah?" Galloway got suddenly interested in Marino. "Let me guess. You speak Spanish?"

Marino nodded. He was looking at Marlene. So was Donahoo. She was a tall, slim blonde, very pretty. She'd be about eighteen. Maybe a college freshman. She had that scrubbed freshman look. Interested and interesting, and vulnerable.

"Tijuana," Galloway said softly. "That fucking pisshole. We lost an agent there a while ago. He was working undercover and nothing ever came out about it because it would have jeopardized the people he was working with. But it was a real cocksucker, I'll tell you. Tijuana."

Marlene was dressed from the waist up. A tuxedo jacket with no sleeves over a frilly white shirt. She did a couple turns and then removed one of the cuff links.

Galloway said, "A slow start," and Donahoo said, "Yeah, but it looks like it's gonna be good," and Marino asked, "What happened to the agent?"

"Huh?"

"The agent. What happened to him?"

"Oh, yeah," Galloway said. "They trashed the poor sonofabitch. You'd think, you know, it's enough to kill a guy, but they gotta get fancy down there, they must have spent a couple, three days torturing him—what's the name of those ants?—and then, fuck, they cut off his dick, stick it up his ass, what's the point here? It's fucking inhuman."

"Whoa." This from Donahoo.

"We know who did it too," Galloway said. He was watching Marlene on her first time out. "But we can't make the case. I'll tell you something, I don't envy you, Cruz, working Tijuana, anything can happen there, you could offend the fucker, he runs the place. His name's Diablo."

Marino gave a Donahoo a little nudge. "Nice try."

Donahoo sighed. He said, "Galloway, you fucking incompetent, I've seen Chuck Norris act better," and Galloway laughed and said, meaning Marino, "He's just too smart for you."

Donahoo didn't think so. If Marino was smart, he wouldn't go back to Tijuana, he'd stay here with Theresa and let her kick the shit out of roof liners and live happily ever after, and that's the truth.

Marlene was working on other cuff link. A slow start but it was going to be good.

Twenty-two

The Battistonis lived in a little Craftsman house on Mission Avenue in University Heights. The old man was a taxi driver and the mother was a baseball fan. Dominic and Gina. They had lived in the same house since the day they got married. A quarter century. Theresa was a graphic designer. How University Heights got its name, there was going to be a university built there, but then it wasn't, yet they kept the name anyway. University Heights. It had a nice ring for a third-class neighborhood.

Marino told Donahoo all this and more as they were driving over from Dirty Dan's in the Toronado to attend The Dinner. Marino had told him so much that now Donahoo didn't want to attend The Dinner. He was thinking seriously of begging off. He was thinking of driving into a telephone pole.

Now Marino was at the part where Dominic's younger brother, Pauly, still a bachelor, incidentally, used to babysit Theresa and have her play with his erection, which he was kind enough to leave in his pants, and Theresa, amazingly, had not suffered any kind of trauma in later life. She thought it was funny. Pauly, the poor fuck, that's how hard up he was, and still was, on account of being incredibly shy.

"Uh," Donahoo said. "Is Pauly going to be there tonight?"

Marino said, "Yeah. That's why I'm telling you. I want you to take a good look at the guy."

"Why?"

"Why do you think?"

Donahoo wanted to abort but he didn't get invited to dinner very often. Hardly at all anymore. Investigator Frank Camargo and the fat, warm Marie used to have him over for dinner, but Frank got killed tracking the Balboa Firefly, and the last time Donahoo had broken bread with Marie, actually it was a sugar cookie, it was at Frank's wake.

170

Monica used to cook him dinner. She considered that one of her wifely duties. At the end, her only wifely duty. She'd cook dinner three, four times a week. She'd start off with a bang on Sunday and slowly wear down. Thursday you could never count on. Friday night she'd want to go to a Stuart Anderson's Happy Hour and fill up on the free hors d'oeuvres. Saturday night she'd want to go to the U.S. Grant Grill and not get seated opposite the toilets.

Presh never cooked him dinner. Didn't get the opportunity. They'd known each other only a few days. Just enough time to get her into bed and teach her how to shoot the Colt Python. To teach her—he had no idea it would turn out this way—inadvertently teach her how to kill a guy. It wasn't something she wanted to do and she never forgave him. Rosie never cooked him dinner either. Breakfast once and they didn't eat it. The Wham Bam Ice Trail was a take-out lady.

Donahoo thought about them a lot. He could imagine what they were doing at this precise moment. Monica was in a rocking chair, looking in a mirror. Presh was handing the *TV Guide* to a quiet man who managed an apartment block. Rosie was on a tropical island somewhere, living in a grass shack, drinking rum out of coconuts, introducing the local boys to the joys of sex, and taking her time spending two hundred thousand ill-gotten dollars. He didn't know that. He was just guessing. But he'd bet his next paycheck he was close.

"Here we are."

Donahoo parked the Toronado. He went way down the block to find a spot. He invested as much time as he could in the procedure without appearing to be obviously delaying.

The mother, Gina, was standing on the porch, welcome party of one, wearing a long white apron. She looked like an Italian mother in the movies. Short and plump. Dark and attractive. Excited. She had her hands clasped together.

Donahoo wondered if she was praying too.

"You brought him?" she said, and then, not waiting for an answer, turned and yelled, "He brought him!"

Marino explained. "They didn't think you'd want to come."

Donahoo followed Marino inside, directly into a small, overfurnished living room that was even more crowded than his studio at The Arlington. Two sofas when there was only space for one. A big outdated console TV. A tea cart in everybody's way.

Gina was burbling. "Cruz's sergeant. He's here." She said, "This is my husband, Dominic." She yelled, "Theresa? Where are you? Cruz's sergeant is here!"

Dominic was on a sofa, watching the TV. He was a tall, dark, intense man, thin and wiry. He was in shirt and suspenders and black pants and black pointed shoes. His suit jacket, waiting to be worn, required, was laid out beside him, draped over the back of the sofa. His black hair was thinning on top and his body was covered with it. Bunched at the throat of his open shirt and thick on his lower arms. Black caterpillar eyebrows hooding his dark eyes. He glanced up as if the distraction was unwelcome. He didn't offer his hand.

Donahoo thought that Dominic would be an unhappy guy, always complaining. He'd bitch if you slammed his cab door too hard. That kind of guy. He said, "Hi."

Pauly came in from somewhere in the back. He was a slightly taller, better-looking version of his brother, perhaps ten years younger; he still had all his hair. He was dressed the same way. The shirt with the half-rolled-up sleeves and the suspenders. The dark pants and black pointed shoes. He was carrying his jacket. He smiled shyly and offered his hand.

Donahoo took it. You're Pauly? He was going to say that. Marino told me all about you. But he didn't say anything. He just nodded.

"That's Pauly," Gina said. "Pauly, why don't you get some drinks?" She yelled, louder this time. "Theresa! Cruz's sergeant is here!"

Theresa, unseen, yelled back, "I know, Maw!"

Pauly got the drinks, which turned out to be red wine, apparently homemade, for everyone. Served in tumblers and dispensed from a tray. Gina went to see about the dinner. Dominic watched the TV. *Wheel of Fortune.*

"Dominic makes this stuff himself," Marino said, meaning the wine. "He and some friends. Every fall, they buy a boxcar full of grapes, do the whole thing. The stomping. Everything."

Dominic said, "It's not against the law. Personal use."

"It's good," Donahoo told him. It was. "What else do you make?"

"Just the wine." Dominic was looking at the TV. "What else would you think I made? The macaroni?"

Donahoo thought Jesus. The guy was a chainsaw. He couldn't believe Marino was thinking of marrying and staying in the area. He ought to make it a condition they move to Switzerland. Someplace neutral.

"So, uh, what do you do, Pauly?" Donahoo asked.

Dominic said, "He helps me with the wine."

Marino explained. "Pauly, he's between positions."

Gina was back. *"Theresa!"*

Donahoo looked at his new watch. The next two hours, they were going to be the longest of his life, he knew that, and there was nothing he could do about it.

"You like garlic?" Gina asked him.

Theresa entered and gave Marino a playful nudge. She was wearing a very severe dark blue dress and a single strand of imitation pearls. Both of them together probably cost fifty dollars and she looked like a million in them.

Donahoo, trying to formulate a garlic answer, was guilty of staring. It was not so much that she was a captivating woman, but that, in his haste to make judgments and draw conclusions, she wasn't supposed to be. She was supposed to be Marino's girl, and, therefore, kind of dumpy.

"Cruz's sergeant!"

"I know, Maw," Theresa said, smiling. She shook hands. "I love that big Toronado of yours." She was still smiling. "Sorry about that."

Donahoo wondered if he was blushing. He felt like it.

"Now we can eat," Gina said.

Dominic got up and put on his coat. Pauly put his on too.

They settled around a big table in a small dining room. Dominic at the head, Gina at the other end, Marino and Theresa on one side, Donahoo and Pauly across from them. The food was ready in covered dishes. Chicken cacciatore, stuffed peppers, green beans. Lots of garlic. Lots of red wine.

Donahoo had trouble not looking at Theresa. She was striking. A model's tall, thin body, maybe a little too tall, a little too thin, fashioned for *Vogue*. A Madonna's face with a flawless ivory complexion. Long black hair, large dark eyes, a sculpted nose, soft full mouth, and perfect, ten-years-at-the-orthodontist white teeth.

Also, the fullest black eyebrows he'd ever seen on a woman and they were perfect on her.

"So, Cruz is interpreting for you?" Gina passed the cacciatore and indicated that it should go first to Dominic. "Is he doing a good job?"

"The best." Donahoo gave the dish to Pauly. He wondered how the hell Theresa could have sprung from the collective loins of Dominic and Gina Battistoni. There was hardly any Gina in her and not much Dominic. She had his wiry frame and his ivory skin and his full set of eyebrows and then the resemblance ended. If anything, she was more Pauly. You could see her bright beauty in Pauly's dark good looks. "Cruz, he knows when to do it word-for-word and when to just summarize. He never tries to inject himself."

Gina said, "He's smart, all right," and Theresa, smiling, said, "That doesn't sound like Cruz." Cruz looked like he agreed.

Dominic helped himself. The cacciatore went back to Pauly and immediately to Donahoo. The stuffed peppers were going down the other side. They were going first to Dominic. Donahoo started feeling comfortable with it. Head of the household being treated with respect. The guy drives a cab but he's the head of his house. It's his house.

"You're in Tijuana?" Gina said.

"Yes."

"Cruz says it's a secret assignment."

Donahoo grinned at Marino. "It's more like a mission of mercy."

"So what are you doing there?"

"Investigating a crime."

Dominic said, "I'm paying your salary and you're working for the Mexicans?"

"Yeah," Donahoo said. "It's a freaking scandal. Tonight I'm gonna give you the police chief's name. I want you to write him a letter."

Cruz said, "Settle down, will you?" and Theresa, smiling, said, "You got a girlfriend?" She said to Cruz, "I was thinking of The Twins."

"They're very pretty girls," Gina said.

Cruz thought for a moment. "Yeah, The Twins." He thought some more. "Which one?"

"I'm not partial," Donahoo said.

Dominic grunted. He said to his wife, "He's a little old, isn't he?"

Donahoo looked at him. He smiled. He said, "Mind your own business."

☐ ☐ ☐

Later, sitting in the backyard, drinking more red wine, Donahoo got to know Dominic the crab and Pauly the babysitter a bit better, and he decided they were going to be okay. They had turned the corner when Dominic offered advice on what kind of car to buy and said not to buy a Ford. He said seventy percent of all cars towed were Fords. He said ask any tow truck driver. Dominic was what his mother used to call the Saul of the earth. Pauly, well, he was just a little shy, that's all. Together with Gina and Theresa, they were a family, rock solid. *E Pluribus Unum.* That kind of stuff. A few flaws. Maybe some things nobody talked about. Or had talked about once and didn't talk about anymore. Anyway, a family, living the good life in University Heights, and Donahoo, full of cacciatore and stuffed peppers and green beans, would just as soon be here with them as with most anybody else in most other places, and he also felt happy for Marino and his choice. Theresa was an exceptional girl.

"You never told me," Donahoo complained once, meaning Marino hadn't said anything about her being exceptional, and Marino said, "Oh, yeah? What did you expect?"

He got trapped into making comparisons. San Diego and Tijuana. Twenty minutes and you were in the Third World. How the hell did that happen? He thought he should have read the article in *The Reader's Digest*. It's our fault? He would like to know how they arrived at that conclusion. He shouldn't have wasted his time with "Humor in Uniform." He didn't remember any of the jokes and he didn't know why we were to blame. There sure was a difference though. University Heights, third-rate neighborhood, was paradise compared to a Tijuana colonia, and Theresa Battistoni, graphic designer, sure as hell carried less of a burden than Catalina De Lourdes Venezuela, lawyer for the oppressed.

She found him alone in a quiet moment. They talked about Marino.

"Cruz, he's a strange guy," she said. "Hard to know at first. You look at him the first time and he's not what you see. You think he's a pushover. He's not. Actually, he's very strong. Maybe not physically. But as a person? He's his own man. He's the strongest man I ever met." She laughed. "One day Dominic says to him, 'You're screwing my daughter,' and Cruz looks at him, he says, 'Of course.'"

Donahoo smiled. That sounded like Marino all right.

"I hope you're with him long enough to know him," Theresa said. "I'm gonna sound prejudiced here. He's worth knowing."

Donahoo smiled some more. He was going to say he'd take care of him but what she wanted to hear was that Marino could take care of himself. He was going to say that but he wasn't absolutely sure yet and he didn't want to in any way mislead a beautiful bride-to-be.

"When this is over—you're through in Tijuana?—I'll introduce you to The Twins. You can have your pick."

"Are they pretty?"

"Prettier than me."

Donahoo smiled some more. If he wasn't such a klutz, he'd be through now, he thought. He wondered what was the big attraction down there. Catalina or Marquisa? Or maybe Diablo? One of them. But he probably didn't have his pick. They were probably going to choose him. For different reasons.

☐ ☐ ☐

Later still, after dropping Marino off at the trolley, after making it almost back to The Arlington, he pulled into the Thrifty at Robinson and Sixth and went to a pay phone and looked up Dr. Sheldon Denke. Board Certified. Cosmetic, Plastic & Reconstructive Surgery. Phone 234-TRANS. He was hoping for an answering machine but got a service and that was probably even better.

"Tell the doctor, this is his last warning," he said. He was trying to sound not too much like Ricky Ricardo. "I'm deadly serious. He is to give back Louis/Lois his four grand right away. Or else he's gonna lose *his* dick. *Comprende?*"

He went back to the Toronado with a better appreciation of Lewis. You grow old and you begin to deteriorate and you retire. It is in the natural scheme of things and not to be challenged or made mock of.

The last thing he had asked Marino was, serious question, because the Third World was twenty minutes away and it was our fault, "What makes America great?" and Marino had said, "The people have a chance."

That was true. Partly true. Like most things, only partly.

Donahoo went home to bed. You can have your pick of The Twins. Yeah, he thought, and garlic doesn't smell on your breath, and babysitters just sit, and the sun shines for everybody.

Twenty-three

It was a mix of excess, worn or outdated equipment. A comparison microscope and a scanning electronic microscope. Liquid chromotographic equipment for detecting gunshot residue and tracking the source of explosives. A Visuprint System for developing latent fingerprints by exposure to chemical fumes and an argon-ion laser for developing invisible footprints. Several kinds of ultraviolet and infrared lamps for the forensic photography of tire prints and the like. What were probably three or four video surveillance cameras piled together in a large box. An infrared camera and two pairs of infrared goggles. And—what was attracting the most attention—a replacement for the identification kit that Grupo Homicidios had worn to tatters.

The LC and the Visuprint System and some of the rest of it would need instruction in use. Donahoo was going to arrange for a lab tech or a criminalist or somebody to come down and do that. For the moment, he just wanted Lewis's voodoo shit delivered, to show what a nice guy he was. No offense at being hijacked and threatened and dumped in the boonies. These things can happen in the best of regulated cities.

"Well—what can I say?—this is very kind and generous of your department," Torres said, Marino translating. "This will be very helpful to us. It fills in a lot of gaps."

They were in Torres's office at Grupo Homicidios. A small cop's office that looked like several small cop's offices that Donahoo had been around. Mostly filing cabinets and piles of paper with a descending turn of yellow. The lingering smell of warmed-over coffee and stale tobacco and unwashed suspects. Posters on the wall. The ambience of the relentless pursuit. Yesterday's hope and tomorrow's despair.

Donahoo and Marino with Torres and a Policia Judicial lieutenant named Jeronimo Herradura. The Herradura who had been on the phone the day before, saying, on behalf of Torres, that the coast was clear. They had already confirmed some things and gotten some business out of the way. Yes, the coast, it was clear, and yes, the discreet bodyguards were still a wise idea, and oh, someone else was looking into the punk kid's story that the cops did it. So Torres had been freed up to concentrate all his attention on the Hernandez murder case.

Torres had said, "It's not something I want to do, investigate fellow officers," and Marino, after translating, had asked, "Well, who is assigned?" and Torres had said, "Actually, I wasn't consulted," and nothing had really gotten settled.

Donahoo had considered making an issue of it but he knew it was useless. Torres with his big hands and his big feet and his big cowboy hat. If necessary he would tell them the big lie.

"It's not why you are here," Torres had said, meaning the punk kids.

Donahoo couldn't quarrel with that. It was one of the few things he was sure about. He might be here for a lot of reasons. But it wasn't because of the punk kids. They weren't expected.

Now Torres was building a face from the identification kit's palette. A wide face with a low forehead. He was pleased with the nose, which was a beak, but he wasn't happy with the eyes, he kept switching them. Herradura was watching with growing concern. He was a small, slight, bespectacled man in a slick khaki uniform with the badge and the patches and the epaulets. Bright and quick. A sharp inquisitive nose over a thin sensitive mustache. They both twitched.

Torres said to Herradura, asking for an opinion of what he had achieved so far with the face, "What do you think? Are the eyes right?" and Herradura, he was nervous now, asked Donahoo, "How should we express our thanks?"

"Your *capitán* just did." Donahoo was feeling pretty good about that part. Torres's appreciation of the donations had been obviously genuine and deep. "That's enough."

"No. I mean in an official letter. From our chief to your chief. Or perhaps it should be from the mayor?"

"I don't think so. I don't even know if our chief knows about the stuff."

Torres looked up, smiling. "You didn't abscond with it?"

"No. It was just donated at a lower level."

"Oh. And they don't need to be thanked?"

"They need to be anonymous." Donahoo thought that wasn't necessarily true but that the idea might appeal to Torres. It was the Mexican way. "I will express your appreciation. Okay?"

"Okay."

Donahoo looked at what Torres was doing. He was putting on a mustache now, a big Zapata. With the slit eyes, the beak nose, the cruel mouth, he had purposely created an evil image.

"Diablo, your nemesis," Torres said softly. He studied his efforts for a moment. "A very good likeness, even if I do say so myself." Now he was looking at Herradura. "Good enough to put on a wanted poster. Well, what do you think, lieutenant?"

Herradura didn't answer. He simply nodded to Donahoo and Marino. Then he quietly left.

"He's one of us," Torres said, again softly, as if to calm them. "There is no need to worry. He is a good man."

Donahoo examined the supposed face of Salvador Urquidez.

"I know how you can thank me," Donahoo said. "I still want to see this guy. Can you arrange that?"

Torres took the image. A movement of his hand and the pieces were scattered and the likeness never existed. "Why do you keep insisting?"

"I don't know." Donahoo thought he should give a reason and all he could think of was nonsense. "It's a part of police work, I suppose. If you see an evil person, then you can recognize evil in others."

Torres looked to Marino. "Does that wash?"

Marino didn't answer. Torres told him, "I think your Sargento has already seen enough evil people."

"I'm talking about degree of evil," Donahoo said, more nonsense. "That's why it's important to look at Diablo."

Torres laughed. He wasn't going to arrange it. He didn't want any part of it. Or so his laughter suggested.

"More important things," Torres told Donahoo. "While you were away, I got a lead on Playa's sister, Cecilia, who is said to live in Colonia X. Perhaps she knows where Playa is. Or something about him. So I thought we'd go."

Donahoo was thinking about Diablo.

"This is your theory that we are investigating, Sargento. That Playa, if he held power once, he might wish to hold it again, or might even, secretly, already hold it, and that is why he has gone missing. That *is* your theory?"

Donahoo nodded. With embellishment, he thought. He was sure that Torres wanted him to pursue Diablo. That could be the only reason for making the likeness and for frightening Herradura. Okay, we do it your way, he thought. At your pace. This was something he knew was going to happen from the start. Torres would find some way to chart the course. And it wouldn't be straight.

Torres found a scrap of paper in his pocket. "Oh. I almost forgot. Catalina called. She wanted me to give you a message. Louis/Lois says thank you." He waited and then smiled. "What is that about?"

Donahoo just looked at the ceiling. There were some odd dark splotches. Maybe blood spilled during interrogations? He was just kidding.

"She says you're fast."

Donahoo still didn't answer. He thought they were all fast. Speedy Catalina and Speedy Tommy Donahoo and don't forget Speedy Jerónimo. You saw the way he got out of here?

□   □   □

Colonia X. It was southwest of the city and beyond El Dompe. Donahoo thought he must be excused for being trite. If you saw one colonia you saw them all. This one was a replica of the others. Dirt roads and paths. Hovels fashioned from scraps. Plywood, tarpaper, corrugated metal, anything. Fastened to the hillside by slanted stacks of old tires. No water. No electricity. No sewer system. No stores and no doctor's office. No police presence.

Torres got directions from a child. He led them to one of the worst shacks. Then he stood aside. He said, Marino translating, "Why don't you talk to her, Sargento? I don't think she will trust me. She may trust you."

Donahoo went in. There were several small children sitting wide-eyed on the dirt floor.

Marino said, *"¿Dónde está tu mamá?"* and the youngest pointed. *"Allá."*

Playa's sister Cecilia was on a dirty cot in a shedlike shelter at the rear. She was pregnant and perhaps soon to give birth. The expectancy was written on her face. It shimmered in the pain.

Donahoo found a stool and sat down. Marino stood beside him on the dirt floor. Donahoo thought that Cecilia had been pretty once, he could see it in the bones of her face, which were delicate and nicely formed and placed, and which showed more than in most faces, she was so thin. She was too thin and that was what made the child appear so large. Actually it probably was a small child inside her.

She looked at them despairingly.

"Tell her," Donahoo said, "who we are and what we are doing and what we want, okay? That, requested by federal authorities, say *federal*, that we are trying to solve a murder, use the name, Deedee Hernandez, and say we suspect someone is trying to frame Playa for it. Playa and—maybe she knows him?—Juarez."

"Tell her that?"

"Yes. Tell her it's an international case under public scrutiny and that not even the Mexican police will harm him while we're working on it. Juarez, maybe, if he's guilty of something, but not to Playa, because as far as we know Playa isn't guilty of anything. He's being framed."

Marino said it all in Spanish. It sounded like a speech.

"What does she say?"

"She understands."

"Will she help?"

Marino asked her. "She says no."

"Why not?"

"She doesn't believe us. She thinks it's a trick."

Well, it is a trick, Donahoo thought. They could offer no protection to Playa. Not for an instant. Like the punk kids, Playa could get a bullet in the back of the head, *coup de grâce*, and there would be doubt about the skill, and the point of view, of the officers assigned to investigate. "Tell her it's not a trick."

Cecilia bit her hand to choke back a scream.

"I think she is going to have the baby."

Donahoo looked at her. Filthy clothes in a dirty cot. "Here?"

"Yes."

"Now?"

"Pretty soon."

"Do you think we should move her?"

"No." Marino was looking around desperately. "Do you think Torres arranged for us to be here now? For this?"

"Absolutely." Donahoo had no idea but he wouldn't be surprised. "He's arranged everything else."

"We're gonna need help."

Donahoo went outside to inform Torres. A small girl was running barefoot down the hillside. She would be seven, perhaps eight years old, a small girl in rags, her long black hair flying. Donahoo recognized her as one of the children in the shack.

Torres, smiling at him, said, *"La partera."*

Marino came out. "She's gone to get the midwife."

Donahoo said, "How can she have a baby here?" and Torres said, *"Lo hacen todo el tiempo,"* and Marino translated, "They do all the time."

"It's not right."

"No. It isn't."

Donahoo reached into Marino's shirt pocket and got his Pacificos. He took one for himself and put the pack back. He went down the hill a bit and sat down on the ground and lit it.

Torres asked, "Are we staying?" He didn't ask if Donahoo had learned anything.

Donahoo sucked in the sweet smoke. "Yes."

The baby, a boy, was stillborn about an hour later. Donahoo didn't see it but Marino did. He said it was deformed anyway.

□ □ □

The midwife looked like a butcher. Her arms and forearms and the front of her dress were red with blood. She was carrying a plastic bag that contained the day's failure.

"There's no water," she said, explaining her condition. "They have no money to buy it." She paused to get her breath. "There's a little. I left it for the children. I will wash at my house."

Donahoo was staring at the plastic bag. It was from Ley's.

"You're looking for Playa?"

"Cecilia told you?"

"No. Luz. The girl who came to get me. She told me what your interpreter said. That you made promises."

"I meant them."

"Yes. But I doubt you could keep them."

"You don't trust me either?"

"No."

Donahoo didn't blame her. "Do you know where Playa is?"

"No."

"Then it doesn't matter."

Torres and Marino were headed down the hill toward the Le-Baron. Donahoo started after them.

The midwife said, "I know why he's in danger."

Donahoo stopped. "Oh? Why is that?"

"Because he is a good man."

Torres and Marino were looking back at him. Donahoo waited.

"Because he is not afraid."

Torres was beckoning. It was time to go. Donahoo waited.

"Because he was going to start a new *colonia*."

Colonia Pompano. Playa was going to give it his name. So he would be remembered forever. They would tear down a statue before they tore down a *colonia* and they had never torn down a statue. Which might or might not be true. Donahoo didn't know.

Torres came back and got all the information from the midwife, whose name was Solace, and the girl, Luz, and an older boy, Ramón, and an old stick of a man, Argyle. After a while they told the story proudly. They said the *paracaídistas*, the parachutists, would descend en masse, as if from the sky, and they would transform the land into a barrio before anyone could stop them. To them, Playa was a hero, even if he'd failed, and maybe he had failed. Nobody knew where Playa was.

Yes, the Juarez question, Donahoo thought, listening to Marino's quiet translation. Everybody's asking it. About Playa and also about Juarez. Tough question. Juarez these guys?

"The new *colonia*? Where is it to go?"

"That is a secret."

"But on private land?"

"It is disputed land."

"Who disputes it?"

"We do."

"That is not a legal claim."

"Who cares? It's not being used."

"How many people to move there?"

"A thousand to start."

"And they all know?"

"Yes."

"And they are waiting only for Playa to lead them?"

"Yes."

Torres was excited. His questions revealed what he suspected now. That Deedee Hernandez, unbeknownst to her husband, Jorge, had been supporting Playa financially in his bid to start the new Colonia Pompano. Someone in power found out about it. It could be anyone. The government. A political party. Perhaps the landowner? Someone found out and decided to get rid of them. They plotted to kill Deedee and blame Playa. Juarez just strayed into the line of fire.

No. Not really, Donahoo thought. Juarez introduced Playa to his friend Deedee Hernandez. The beautiful rich lady he met . . . where? Maybe in his taxi after her Mercedes broke down? Maybe by chance at El Dompe? Anyway, he met her, introduced her, and then he strayed.

"Do you think there'll be a new *colonia?*" Donahoo asked this one question. He asked the girl, Luz.

"How can there be?" she said. "If Playa is dead?"

"How do you know he is dead?"

"Then where is he?"

Donahoo took the question back to El Greco. He went to sleep with it. He had thought they would find Playa with Juarez. He still thought that, but now he believed, like Luz, that they would be dead. They ran away because they knew they were in danger. They had decided, correctly, that they couldn't win. If Deedee couldn't, they couldn't. Deedee had done too much and Playa intended too much and Juarez knew too much. It marked them for death. If they weren't dead now, they would be dead soon. Torres had said as much. He had said, "There is no time to waste, we must find them, Sargento."

Marino wasn't going to go to sleep for a while. His role with the midwife was too fresh in his mind. He wanted to talk. He said, "God. I wish you had seen that baby."

Donahoo wondered when Marino was going to learn. "I don't like to look."

Twenty-four

They went looking for corpses. Torres seemed to have lost all hope that next morning. He didn't say so but Donahoo could see it in his face. The weary resignation as plain as the furrows. All the spirit seemed to have been drained from him. He moved slowly and didn't lead. At first, Donahoo thought there might be something else causing it, something to do with the four punk kids, but whenever Torres did speak with any sense of urgency, it wasn't about them, it was about Playa and Juarez. Donahoo decided that Torres must have some fresh information. He must have heard something. Perhaps some scuttlebutt at Policía Judicial. Or perhaps some word from an informant. Donahoo was content to wait to hear what that was.

Torres might not appear to lead, but only he knew the way, Donahoo thought. He would get them there eventually. Donahoo was convinced now that there was an agenda and that it was no longer hidden. It was unfolding and you could see it. In every little piece of the puzzle that struggled into place too late.

The place now was called La Metrópoli. The piece was not yet apparent but it would appear. La Metrópoli was a hotel with a restaurant and a bar and a whorehouse. Torres said they were all one and the same. The single enterprise. So, yes, the piece would be here, Donahoo thought, which was the best he could manage before breakfast. She would be along maybe when Torres got back from the toilet. He had directed them to a table and then disappeared with the bartender/waiter. The table was in the center of a bunch of other tables that were in a kind of shallow semibasement square pit. The bar was above it, along one wall, and there was a kind of balcony, a long, narrow walkway, along an adjoining wall. The other two walls were street walls with high windows. La Metrópoli was on a corner.

"There's an agenda, you know that?" Donahoo said now that he was alone with Marino. There were only a few other customers and they were in a corner. "We are doing one thing, investigating Deedee's murder and the complications arising from it, the disappearance of Playa and Juarez, but it's not the main reason we're here."

Marino was having a bad morning. He said, "Please."

"You don't see it?"

"No."

"Yeah, well, I do," Donahoo said. "Nobody much cares whether we solve Deedee's murder or not, including her fucking husband, he's happy she's gone. Torres didn't get into gear until we connected Juarez to Playa and then only when we found about the new colonia. Now look at him. He's given up on them. He's just going through the motions."

"And?"

Donahoo thought it was there in front of them. The motions, as always, relentlessly, were taking them through the slimy underbelly, from El Dompe to La Mesa and Dios Mediante. To Colonia X and now here to La Metrópoli, which was yet to reveal itself, but would. "You said so yourself. Torres is always showing the bad side. There's a good side. You'd think he'd show it too."

"He's a cop."

"So am I."

Marino considered. He was tired and cranky. He hadn't slept well at all. He had twisted his sheet into a rope. He had a headache and the aspirin hadn't worked. He'd been complaining about all these things.

"Don't you ever wonder why?"

"An agenda," Marino said. "What is that? A plot?" He got out his Pacificos. "I don't see a plot here. I see a lot of shit." He lit up, his pudgy face, if that was possible, drawn. "You can make a plot out of shit? I guess that's why you're the sergeant."

Torres returned from the toilet. He looked at them suspiciously. He apparently thought, correctly, that they were talking behind his back, discussing the case and maybe keeping something from him. He said, "What have you got?"

"No respect," Donahoo said. He felt like giving Marino a whack. He wondered if he ever would. Probably, he thought. One of these days.

Torres sat down and they ordered *huevos rancheros*, for breakfast from the bartender/waiter and then the whores came out.

They came out on the narrow balcony, five of them, and they stood with their backs to the wall, facing the pit, as if they were in a police lineup. They had cardboards with numbers which they held up briefly.

Donahoo thought they were the worst whores he had ever seen. They were ugly, hard whores. He thought, Jesus Christ. Marino, the Far East Marino, the Philippines and beyond Marino, looked like he was thinking much the same thing.

"I recommend you should choose the blonde," Torres said, looking at Donahoo, "Number Two," and Donahoo said, "Tell him he's out of his fucking mind. Tell him I would rather catch my dick in a zipper."

Torres smiled. He looked for the bartender who was also the waiter. The man was going through a door with a porthole. Presumably into the kitchen. He looked to the other customers, the men in the corner, three at one table, two at another. They were not paying any attention.

"This is how we must do it," Torres said softly then. "Otherwise you may compromise her. It's like the 'French Connection.' Popeye takes the stoolie into the toilet and slaps him around so the other criminals won't be suspicious. In the same way we, you, have the woman here at our table, to see how much she charges for what, but the thing we actually are doing is questioning her about Juarez. You see?"

"I don't see why she can't come here to see Cruz."

"Cruz?" Torres laughed. "What would a man such as Cruz need with a whore? He is young and handsome. He can have any woman he wants. He doesn't have to pay."

"And I do?"

"I'm sure not." Torres was still laughing. "But I'm also sure this way is more plausible."

The waiter came with their coffee. Torres said, *"Por favor, también mandenos el número dos."* Marino was too distressed to translate but Donahoo knew what Torres had said. He had asked Number Two to join them.

"Has anybody got a twenty?" Torres said when the man left. He took one of Marino's Pacificos and gently rolled and squeezed the tobacco out of it. "Anyone? Someone?"

Donahoo gave him a twenty. Torres took the bill and rolled it up tightly and inserted it in the empty tobacco tube. He put it aside.

"Tell me about these women," Donahoo said. "Why are they . . ." He searched for a polite word. "So disreputable?"

"Fate," Torres answered. "They were born ugly and for whatever reason they have no education and no skills and so little choice but to be beggar or whore and there is small call for a truly ugly whore. So they end up here in bondage at La Metrópoli."

"Bondage?"

"In the sense that there is no place lower that they can go. They could leave if they want but no other whorehouse would have them and they couldn't make a living on the street."

"What makes La Metrópoli different?"

"Its reputation. Which is that a whore can be knocked around and no one will complain very much."

Number Two came over in answer to some unseen signal. She was bad at a distance and worse up close. She was an ugly slut that no amount of thick makeup and heavy perfume could disguise. A peroxide blonde with big hurt brown eyes sunk deep in her face and a broken nose and decayed teeth. She'd be in her mid-twenties but looked more like forty. She had been used harshly. There was a lot of scar tissue. Lumps that had become permanent.

"What is your name?"

She smoothed a pale green satin dress that had crept up on her long walk over. "Desmonde."

Torres pushed out a chair for her to sit down across from Donahoo. He got Marino's Pacificos again and knocked one out for her. He lit it and then gave her the tube with the hidden twenty. *"Para luego,"* he said, winking, meaning for later, and she nodded through the smoke, showing no thanks or pleasure. She said only, *"Cuanto?"* and when he said, *"Veinte,"* she said, *"Bueno."*

"We have some questions which only you will hear and no one need know we asked," Torres continued in Spanish, and now Marino was belatedly translating, most of it, as required. "The same goes for your answers. This is a private conversation we are having."

"Es la policía?"

"Sí."

She shrugged slightly. *"Siga."*

"This is about Pedro Juarez. We know he is your cousin. We know you know he is an escapee from La Mesa. That he is a suspect, not yet charged, in a woman's murder there, and also as a material witness in another murder, the slaying of Deedee Hernandez. We know you know this but what we don't know is if you can help us find him."

"*No creo.*"

Marino translated. "She doesn't think so."

"We want to help him."

"*No creo.*"

"She doesn't think so."

"That big shot," Desmonde continued bitterly. "He thinks he's in politics? He wants to be a lawyer and he's a cab driver. He's a *basurero.*"

Torres pounced. "He worked at the dump?"

"For a while. Last year. He's so important."

Donahoo listened to Marino's translation. Rosetto had been right about Juarez, he thought. Partly right, anyway. He knew Deedee Hernandez. They'd met at El Dompe. Whether they were friends, though . . . ?

Torres said, "We must have your assistance."

"*No creo.*"

"Tell her," Donahoo suggested, "that Juarez has fallen into unfortunate company, with Playa Pampano, and that unless we get to him first, he is going to get what Playa gets."

Desmonde's eyes widened at the mention of Playa's name. Marino, on an indication from Torres, told her what Donahoo had said, and now fear showed in her eyes.

"Does she know about the new *colonia?*"

Marino translated and she nodded.

"Does she know who wants to stop it?"

Desmonde hesitated, then said, "*Lo siento. Debo irme ahorita.*"

"She is sorry but now the interview is over."

Torres told her, "Here maybe. But not at the police station. That is where we are taking you now."

She shrugged.

"No," Donahoo said. "Tell her instead that we will make it impossible for La Metrópoli to keep her here. Tell her that we will put her on the street and she will have to stay there."

Desmonde could suddenly understand and speak English. "You gringo prick," she exclaimed sharply. It took her a moment to compose herself. Then she stood and put her cigarette-for-later in her bra. She glanced at her sisters still lined up against the wall. "Why don't you look at our old house? We all lived there together once. My family and Pedro's family. The house no longer exists but maybe the root cellar is still there. Pedro used to hide there. He called it his fort. Maybe he would go back there. I don't know."

Torres asked, "Where was the house?"

"On Calle Montayo in Pueblo Sorrento. Where it ends at the edge of the mesa. All the houses there were razed for a *maquiladora* but it still hasn't been built. So it is just a wasteland now."

"Thank you. We will look there."

She glanced again at her sister whores. "Well, now, you seem in a hurry, gentlemen," she said more loudly. "But maybe you will come back later? My price is twenty dollars. That is for straight. To ass fuck is thirty. For fellatio only is fifteen. I can give a group rate on fellatio. The three of you for thirty." She smiled grimly. "Or, of course, there are other girls, and we could party."

They watched her go. Marino said, "She knows we're not coming back, right?" and Donahoo told him, "I don't think that's going to disappoint her."

□ □ □

The house, as stated, no longer existed, but the root cellar, as predicted, was still there. It was at the back of what had been the lot, still defined by bits of fence, a hole in the ground with a rough plank door, and difficult to locate because it was on a hillside and facing away from the property, looking out over a slum valley.

Torres found it. He yelled, *"Allá abajo!"*

Donahoo and Marino went down the hillside. Torres waited for them and then pulled the plank door aside dramatically. It was just a hole and there was no one in it.

"Mierda," Torres said. He had brought a flashlight, which he played on the dirt floor, the walls. It illuminated an old mattress, broken bottles and rusty cans, scraps of yellow paper. *"Nada."*

Donahoo took the flash and crouched down and went inside. He checked around thoroughly and there was nothing. Then he lifted the mattress and found a section of folded newspaper that looked fresh. He took it outside and gave it to Torres.

"La Mejicana." Torres read the date and grinned. "This has that gossip column about you dancing for Marquisa. Would you like it for your files?"

"No."

Marino said, "Maybe Marquisa was hiding here?"

Torres shook his head. He showed a small story he had found.

Marino translated the headline. "La Mesa Murder. Escapee Sought." Torres said, "I think Juarez, huh?"

Yes, Donahoo thought. But now he's run away from here—maybe. He was changing his mind. The hillside had been disrupted recently by someone's hurried passage. If Juarez had been here? If someone had come from above to harm him? Where would Juarez go?

Donahoo started down the hill.

"Dónde vas?"

"To look."

Donahoo kept going. There was a kind of path he was following. Dislodged dirt. Upturned rocks. Broken twigs. Two rough trails. Where one man ran and another man chased him?

"No hay nada allá abajo!" There is nothing down there!

Donahoo didn't answer. He went down the hillside, following the two paths which sometimes paralleled and sometimes ran over each other, indicating, he thought, rough pursuit.

"Está perdiendo tu tiempo!" You're wasting your time!

Donahoo smelled them first and then he saw the flies. He got his handkerchief and put it over his face. He moved closer reluctantly. Two bodies face down in the weeds. Both shot in the back several times by what appeared to be a high-powered rifle. They had been trying to escape and they had been shot like animals.

Juarez and Playa, Donahoo thought. He didn't look.

Torres surprised Donahoo on the drive back to El Greco. Before, in the morning, Torres had been depressed, and Donahoo had thought it was because Torres feared that Juarez and Playa were dead. Now, it seemed, and it was difficult to imagine, let alone comprehend, Torres seemed somehow elated by their deaths. It was as if a burden had been lifted from him.

Donahoo couldn't get that idea out of his mind and at last he had to ask Torres about it.

"What has relieved him?" Donahoo said to Marino, putting the question as delicately, as diplomatically, as he could. "What has happened here?"

"What do you mean?"

Torres had understood most or all. He slowed the LeBaron. He thought for a moment. Then he pulled over, parked. He got one of Marino's Pacificos.

Donahoo took one too. They were all smoking now. Marino's Pacificos. Fuck the Surgeon General.

"We've come to the end, I think," Torres said, Marino translating. "It is a kind of closure. Deedee is dead and Juarez is dead. The victim and her killer." He raised a big hand. "Which we know is not true but the truth doesn't help us and a lie does. It permits Jorge Hernandez to go to the District Federal and sit at the right hand of El Presidente."

"There is no longer a need to frame Juarez?"

"Yes. We are excused of that despicable act."

Donahoo puffed on the cigarette he didn't like but liked a lot more than a Marlboro. "What about the real killer?"

"Do you think you can find him?"

No, Donahoo thought. Not here, anyway. In San Diego, with time, yes. He could find a killer. But here? No. That was a joke. It had always been a joke.

"I don't think I can find him either," Torres said, and now he sounded depressed again. "Maybe, someday, I will find him, and I hope I do, but it will be for something else. That would be my only chance, I think. If he is an assassin, he will kill again, he will kill often, and maybe, one of those times, he will come to me, huh? Perhaps."

Donahoo said, to Marino, "What do you think?" and Marino said, "I think the whole thing is fucked."

□   □   □

The whole thing? Donahoo wondered about that later at dinner with Catalina. She had called him and said it was her treat. To say thanks for getting Louis/Lois his money. They went to a new place, it was very romantic, a strolling violinist, not a *mariachi* band. It was called Marfil. Which meant ivory.

She was as beautiful as ever and just as mussy. She made him happy. He delighted in her. Then, as he knew he would, he confided in her, and soon he had made them both sad. He told her more than he meant to about Juarez and Playa and possibly more than he should have about Torres. He was not at the point where he cared much about the niceties though. He too felt that it was over. There was nothing more he could do except go home. They had achieved—how did Torres put it?—a kind of closure.

She had also told him too much. She had a younger brother, Manuel, who had been (this is what he said) falsely accused of drug possession, marijuana for his own use, and he had been attacked in jail, by men who were going to rape him, and he had killed one of them, protecting himself, and now he would spend most of his life there. It was a horrible injustice, and one of the reasons, perhaps the main reason, she was a lawyer.

Donahoo had said, it was a stupid thing for him to say, "How can I help him?" and she had smiled sadly and answered, "I think only I can help him. Or, if he is a lost cause, maybe he can be of service?"

How? He was going to ask but didn't. He thought that maybe he already knew too much and anyway they had reached closure. The intimacy he had hoped for wasn't between them tonight. There was too much sadness.

Maybe some other time? He hoped so. "Well," he said. The word was like a rock in his throat. "Closure?"

Catalina smiled carefully. Then she said, "I think you're wrong. I think, tomorrow, you may change your mind." She said, "It's not over until the fat lady is buried."

He didn't correct her. It was, he suspected, the Mexican version.

Twenty-five

Donahoo thought about that all night. He took it to bed with him and he woke up with it. Found it still with him as he kept his eyes closed because he was dimly aware of the sun at the window and he wasn't ready for the sun. He was taking a lot of things to bed these days, he thought. Not anyone interesting or desirable. Certainly not Catalina De Lourdes Venezuela. He was taking dark thoughts and bad choices and dead ends. He lay there a moment longer and made up his mind. He was going home.

He reached over blindly for the cellular. He didn't open his eyes until it was absolutely necessary. The sun was slanting in between drapes that hadn't been fully drawn. He turned away from it and punched in Lewis's number.

Marino was still asleep. Donahoo didn't know how anyone could sleep so long and so soundly. Marino had been asleep when he returned home from dinner with Catalina. That—Donahoo checked his new watch—had been just after ten o'clock. Now—needlessly, dumbly, he checked it again—it was almost nine o'clock. So what was that? Eleven hours? Who slept eleven hours? He had no idea when he had fallen asleep himself. Sometime in the middle of the night. The last time he had looked it was two-thirty.

The switchboard, and then Lewis said, "Yeah."

"It's me." Donahoo got up on an elbow. He had made up his mind. "We've got a wrap here. We're closing down and we're coming in."

"A what?"

"A wrap."

"What the fuck is a wrap?"

Donahoo closed his eyes and fell back on the pillow. All he wanted to do was go home. How could that be difficult?

"What are you saying? You solved the case?"

"No," he said. "It's hard to explain, but it's over, okay? Juarez, the material witness, he's dead, murdered, and his political friend, Playa, who got him into this mess in the first place, he's dead, too. Both of them murdered. Together."

"And that's a wrap?"

"Yes."

"It sounds like an *un*wrap to me."

Yeah. Donahoo had to admit that was true. It had spilled out all over the place. It was scattered from here to there. But he still wanted to go home.

"I don't get it. You're settling for this?"

"Yes."

"You're down there on a murder and now you've got two connected murders and you're through?"

"Yes."

"What did you say your name was?"

"Listen," Donahoo said tiredly. "I'm not sure anymore why we're here, if I ever was. Maybe we're looking for the ancient astronauts or flying humanoids. It could be cattle mutilations or the giant squid. I don't know, Lewis. We could be checking on the goblin universe. Listen to me. I want outa here."

"Is it something you ate?"

"I'm coming home, Lewis," Donahoo said. He looked at the sleeping Marino. *"We* are coming home. We've got a wrap and we're coming home."

"Okay. Shit. It's your case. Who gives a fuck? Just tell me. What did they say?"

Donahoo wondered. About what? The donations? "I thought you didn't care?"

"I don't. I'm asking for Saperstein. He cares."

"About the donations? He knows about them?"

"He knows about everything."

No, he doesn't, Donahoo thought. He doesn't know about this shithole. "They're grateful. They said thanks."

"I'll tell him."

Donahoo said good-by and hung up. He wondered why Lewis hadn't had asked about Diablo. Whether he had forgotten or was just being polite. He decided he had forgotten.

Torres was knocking on the door. He was yelling, "Sargento?" and yelling, "Cruz!"

Marino didn't blink. Donahoo got up and went to the door. He unlocked it and went immediately back to bed.

Torres finally pushed the door open and entered. He looked at them and smiled. He took off his cowboy hat and sat down.

Donahoo knew that he was trapped. He didn't even argue.

"Have you ever been to a donkey fuck?"

"No. As a matter of fact I haven't."

"Would you like to go to one?"

"Will I see Diablo there?"

"Yes. Most likely."

"Then let's do it."

The donkey fuck was in the dank back room of a seedy bar in Zona Norte called Club Plus.

The guard at the heavy door knew Torres. He had only to say, *"Están conmigo,"* meaning, "They are with me," and the guard said, *"Pase,"* and opened the door on a clamor.

Donahoo took a last clean breath. There were perhaps two dozen men crowded into the small smoky space. They were drinking and laughing and visiting with each other. They were mostly well-dressed men in their thirties, forties, and fifties. There were no young men and only a few old men. Some glanced their way but no one showed any real interest.

The donkey—actually, it was, in this instance, a burro—had been put atop a large wooden table with its legs spread and tied in place in special blocks. It was tied so securely there was no way it could move or kick.

One of the men was sitting on a rubber donut cushion on a low stool and playing with the animal's genitals. He was making it have an erection.

Donahoo thought he recognized the man from the identification kit picture Torres had made. A smallish man with a big round head and a low forehead. Slits for eyes and a beak nose and cruel mouth and a Zapata mustache. It could only be Salvador Urquidez. He'd finally met Diablo.

An unexceptional man, Donahoo thought, oddly disappointed. He had expected that Diablo would exude evil. That it would be palpable here in this evil room. But he was merely a smallish man playing with a burro's cock. He was repugnant and sickening but he did not look like the devil.

"Is that him?" Donahoo asked softly, and Torres, not waiting for Marino, said, *"Te decepcionaste?"*—are you disappointed?—and Donahoo, practicing his Spanish, said, *"Muy desilusionado."*

Now Marino was translating for Torres. They were standing in a vacant corner and no else could hear. "Everybody is. It is the nature of man. He saw the Son of God and he was disappointed. He sees the Devil and it is not enough. He must have horns and a tail. Hooves."

Yes, Donahoo thought. Where is the pitchfork? Urquidez was tugging on the burro's cock. It was getting enormous.

"Why the cushion?"

"Piles."

Donahoo thought that the guy looked silly and oddly effeminate. He wasn't wearing the khaki mufti often opted for by ex-army officers but was dressed instead in a sleek brown leather jacket over a teal silk shirt. Blue jeans and thick white socks and rich tan boat moccasins. All he needed was a scarf. Then he'd be suspect.

A waiter came around asking what they wanted to drink.

"Coronas," Torres said, without consulting. "Trust me."

The waiter smiled and went away.

"What do they do?" Donahoo asked, meaning what would the woman who was coming do with the burro who was waiting, he had a pretty good idea but he wasn't absolutely sure, and Marino said, "They just hug and kiss a lot," and Donahoo thought he was getting pretty fucking tired of Marino. The guy slept in and then he got fresh.

The woman came now as a cheer went up. She looked like one of the whores in the lineup at La Metrópoli. A hard slut with a fighter's face and a wrestler's body. Big silicone-bag breasts and thighs that hadn't required any outside assistance. She came eager and smiling and twirling flat-footed through the men in a tight pink ballerina's costume.

A man started chanting her name. "Ella, Ella, Ella!"

Donahoo wondered who the woman was and what had brought her here. How could she have sunk so far as to be with a beast?

He said, "Why does she do this?"

"She is Diablo's wife."

"Be serious."

"I am."

Donahoo realized that he was speaking directly to Torres and without any need of Marino.

"His wife?"

"Yes."

The waiter came with the Coronas. They were five dollars each. Donahoo gave him a twenty.

"It's so . . ."

"Bizarre?"

"Yes. I can't explain it."

"I don't want you to try."

Ella took the burro's cock from Urquidez. Either she had a better touch or the burro had a fond memory. He became noticably bigger.

"Ella! Ella!"

Donahoo decided that he didn't want to know anymore. That there was nothing more he wanted to hear. Nothing more he wanted to see. He left with his beer.

Torres called after him in surprise, "Hey," and Marino, apparently thinking he was out of earshot, said, "Forget it, he doesn't like to look."

Donahoo waited outside in the hot sun. There was shade available in arcades and on doorsteps and behind pillars but he preferred the sun. He hadn't wanted it in the morning because he didn't want to see the morning. He wanted it now to bake out the sorrow.

He was so full of sorrow, he thought. For Juarez and Playa. For Deedee Hernandez. For the four punk kids. For all the prisoners at La Mesa and the Tijuana Jail. For Cecilia and her dead deformed baby and barefoot Luz. For Torres and Catalina and Louis/Lois and Desmonde and Ella, Ella, Ella. For all those little cocksuckers at Dios Mediante Orfanato y Refugio. He even felt sorry for himself. He couldn't go back in there and whack smartass Marino. He couldn't do that because Marino's indiscretion was inconsequential compared to Salvador Urquidez's crimes. He couldn't hurt Marino and not punish Urquidez and he didn't know how to punish Urquidez.

So he baked in the sun. And he wouldn't have seen it if he hadn't been doing so. It was only there for a split second but unmistakable—the glint of a highly polished gun barrel.

Firearm, he thought, that kind of instant, flat warning inside his head. The glint had come from across and down the street. Where two men were changing places. One was getting out of a trashed Ford Tempo. The other was getting in.

The bodyguards? Torres had mentioned them being in the street when they entered Club Plus.

The Tempo pulled out and headed his way. The man who had been left behind went into a restaurant.

Donahoo walked out into the narrow street and blocked the path of the car. When it stopped he smiled and shrugged and pretended he was stupid. He got out of the way and let the car start up again. He wanted it to pass slowly. He wanted to get a good look at the driver. Wanted to know what quality of cop was guarding him. The man looked at him quizzically. He was trying to hide something between his legs. A sawed-off shotgun.

Donahoo had his Python out. He put it in the man's face. He said, "Stop."

The car stopped. Donahoo got in the back. All the time he was careful to keep the Python only inches from the man's skull. He got settled and looked around. No one was paying any attention except the man who had gone into the restaurant. For some reason he had come out and he was staring uncertainly.

"Do you speak English?"

"Yes."

"Is that your shotgun?"

"Yes."

"Do you know how many there are like it in the world?"

"No."

"There are none," Donahoo said, certain of that. "Because it's a Woodward-Purdey vertical double and it's virtually impossible to make an over/under with less depth and more elegance and because only an utter asshole would saw it off."

The man said nothing. He sat at the wheel. With the Python's muzzle pushing at the base of his skull.

"We've done this before," Donahoo said. "You know the place. It's a side road and eventually it ends in wasteland outside the airport. We'll go there and we'll do it again."

"I'm a cop."

"Why doesn't that surprise me?"

☐ ☐ ☐

They arrived at the empty field without incident. Nothing had been said between them the whole time. The man had started to speak a couple of times and Donahoo had silenced him with a nudge of the Python. He wanted the man to talk. He wanted that very much. But he wanted to prepare him first.

The Tempo stopped. Donahoo ordered the man out. He ordered him to stand at a distance with his hands clasped over his head. Then he got out himself and took possession of the Woodward-Purdey. He snapped it open and confirmed that it was loaded.

"How does it go now?" he asked the man. "We can do this your way. Is that how it goes?"

The man didn't answer.

Donahoo went to him with the Woodward-Purdey. He cocked it and stuck it in his face. When the man closed his eyes, Donahoo raised his left foot and sliced down with the outer edge of his hard sole along the man's shinbone, crushing his instep. The man screamed in agony and hopped around wildly. Donahoo waited for the right moment and kicked him viciously in the balls. The man screamed and doubled over. Donahoo kneed him in the face with all the force he could muster. There was a loud snapping noise and the man collapsed without another sound.

"I still want to talk," Donahoo said, breathing heavily. He had hardly exerted himself but still he was short of breath. "We'll talk later."

He went back to the Tempo. He got himself settled. He sat waiting for the man to revive.

□ □ □

Torres and Marino showed up before that happened. The LeBaron came boiling across the field and stopped at the man's crumpled form. Torres got out greatly agitated. He bent over the man and felt for a pulse. His relief showed when he found it.

Marino said, "I thought you might come here."

"We'll make a detective of you yet."

Torres came over. He was again greatly agitated. He got himself in Donahoo's face.

"Fuck off," Donahoo told him. "The guy is a cop. You know he is a cop. You also—I only suspect this but I suspect it very strongly—you also know that he was in the gang who hijacked us the other night. So all I have to say to you is fuck off."

Torres stared at him. "Okay," he said finally, and then, "Wait here, I will be back in a moment," and then, "You don't have to talk to this man, you can talk to me, Sargento. We can talk together."

Donahoo thought that he had finally gotten rid of Marino. Torres could speak English as well as Marquisa.

Torres went back to the man on the ground. He picked him up and put him in the back seat of the LeBaron. He spoke then in rapid Spanish to Marino. Donahoo got only a bit of it. Marino was supposed to take the man to a doctor. Then he was supposed to take him to a dentist.

Donahoo went over and got Marino's Pacificos. He took the whole pack and sat in the Tempo.

Marino drove away with the man in the LeBaron. Torres waved him good-by. Donahoo lit two cigarettes. He had one ready for Torres when Torres joined him.

"Well," Torres said wearily. "Where do we start? I pretend not to speak English because it helps me in my police work to offer that ignorance. People will say things and think I don't know anything and of course I know everything and sometimes that can help. But I have to pretend all the time or else my guard will drop and I will respond to something in English and I will be caught, huh? So I have to try to fool everybody."

Donahoo said, "Okay."

"The rest might not be," Torres admitted. He looked at his cigarette and seemed to approve. "This is hard for me. I wasn't going to tell you this until we knew each other better. I wanted you to be here a month or so. To know and understand the situation better. Maybe come to a conclusion about it. But now you have accelerated my timetable. So I have to take a chance. To trust you when I don't know you very well. To hope that whatever you decide, you won't do us harm. We didn't ask you here to solve the murder. El Presidente doesn't know you from a woodpecker's ass. Jorge Hernandez will get in the cabinet when I fuck Madonna."

"Go on." Donahoo checked his cigarette too. "I mean, continue."

Torres smiled. "The only truth here? Maybe you really are the best homicide detective in the land. I've seen no evidence of it but I am not the one to judge and so I happily accept the verdict of others more qualified. We asked you here to look at what you are fond of calling the slimy underbelly. We kidnaped and threatened you to see if maybe you had some fire in your belly. We asked you here not to solve a murder but to help commit one."

Donahoo had seen that coming for a while. He had started to tumble back where the Presidente didn't know him from a woodpecker's ass. "Diablo."

"Yes. He truly is a monster and he truly should die. We were making progress in Tijuana and now he is dragging us back. He is dragging us down and if we let him we may never be able to get up. I compare him to a Hussein or a Khadafi. You look at those men and you wonder why someone doesn't shoot them. I look at Diablo. I wonder why someone doesn't shoot him."

"Why don't you shoot him yourself?"

"Because I would be immediately suspect. Because, probably, I would be caught, and because I don't want to be caught. I want to help rebuild this city and this society. I don't want to rot in jail. It is to nobody's benefit if I become Torres the Martyr."

"Ah," Donahoo said. "Now I understand. You want the perfect crime. Diablo dies and nobody knows why or how. He just dies."

"Yes. The perfect murder. By some unusual, subtle means that we don't know about. Not committed by, but the method supplied by, *proposed*, by a master of the art."

"That's why you asked me to come here? To show me how fucked you are and to blame it on Diablo?"

"Yes."

"Goddamn," Donahoo shouted. "You're *all* to blame! Diablo didn't do this alone. You're all to blame. Every fucking one of you. You let it happen."

"Yes," Torres said. "That is true. Partly, anyway. But now—some of us—want to do something, and we think this is the way. The Diablos of our world cannot be removed by an election. They have to be torn down. Diablo and others like him. We think we have to do it this way, selectively exorcising the cancers at the top, or else, in time, there will be a mass uprising, another revolution, and it won't accomplish as much as our way, if it accomplishes anything. Ours is actually a simple proposition when taken to its conclusion, and hundreds of thousands don't need to die to achieve it. When there are no evil men at the top, then finally there will be room for good men." He said, "We are not inventing this procedure, okay? Here many things are settled by the gun. We simply want the gun in the right hand for a change."

Donahoo flicked away his cigarette. He said, "You've just

touched the world's heart and I can't get laid. I am going to think about this and then I am going to tell you what I told you at the start. Fuck you and fuck off. Get out of the car."

Torres looked at him. "You want me to leave?"

"I want you to stay. I'm leaving." Donahoo waited for a moment. "Carlos. I can make you get out."

Torres pushed outside. He backed off several steps. He stood there wondering. He seemed about to reach for his gun but he didn't.

Donahoo drove away and left him standing alone in the empty wasteland with his cowboy hat at his side.

Torres shouted, "You're wrong, you know!" and Donahoo thought yes, perhaps, and that he had been wrong before.

Then he circled back. He had to know. He had to ask. He shouted as he drove by. "Catalina?"

"She is one of us!"

Twenty-six

Donahoo was throwing things. He was throwing them at his two-suiter and mostly missing. He was filled with unspent anger. He was afraid it was going to stay in him forever.

Marino, watching from the other side of the motel room, said, "You almost killed that guy."

Donahoo flicked a look at him. So?

"The doctor called the cops. They made me give a statement. They're gonna want one from you."

"Fat chance. Unless you told them I was here?"

"No. I said you'd gone back to San Diego."

"Then I guess they won't get their statement."

"I guess not."

"Look," Donahoo said. He stopped throwing and started packing. "Torres will take care of it, okay? The guy will live and it is not a big thing."

Marino sat down on his bed. He was already packed because he had proceeded more carefully. Donahoo stared at him unsurely. He had told him everything and Marino didn't share his anger. He was, if anything, merely more subdued.

"This place," Marino said, meaning Tijuana. "It forms you in its image. You become, very quickly, what it is."

"Yeah. I think that's what those Nazi Youth kids said."

"You can't see it?"

"In myself?" Donahoo gave up. "No. You haven't been listening. I reject it, Cruz. All of it. I'm getting outa here."

"That's how you solve it?"

"Yes."

Marino pushed up and got his gym bag. He took the car keys off the bureau and went outside.

Donahoo pulled himself together. He continued packing his

suitcase. Piling in his slacks and shirts. Stuffing them in. He couldn't get away fast enough.

Marino came back inside. He said, "She's here."

Donahoo stopped. He didn't look. When he did, Marino was gone again, the door ajar.

"Tell her . . ." Donahoo began. He was so used to starting with that kind of instruction. "To go away."

There was no answer. Donahoo continued to pack. Nothing happened. After a while he went outside.

Marino was sitting in the Toronado. He was smoking.

Catalina was standing down the block and across the street in front of the Catedral de la Virgen of Guadalupe. When she was aware that he had seen her she turned and went inside.

Donahoo almost called out to her. Then he almost went back to the motel room. Finally he went across the street and into the church.

It was empty save for a few women scattered about. Catalina was kneeling, head bowed, in a back row, a shawl that had been around her shoulders now over her head. He recognized her from the shawl. Otherwise he would not known it was her. She would have been just another bent woman.

He made the sign of the cross with holy water. He thought that was something he hadn't done for a long time. Mostly, he thought, because the water wasn't holy, and, in this instance, it probably wasn't clean. He went down the aisle and moved into the row behind her. He sat directly back of her. He didn't want to see her face.

"How can I explain?" she asked softly. "There are not very many of us. There is not much we can do but we all try to do something. I try, as best I can, to defend the unjustly accused, and Carlos collects *mordida* to help pay the court costs, and others do their part in other ways."

He didn't say anything. He was looking at the back of her bowed head.

"I am telling you this because I need you to understand and because I want you to keep our secret. You know what will happen to us if we are found out. We are a cell and there are other cells in other places. We don't have a name yet. We don't want one until it is time."

He still didn't respond.

"The time will be when we kill Diablo. That is still going to happen. Only we need to find a safe way of doing it."

"There is no safe way of killing somebody," Donahoo said finally. He wanted to touch and comfort her but he couldn't. His hands were like stones in his lap. "There is no good way either. This is what I wanted to say to you. That whatever the provocation, it is still wrong. It's why I can't help."

"I know," she told him. "I think I knew that from the start. When I first saw you, I thought, he is the wrong man for this, he won't do it, and then I came here every day and prayed that you would be the right man, but it didn't help. That is the thing about prayers. Sometimes they aren't answered."

"Yes. I've experienced that."

Donahoo got up and went outside and crossed the street to the Toronado. He got behind the wheel and got the key from Marino. He started the car and backed up, tires squealing. Neither of them said anything. Donahoo knew that Marino was going to remind him about his suitcase and then had decided not to do that. Marino had to know that the suitcase was the least of what he was leaving.

□   □   □

He had to either laugh or cry and somewhere across the border and up the freeway he started laughing. He knew it for what it was, a release, an escape, and he was glad to have it, because he didn't want to cry in front of Marino. He didn't want to do a lot of things and crying was way up there on the list. Along with not going back to Tijuana and not killing Diablo and not thinking about Catalina.

When he had stopped laughing, he said, "There is a way of doing it, you know," and Marino, smoking his last Pacifico, said, "Oh, yeah? How?" and he said, "Here."

"Here?"

"Yeah," he said. "In San Diego." He was making it up as he went along. It was another form of release. If he could kill Diablo in his mind then he wouldn't have to agonize about not killing him with his bare hands. "Torres is right. If Diablo is killed in Tijuana the crooked cops will round up all the decent cops as suspects. But if Diablo is killed in San Diego none of the cops here will much give a shit and they certainly won't go down to Tijuana looking for suspects. The case will go into fucking limbo."

Marino was carefully smoking his last Pacifico. It had burned dangerously low. "Who would kill him?"

"Somebody from one of their cells. They're supposed to have several cells. So they can recruit from one of them. Preferably from a distant city in the interior."

"How would they get Diablo here?"

"Lure him."

"How?"

Donahoo didn't know. He was making it up. He was winging it. "He's a greedy fuck. So he'll come if the price is right. Offer him a big piece of some criminal operation and he'll come up to talk about it. He's a degenerate. Offer him some sort of kinky white slave deal and tell him he can experiment with the girls and he'll coming running."

Marino looked doubtful.

"You saw that beak?" Donahoo said, getting silly. "It looks like a bad carrot. Fix him up with a free nose job from Dr. Stanford Denke. The doctor gives him a cushion to sit on. He goes out of the room and the cushion explodes. Juarez your ass, Diablo?"

"Denke?"

"He's this plastic surgeon here. He'll do anything I tell him."

Marino still looked doubtful.

Yeah, well, Donahoo thought, but he had gotten it out of his system, and that was the whole point.

Twenty-seven

Donahoo had thought that he would never see her again. Then one morning she was at his door. He opened it and she was standing there. Almost defiant with her proud profile and long neck and mussy piled auburn-black hair. With her dark slanted eyes and cocktail-sausage lips. He thought also that she seemed sort of trollopy in an understated way. She was wearing the same dress she had been wearing when he first saw her. Plain blue with white piping at the neck. The same flat-heeled plain blue shoes. Still, the plainness of them couldn't deny her full, ripe body. A peasant courtesan's wanton simplicity, he thought. She was the same woman who had walked into The Desperate Frog with her plastic LEY's shopping bag in order to spoil him for anyone else.

He had rehearsed this many times. What he would do if she came to visit. What he would say to her. How he would send her away.

"Do you have company?"

"No." He stood aside to let her to enter. "There's just me."

"It's Saturday so I didn't think you would be working but I did think I might be interrupting."

"No."

"I should have called," she said, slipping past him. "I started to several times and always hung up. I thought I should come here and knock because you can't hang up on a door." She stopped and turned when she reached the middle of the room. "Also I wanted to see you. I wanted to see your face when you told me to go away." She was looking at him with a half-smile. "Are you going to tell me to go away?"

"No."

"Good."

She chose the ottoman and sat down and put her big burlap bag purse alongside. She stretched out her long bare legs.

"How did you come?"

"The trolley. Then the bus. I got off too soon though and had to walk. I'm not used to walking that far. Do you have something to drink?"

"You can have a Coke. Or would you like a beer?"

"No. Just a glass of water, please. Who is this?"

"Oscar."

Donahoo went to the kitchen bar and put ice cubes in a tall glass and filled it with bottled water and took it to her.

Oscar was in her lap.

"What's wrong?"

"Nothing." He gave her the water. "Normally, he doesn't like people, that's all. Especially women. He once bit Vera."

"This pussy cat?"

"Yes, but Vera was picking on Cody, so there was provocation, I guess. Why are you here?"

She was stroking Oscar and drinking the water as she was looking around the studio. She seemed to have figured it out. Most of it anyway.

"Where do you sleep?"

"There's a Murphy bed."

"Oh? Let me see."

"Why are you here?"

She let Oscar down and rose slowly from the ottoman.

"I don't know," she told him, putting the glass aside. "I should know but it eludes me. For a while I thought I should come to apologize to you. But why should I apologize when I feel I have done nothing wrong? Then I thought perhaps I should ask you to forgive me. But then again what is there to forgive? What sin was committed?" The half-smile returned. "Most of the time I just want to tell you that I miss you. So perhaps that is why I am here. But there could be another reason."

Oh? Donahoo was afraid to ask what that might be. He had spent a very rough week trying to hate this woman. He hadn't succeeded. He hadn't come close. But he thought he should keep working on it. There were times when he thought it was his only salvation.

She looked away and pretended to examine the studio. She touched a few things. A lamp, a book, a photo. She said, meaning the studio, "It's small."

"You're kind. Monica. She was my wife? She came over to in-

spect it after we went our separate ways. She called it inade-
quate."

"Do you think it is?"

"Not anymore."

"Good."

He looked at her. He wondered why she kept saying that. It
wasn't good, for God's sake. It was awful. This whole thing was
awful.

"Do you have plans?"

"What? For the day?"

"For now."

Me? No, no plans, he thought. He went to work and he came
home and he drank his Old Crow and watched his TV and argued
with Oscar. Then he pulled the covers over his head and pretended to go to sleep. He did all that with no plan whatsoever. He
just did it. He had no plans.

"I thought we might go on a picnic or something." She was
looking out the sliding glass doors. "You have such a lovely park.
That's Balboa Park, isn't it?"

"Yes."

"Do they allow picnics?"

"I imagine so."

"Then let's do it."

□ □ □

There was a place he knew that was perfect. He left her to freshen
up and to make sandwiches and he went next door to borrow a
picnic basket from Cody. It had a false bottom that could hold
two bottles of vodka.

"Don't tell me," Cody grumbled. He was hung over and still in
pajamas. An old Navy guy with the crewcut and the aviator
glasses and the hollow leg. He'd crashed and burned a long time
ago. He refused to be buried. "Let me guess. You're collecting
Easter eggs."

Vera screamed from the bedroom, "Who is it?"

"I've got a date," Donahoo told him.

Then he went upstairs to see his rooftop gardener neighbor
Barney. Because it was Saturday she was wearing bib overalls
and an engineer's cap. It was her gardening outfit and she liked to
think that she looked like a gardener. Actually, she looked like the

Campbell's Soup girl used to look. The same kind of curly red hair and big rosy cheeks.

He borrowed a bottle of wine from her, a California chardonnay he'd never heard of, and a half round of yellow cheese, a sharp cheddar, and some Dijon mustard. He didn't want to waste time stopping at a store. He wanted to get there.

"You know those little ducklings you bought for your niece? Your sister said not to give them to her? They'd crap all over? Have you given them to the zoo yet?"

Barney looked at him. "What? You want to cook them?"

"No. I thought I would take them for you."

"Are you going to the zoo?"

"I'm going to the park. I can stop by."

"Good. Then you can take them. They're crapping all over."

She went away and came back with a wiggling bleeping paper bag. He put it in the picnic basket with the other stuff.

"You know those elastic bands you wore when you were getting your teeth pulled together? Do you think you have any left?"

She looked at him again. "Okay. What's going on?"

"I've got a date."

Halfway downstairs he stopped and took the ducklings out of the bag. He put the elastic bands around their bills so they couldn't quack. Then he put them out of sight in the picnic basket's false bottom with the crumpled-up paper bag between them so they couldn't move around too much.

Catalina had the sandwiches made. Deviled egg on rye and roast beef on sourdough. She'd made them one of each.

He got her a jacket of his that she could wear if it got cold. He also got the blanket he used to take to Chargers tailgate parties.

"You ready?"

"Yes."

They were going out the door when the phone rang. He kept moving. He hadn't been answering the phone for a while. He listened to the messages and, sometimes, not very often, he called back.

"You want to get that?"

"No."

☐ ☐ ☐

He chose the long way around and went down Sixth Avenue and took her into Balboa Park via El Prado. He drove the scenic circle that twisted past a couple miles of lush lawns and stands of tall eucalyptus. Then he took her across the long narrow aqueductlike bridge and past the rococo tower of the Museum of Man. Past the Old Globe Theatre and the House of Charm and the Alcazar Garden. El Cid Campeador on his steed, heroic in armor with banner. The Spreckels Pipe Organ Pavilion. He was proud of the vast thickly treed park and its Exposition architecture and he wanted to show it off. He felt strongly that the park, rather than the downtown it overlooked, was the soul of the city. The heart might beat in those gleaming towers. But the soul was kept here in this green sanctuary.

They parked the Toronado in the lot behind the pavilion and walked back to where wooden stairs led steeply down into Palm Canyon. It had been planted eighty years before with a wide variety of palms that were now specimen giants. A concrete path turned to dirt and narrowed and finally they were in a jungle. Elephant ear plants stood as tall as they were.

Donahoo found the place. It was patch of grass near the small winding stream created by the rows of sprinklers high on the canyon wall. The stream puddled near the patch of grass.

She said, "This is perfect."

"I was hoping you'd think so."

While she was busy with the blanket he unpacked the picnic basket and got the ducklings out of the false bottom. He took off the rubber bands and tipped the basket. The first time she saw them they were just leaving it. They were quacking and heading for the water.

"Oh," she said, and her face was filled with joy and he forgave her for everything.

□ □ □

It had been a long time since a woman had taken him to bed. Not since Presh. He had taken a few women to bed but none of them had taken him. He thought of this when they returned to his apartment. He wondered which way it was going to be. It was going to *be*. He was pretty certain of that. He just wasn't sure which way.

He left the basket at the door and put the folded blanket on the fireplace mantel. The red light was blinking on his answering machine. He moved a photo and it was no longer visible.

She shook off the jacket he had put over her shoulders. It fell to the floor and she left it there. She stepped out of her shoes. She undid the mussy bun and her hair fell in a soft whoosh. She turned to show that it was halfway to her waist.

"Do you like it this way?"

"Yes. Very much."

"It's long, isn't it?"

"Yes."

She came to him and put her arms around his neck. She kissed him tenderly. She looked at him with her half-smile.

"Was that nice?"

"Yes."

"Is that all you can say, yes?"

"Yes."

"Very well. I don't want you to say no."

She kissed him again, tenderly at first, but then passionately, and, before she released him, quite fiercely.

"I think I would like to see your Murphy bed now," she said, long fingers brushing her bruised sausage lips. "I'd like you to make love to me. Would you like to do that?"

"Yes."

He moved the ottoman and a coffee table out of the way. He worked in a kind of slow motion while not daring to look at her. This wasn't something he wanted to hurry, he thought. He wanted it to last a long time. He moved her purse and saw that its contents included her rose silk pleated dress with the buttons all the way up the front. He thought that he liked it a lot but that he liked the plain blue dress better. He reached up and turned the latch and the bed fell out of the wall and lowered creakily. When it touched down it took up all the open space. The whole floor was covered by it. She would have to get on the bed to go anywhere.

"So this is how you trap us?"

She sat on the side for a moment, testing it and testing him, and then she slowly surrendered to it, stretching out full length.

"It's big."

He stood looking at her. Slowly, he told himself. Go slowly. He removed his jacket and toed off his loafers. He waited for a smile, a full smile, to give him permission, and then he settled in beside her. He stretched full length as she had done. He could feel the warmth of her. She had been cold in the park but now she was warm.

"Can we talk first?"

"What about?"

She laughed. "You mean it depends?"

"Yes." He was thinking about Torres and Diablo. She hadn't talked about them so far. He hoped she had the good sense not to start now. Already the idea was intruding. "There are some topics that don't appeal to me."

She got up on an elbow so she could look into his face. "No. What I meant, we don't know each other very well, so I would first like to hear more about you, Sergeant Donahoo. This man who is going to take me. And, maybe, you would like to know more about this woman who is going to give herself to you. Maybe there are some happy secrets we can share or some special requests. Things that we can tell each other that will make the moment even gladder."

Donahoo felt ashamed. Jesus, he thought. He couldn't think of anything to say.

"You start."

"I can't."

"Okay. Then it's me." She fell back. "My first special request is that you should be careful with my dress. It is an old dress but if you tear it you will of course have to buy me a new dress. Can you afford that?"

Donahoo found his voice. "Yes. But I'll be careful with it because it may be more special to me than it is to you."

"You don't have to buy me a lobster dinner. You don't have to buy me dinner at all. The sandwiches were quite sufficient. But maybe you could buy me a drink in some romantic place. Maybe, you've mentioned it, Mr. A's? It doesn't matter. You can pick. That would be another special request. Can you afford that?"

"Yes." He made a joke. "If it's Happy Hour."

She was serious. "I'll be happy if I'm with you." She looked at him. "So now it's your turn."

Donahoo didn't know. His mind was a blank in the secrets and special requests department. All he could think of was that she might want to do something now. Some sort of preliminary exercise in the bathroom. Something she might want to put in or take out or whatever. He was thinking of this to be considerate and polite and an intelligent lover and he also was thinking fuck it.

"Well?"

He turned toward her and kissed her. It was the first time he had taken the initiative in that. He kissed her for a long time and he thought that Marino might be a lucky man to have Theresa but not so fortunate as he was to have Catalina. He had thought that she was going to take him to bed but now he thought that he was going to be the one. After a while he turned her over and undid the buttons at the back of her dress. He undid her brassiere. Then he rolled her over and pulled the dress down and her light chocolate breasts spilled out.

Catalina rose up to him. She took his crotch in both hands.

"We're going to have a good time?"

"Yes."

☐   ☐   ☐

The phone was ringing. Donahoo wanted to let it ring. If he did, though, the machine would pick up, and he'd have to listen to someone's message. He was afraid it might be the wrong message. It might be Millie from Bully's.

He turned over and against Catalina. She was face-down, nude, asleep. They had made love and they had slept for a while. They had made love again and slept for a longer time. He reached across her too late.

Theresa, being recorded, was saying, "Damn! Where *are* you?"

He turned down the volume. "Hi. It's me. What's up?"

"You didn't get my messages?"

"No." He carefully maneuvered over Catalina. He got off the bed and moved away with the phone. "What's going on?"

"Cruz has gone away. He left a note."

"Cruz?"

"Yes. I was supposed to spend the weekend in LA. The plans got changed. A girlfriend got sick . . ."

"What happened?"

"I came over to his place this morning. I was going to surprise him. I'm scared. He's taken all his stuff."

"What stuff?"

Now she was crying. Donahoo didn't want to awaken Catalina. He looked for his shorts and couldn't find them. He opened the heavy glass slider and went out on the balcony. It was getting dark and there was a high railing. No one was going to see that he was naked.

"Theresa. Get ahold of yourself. What stuff?"

"All the things he treasures. Photos. Keepsakes."

"I don't understand."

"He left a note. It's like he's not coming back."

"Well, fuck," Donahoo said. He was still half-asleep. "Where was he going?"

"I don't know. All I can think of, to do his duty."

"What?"

"He was talking a few days ago. He said he had to do it. Nobody else would, so it was up to him."

Oh, shit, no! Donahoo thought. No, no, *no!* He couldn't believe it. Not Diablo.

"Is there something you can do?"

"Where are you?"

"His place."

Donahoo glanced up. Catalina was off the bed and coming towards him. She closed the slider and locked it.

"Hey!" He tried the door and then hammered on the glass. "Catalina. Open this thing!"

She was pulling on her dress. In such a hurry that she had ignored her panties and bra.

"Catalina!"

She looked at him briefly and ran.

"Sergeant Donahoo?" Theresa was yelling. "What's wrong?"

Donahoo hammered uselessly on the slider. Finally he picked up his hibachi barbecue and slammed it with all his strength. The whole sheet of glass shattered and fell out of the frame.

"Hello?"

"Don't hang up. I'll be back."

He tried to pick his way through the littered shards but still cut his foot badly. There was blood all over by the time he got inside. He tore a pillowcase into strips and bandaged the wound roughly. He found his shorts and pulled them on.

"Catalina!"

He ran out into the hall and down the stairs and into the street. There was no sign of her. She was gone.

He went back to his apartment and picked up the phone. He thought that there had to be a car waiting for her. She couldn't have disappeared that quickly otherwise.

"Theresa?" He sat down on the ottoman. His foot hurt and his head and his heart. "I need a clue. Give me a clue."

Twenty-eight

There weren't any clues. Donahoo went through Marino's apartment in El Cajón like a dog digging for a bone and couldn't find a thing. No names. No numbers. No diagrams. Nothing that might help him.

There was only the note that didn't help Theresa.

I'LL ALWAYS LOVE YOU. DON'T WAIT. CRUZ.

She was slumped at the phone. She had been calling everybody she could think of. Cruz's friends and relatives and the places he frequented. She hadn't come up with anything either.

Such a pretty girl, and it was a shame, a pity, a fucking tragedy what Marino was doing to her, Donahoo thought. He had seen her only once since The Dinner but he had again been very impressed. He had thought then that she was a real sparkler who could light up any man and he had been happy for, and a little amazed by, Marino. The guy had sure gotten himself a marvelous woman. But now she was just an absolute uncombed wreck in a worn man's shirt and out-at-the-knees Levis drooping over new Reeboks.

"It doesn't make sense."

"No."

Donahoo tried to think what else he could do. He had alerted Lewis. There was a citywide stop-and-detain order for Catalina. He had tried, unsuccessfully, to reach Torres, and the little Grupo Homocidios lieutenant who, Torres had said, was one of them, Herradura. He had ascertained—Cominsky had already been to see him—that Dr. Sheldon Denke didn't have any suspicious whoopie cushions for a patient named Salvador Urquidez. If Donahoo had known of any way to reach Urquidez, he would have sent Cominsky to look for him too. He had done everything and nothing.

It's going down, he kept thinking. It's going down. He looked around the cluttered apartment for what seemed like the hundredth time. It was almost as small as his own at The Arlington. Not really an apartment so much as a couple of rooms in an illegally divided private home. A living room and a large walk-in closet that served as a bedroom. Furnished mostly with garage sale junk. Marino was saving his money.

"I don't understand," Theresa said brokenly. "We were going to get married. It was all planned." She looked at him. "What went wrong?"

Donahoo thought that he had to tell her what he suspected. What he *knew*. He'd been putting it off but now he had to tell her. Maybe it would prompt some helpful recollection.

"Everything," he said, meaning what went wrong. "The secret assignment in Tijuana? It was just a murder case. But the cop we were working with started giving us the tour. He kept showing us all the terrible shit those poor people have to go through." He found a place to sit down. "And, you know, after a while, it started to make an impression."

"Yes. He told me some of that."

"Okay." He took a deep breath. "There is this particularly twisted bastard there. His name is Salvador Urquidez. Diablo. They blame him for much of what is wrong. They want to kill him and they asked me to help. I refused and we came back."

She looked at him. A bright girl with bright fear in her eyes. "And now Cruz is going to help them?"

"Yes. I think so."

The tears started. "What are you saying? That he's going to be a murderer?"

"Maybe."

"Oh, Jesus," she cried. "Jesus, Jesus." She put her face in her hands. "The fool! How could he want to do something so crazy? He's ruining our lives."

Actually, he thought, it was *why?* The how was his problem. He had to figure out how they were going to do it. Marino and—he had been thinking this for a while—Marino and Catalina.

"Theresa. Maybe we can stop him."

"How?"

"I don't know. Maybe he said something to you?"

"What?"

He said sharply—he wanted to shock her out of it—"Theresa! Stop your goddamn crying. We haven't got much time."

In a moment she had composed herself. She rubbed the back of her hand across her mascara-smeared face. "What do you want me to do?"

"Think."

Lewis was at the door. He bulled in without knocking. He was wearing an orange Hawaiian shirt smeared with barbecue sauce and dirty shorts and zoris. Gomez and Montrose were right behind him. Gomez in a sharp pinstripe suit with a fresh white shirt and shiny black shoes with pointed toes. Montrose in a tank top and baggy khaki pants with too many pockets and scuffed court shoes.

Donahoo thought that they had come as they had been found. A measure of the urgency when it is feared that a cop may have become an assassin. They were already pulling on rubber gloves.

"You sure know how to ruin a Saturday night, Tommy," Lewis said. He looked at Theresa. "You're the fiancée?"

Donahoo said, "Yes. Her name's Theresa."

"You finished with her?"

"Not yet."

"When he is, stay," Lewis told her. The rest was for Donahoo. "We've got a warrant. We're taking this place down to the joists. What have you got so far?"

"Nothing. Just the note." Donahoo pointed to it on Marino's computer desk. "He's traveling light with the things that we know are missing. A knapsack and rough clothes and sneakers and . . ." He took Theresa's hand and pulled her up. "Those few personal items that could be called keepsakes."

"The things that he would treasure?"

"Yeah. The treasures."

Donahoo finally had the chance to acknowledge the presence of Gomez and Montrose.

"This is fucked, huh?" Montrose said. He looked at the computer. "You been through it?"

"Yes. But try again."

Gomez said something with his eyes. It looked like hello and sorry.

"I finally got Saperstein," Lewis grumbled. He tucked in his Hawaiian shirt. "He's driving down from Julian. We've got a meeting in his office at ten. Be there."

Donahoo nodded and steered Theresa outside. He sat her down on the front step. He thought she would talk more freely in private.

She had taken a pack of cigarettes from her purse. Pacíficos. "Where did you get those?"

"From him."

"When?"

"Yesterday."

"Did he have any before that?"

"Yes. Earlier in the week. But then he ran out."

Donahoo thought that meant at least two trips to Tijuana. Marino had smoked his last Pacífico when they drove back together. So he had to have gone back at least twice. They weren't sold in San Diego.

Or. Or, he thought, someone had come up yesterday to meet with him, and they, this was something Marino would ask, they had brought him a few packs? Maybe—who might do that—Catalina?

He took one of the cigarettes for himself. He lit hers and then his own. He was talking to himself. "How much would they fiddle with it?"

"I'm sorry . . . ?"

He was trying to think. He again went over the stupid how-to-kill-Diablo plan he had proposed to Marino. That Diablo be lured by money or sex to San Diego. That someone from a distant cell be brought in to kill him. How much would they fiddle with that?

Now he didn't want to think. He had thought—this is what he had first thought—that Catalina's purpose was to sit on him while Diablo was killed. To come up and distract him for the day and take him to bed and out of the way. But now he thought that Catalina might also be the lure.

"She could be both."

"Huh?"

Donahoo shook his head. Why not? She could leave him whenever it suited her and then go on to be with Urquidez. She could leave him asleep in his bed, sated, satisfied, happy, out of the way, and she could go with Marino to kill Urquidez. She could be the lure.

Who better?

He pushed up. He didn't know how to find Marino. But perhaps he did know how to find Catalina. He took Theresa by the arm and stood her up. He quietly took her down the stairs.

She said, "I'm supposed to stay here," and he told her, "No, you're supposed to come with me," and she said, "Won't we get in trouble?", and he said, which he thought was pretty obvious, "We're already in trouble."

☐ ☐ ☐

Donahoo got on Interstate 8 and then he got on his cellular and got Lewis.

"I always knew you were going to do it," Lewis said. "Now you've done it. You've crossed the line."

Donahoo thought that maybe he had. He had just crossed into Grossmont and pretty soon he'd be crossing into La Mesa.

"Yeah," he said. He was feeling pretty good. It was the first time he thought he might have a shot. "You know how hard it is to get good help these days. I have an idea. You want to hear it?"

"No."

Donahoo grinned. Lewis would always be Lewis. He said, "Catalina De Lourdes Venezuela. If there is one thing I know for sure about her. She loves lobster."

Lewis said, "Don't do this to me."

"Lobster." Donahoo repeated. "She loves it. So, what I think . . ."

"I know what you think."

". . . if she was going to lure Urquidez to San Diego she would would start by luring him to a fancy restaurant that served lobster. So I want . . ."

"I don't give a fuck what you want."

". . . a plainclothes cop with a description of them at every fine restaurant where there is the remotest chance of getting lobster."

"No."

"Why not?"

"Because that is the dumbest and slimmest lead that I have ever heard of in my life."

"No it isn't. It is the *only* lead you have on this case, and your life is gonna be shit if you don't act on it, Lewis. If it turns out I'm right and you're wrong, you're gonna retire in disgrace. You're gonna die as the guy who dismissed the lobster lead. They're gonna talk about it at your fucking funeral, Lewis. They're gonna make lobster jokes. Claw your way outa this one."

Donahoo clicked off and looked at Theresa. "I'm sorry. You can't ask him to do something. You have to provoke him."

She nodded tightly. "I understand."

The cellular rang. He picked up. "Yeah?"

It was Lewis. "Where are you?"

"La Mesa."

"Where are you going?"

"In circles."

"Good. Tell me what they look like."

"You've got a file photo of Urquidez."

"And no time to circulate it. What does he look like?"

"Okay. He's about fifty. Graying. Pretty short. About your height and your gut."

"You're crossing, Tommy."

"A round head with a low forehead. A bad nose. It's a beak. Slit eyes. Cruel mouth. Oh, and a mustache. A big droopy Zapata."

"Anything else?"

"A sharp but casual dresser. He may be in a dark brown leather jacket. The bomber type."

"And?"

And Catalina. Donahoo didn't know where to start. He said, "Okay." He looked at Theresa. For some reason he was hesitant on account of her. "She's kinda tall, five foot seven, eight. Dark complexion. Actually, more a light chocolate." He stopped for a moment and tried again. "What they should look for, a very striking, beautiful woman, Lewis. She's just a fucking knockout. Big, slanted dark eyes, and a pouty mouth, this is gonna sound ridiculous, but, you know, like those little cocktail sausages?"

"Those are weiners."

"Okay. Weiners. Have it your way. And she's got long auburn-tinged black hair which she usually wears in a mussy bun and I wouldn't expect her to be dressed any too fancy. Maybe a plain blue dress with white piping on the collar. Maybe a rose silk pleated dress that buttons all the way up the front. Probably flat or low-heeled shoes."

"Anything else?"

"Yeah. She's a lawyer and a liar and a slut."

He switched off. Theresa was looking at him. "You know your women."

"Oh, yeah," he said. "But not soon enough."

Twenty-nine

He had to take her somewhere, so he took her to Mr. A's. He had always thought that the rooftop restaurant made a good killing floor. He imagined business executives bringing their victims here to buy them a drink and break the bad news. "Hell, I don't know how to tell you this, Harry, but the promotion didn't come through." He could hear the axe fall. "You want a raise? Fuck, Al, I want my dick pulled by Waitress Number Two, but that don't mean it's gonna happen." He could see metaphoric blood staining the carpet.

Theresa, embarrassed in her worn shirt and out-at-the-knee jeans, said, "What are we doing here?" and he said, "Killing time."

It was true. He didn't want to wait in the Toronado. It could take hours for a call to come. If one came. So he preferred to wait here in a central location with the car less than a minute away in the basement garage. Also, Mr. A's served lobster, every day. So this was one of the places a cop should be waiting. Actually, one of the best places, because he had mentioned on occasion, to both Catalina and Marino, that Mr. A's, with the view, with the fancy-wancy hors d'oeuvres that appealed to the ladies, was the best Happy Hour in town. Also—another also—Catalina had made mention this afternoon. Maybe to throw him off? Or maybe to lure him here and get him involved by default? They could be sitting here together and she could excuse herself to go to the bathroom and instead go downstairs to meet Urquidez at an appointed time. She could come back up and ask him to say that she'd been with him the whole time, and she might think that he would agree, and perhaps he would. Maybe.

Donahoo showed his badge to an empty maitre d's station and said needlessly about his disheveled companion, "Make an exception." He steered Theresa to an empty table in an all-glass corner and put her in a chair with an unobstructed view.

224

She was distraught but still aware of it. The restaurant was atop the Fifth Avenue Financial Center on San Diego's Bankers Hill. It was only a twelve-story building, but because of the hill, it seemed much higher. The view facing south swept from the jungle of Balboa Park to the downtown's gleaming towers and then across the busy harbor and Coronado to the long hump of Point Loma. The wind-whipped waters teemed with pleasure craft scuttling around Navy ships. Airliners brushed by on their descent to Lindbergh Field.

"Do you come here often?"

He got settled across from her. "Between four and seven. Then the prices change."

She tried to smile. "I can't believe we're doing this."

"I know," he said, looking at the Happy Hour drink menu, which was always the same, but he lived in the hope that some day Old Crow would be there in the place of Jim Beam. "We should be doing something and maybe we are. I've recommended the place to both Catalina and Cruz." He was starting to feel stupid. "They serve lobster."

That started the tears again.

"Don't. There's no sense chasing around, okay? We can be the reserves. We don't go in until we're needed."

She still wasn't satisfied. And she was still crying.

"We go in prepared," he added. "We have a plan."

"What kind of plan?"

The list said Jim Beam. He told her, "Jesus, I don't know, Theresa. Maybe we should talk about how you're going to conduct yourself if we should ever catch up to them. What you're going to say . . ."

"To Cruz?"

"Yeah. I thought, you know, if we got lucky, if we got the chance to talk to them before they do something really dumb, you could talk to Cruz and I could talk to Catalina. Maybe you could talk to him better than I could."

"You really think I could change his mind?"

"Yeah. You could tell him what he's throwing away here. Not just his own life. But you."

"That's why I'm here?"

The waitress came. He thought fuck it and ordered an Old Crow. In a chilled glass. No ice. Theresa didn't want anything. He ordered her a Jim Beam. If she didn't drink it he would.

"Yeah," he said. "It's why you're here. But you don't have to be here. You can wait in the car. Or go back to Cruz's place. Or you can go home. It's up to you. Do what you like."

"Don't be cruel."

"Okay. But don't be dumb. What you must know by now, this is tough for me too, and I'm not asking why I'm here, Theresa. I'm here because I've got to be somewhere and it's as good a place as any. If you've got a better place, go to it. That's all."

"That's enough."

"I'm not finished. We've got about a jillion-to-one shot here. If it happens we're gonna be the luckiest people in whole world. For a while."

She looked away and at the downtown towers. She said, "Cops."

"You know some?"

"Besides Cruz, you mean? Yeah, a few. I used to be a cop groupie. I never told Cruz this but I got off on cops when I was a kid. I had my first cop when I was fifteen. In the backseat of a patrol car."

"Tell me it was in Chula Vista."

"It was in National City."

"Okay. That's just as good."

"Better. I tried 'em both."

He laughed. "Fifteen?"

"What's wrong with fifteen?"

Nothing, he thought. The drinks came and she accepted hers.

"Excuse me," she said. "But I'm getting mad at him. Really pissed. He's got . . ." The tears started again. ". . . no right . . . to do this to me."

Donahoo took a long pull on his Old Crow.

"You wanta run a tab?" the waitress asked.

"Yeah," Donahoo said. "We'll be here awhile. We're killing time."

The waitress said, like she knew something, "This is the place for it," and then she said, smiling, "Actually, I think they mutilate it," and then she went away, a tall, thin, not-too-bad-looking blonde in a long red backless dress.

Donahoo looked around. Now, at Happy Hour, the place, as always, was exceeding the seating limit. The patrons, talkative, laughing, were mostly regulars, a mix of business types and on-the-make women. The rich little-old-lady dinner crowd was starting to totter in to replace them. The ebb and flow of two distinct social levels. And the lamb chop special was twenty bucks. All very boring, but kind of classy too, Donahoo thought. Mr. A's must be one of the few places left that still asked men to wear jackets. It wouldn't always insist. But it would ask.

"Help me here," Theresa said. "There is something I don't understand. Marino isn't crazy. So what the hell is he thinking? How is it going to help if he kills one guy? How does that make any difference?"

"That's what I thought," Donahoo admitted. "But they killed Colosio in Tijuana. The presidential candidate? And that made a difference. The guy who took his place wasn't a Colosio. Dan Quayle isn't a John Kennedy and the guy who got elected instead isn't a Colosio. They want to give him the Nobel Prize for chemistry. He turned the peso into shit."

"Diablo isn't running for President."

"No. But he holds immense power in Tijuana. Holds it and misuses it. He is responsible for a lot of pain and suffering."

"So won't someone just as bad take his place? That is like a tradition there. Nothing ever seems to get better."

Donahoo had to admit that too. He said, "Maybe. But then maybe a Colosio will take his place." He thought for a moment and said, "Maybe, if the wrong man replaces him, they'll have to kill him too, and keep killing until they get a Colosio."

She looked at him in alarm. "Jesus Christ. You're condoning this?"

"No. Trying to explain it. I'm trying to tell you what may be in Cruz's head. I think he may have seen some things that profoundly disturbed him and then he multiplied them by millions. This may have been Cruz's real discovery in Tijuana. That he couldn't live with himself unless he did something about it."

Theresa was silent for a time. Then she said, "I never saw that in him. I thought, you know, he was just a cop, okay? I never thought he wanted to save the world. I didn't know him."

Donahoo drank the last of his Old Crow. "Neither did I."

They were on their third round when the cellular rang. Donahoo let it ring a couple times more before he answered. He didn't want to hear Lewis saying, "Well, it didn't work, maestro."

He said, "Yes," and Lewis said, "Well, I guess you were right,

Tommy. We've got a massacre over at Anthony's Star of the Sea. Some guy went in with an Uzi. They've got bodies all over." He said, after a breath, "It looks like a gang thing. Mexicans."

Donahoo could barely speak. "Some guy?"

"Some little fat guy."

Theresa was saying, "What is it?"

"The victims? Any IDs?"

"No. It just happened. I got it from nine-one-one. You know what I know. We haven't even got an officer on the scene."

"Uh," Donahoo said. He was afraid to ask. "Were any women killed?"

"Tommy. I don't know. I'm sorry. You're gonna have to go over there and find out for yourself."

He said, barely audible, "Okay," and Lewis told him, "Tommy, if this is Marino, if he did it, you have my permission to kill the sonofabitch."

Donahoo switched off. Theresa was staring at him with bruised eyes. He found his wallet and left a twenty. He said, "We may have something. Let's go."

They went to the elevators and got a car and went silently down. Theresa didn't say anything the whole ride. Donahoo thought she might have heard something of Lewis's side of the cellular conversation. Or maybe she had guessed enough. He didn't know what to tell her anyway. He was trying to focus on Marino. If Marino had done it? If he'd gotten away? Where would he go? Donahoo thought that if Marino had somehow put Catalina in the crossfire maybe he would kill him.

Garage level. They got out. Donahoo started for the Toronado. It was parked nose-out in a nearby stall. The key was under the mat. He had made an arrangement with the valet. It was prepaid and ready to go.

He went past the last elevator. The door was closing. It was just for a split second. He saw Salvador Urquidez and he saw Catalina. In that briefest of moments he saw her anguish and then he saw her face become a mask.

He swung around and ran for the elevator he had vacated. The door had already closed. It was going back up.

He got his cellular and punched in Lewis's number.

Theresa said, "What's wrong?"

He held up a hand telling her to wait.

"Lewis," he said, riding over whatever Lewis was saying. "It's not Star of the Sea. It's Mr. A's."

"How the hell . . ."

"Lewis. Listen. I'm in the basement. The garage. Diablo just went up the elevator with Catalina."

"Shit. We're gonna have two fucking bloodbaths?"

"Not necessarily." He was frantically pushing the elevator button. "Let's figure this out."

"How do you know they're going to Mr. A's?"

"It's Saturday. The building is a tomb. Where else are they gonna go?"

"It's not a seafood restaurant."

"Goddamn. They're *here!*" He was trying to work out something. "Lewis. We need a distraction. Phone Mr. A's. Tell them they've got a bomb threat. Tell 'em they've got to evacuate. They've got to clear the place out right away."

"Wait a minute. We're gonna have people jumping off the fucking roof."

"Lewis. *Do it!* Marino could be up there waiting for them."

"Okay."

"I also want wailing sirens and a chopper."

"Everybody's at the Star of the Sea."

"Move 'em over. Do it!"

The elevator came back with an elderly couple in it. They looked confused and unsure of the floor. Donahoo pulled them out roughly with no explanation. He was trying to figure Marino. Was he waiting up there? Or was he still to come?

Theresa squeezed on just before the door closed. He pushed twelve. They started up. He changed his mind. He pushed eleven. If Marino was there, he might be watching the elevators, but he couldn't watch the stairway, which was concealed from the restaurant and bar.

"Lewis?" No answer. Lewis had hung up. Donahoo thought fuck. The guy was getting old. He should have kept the connection open and used a different phone. "You okay?"

Theresa nodded numbly.

"Cruz is around here somewhere. If we get to him in time maybe you can talk some sense into him. But I don't know. It could be dangerous. You tell me. He's your guy."

"I'm okay."

"Good."

Donahoo looked at his new watch. Lewis should be making his bomb threat call to Mr. A's. If he did it right there would be a reasonable amount of subdued panic. The restaurant would not be the time and place for an assassination. There would be a lot of people milling around. It would be hard to get off a clear shot.

The elevator was stopping. Fifth floor. Donahoo couldn't believe it. Somebody working Saturday.

Thirty

The elevator door opened. Salvador Urquidez had Marino on his knees in the corridor. He had a Luger pistol stuck between Marino's eyes. Marino was bleeding from a gunshot to the left shoulder. Catalina was standing against the wall in a state of shock. Halfway down the corridor a redheaded man was sprawled dead in a pool of blood. A big black automatic was near his right hand. Marino's .38 Special—it looked like Marino's Special—was farther down the hall.

"Join us," Urquidez said. "Do it now. Otherwise I will kill this bastard."

Donahoo left the elevator. Theresa screamed, "Cruz!" and stumbled out after him, trying to reach Marino. Donahoo held her back.

"I want your weapon," Urquidez ordered. "Hand it to me. Butt first. Otherwise I kill him."

Donahoo got the Python and passed it over. Marino's wound didn't look too serious. He had been winged.

"So what is this foolishness?" Urquidez asked Donahoo, strangely calm. "I thought I recognized you. The Club Plus."

"Take it easy. We're cops."

"Yes. I know. This bastard who is praying told me that. What he hasn't told me is what is going on."

"I think a mistake," Donahoo said. "A big mistake." He looked down the corridor to the man in the puddle of blood. "Who is that?"

"My bodyguard." Urquidez glanced there too for an instant. "Don't let the fact that he is a Dutchie fool you. It didn't fool this bastard. He took him out first. No warning. I don't think it was a mistake."

Catalina said, it was the first time she had spoken, "He had to. It was shoot or be shot."

232 □ JACK TROLLEY

"Well," Donahoo said, looking at Marino. He had his eyes closed and maybe he was praying. He had a pack of Pacificos in his shirt pocket but the cancer wasn't going to take him. He'd gotten the Pacifico habit too late. "Not a mistake then. But don't you make another one. You've done nothing wrong. Let me have this man. I'll turn him over to the authorities."

"A cop who is your friend?"

"Yes. I don't have a choice."

Urquidez's smile was a sneer.

"You can leave," Donahoo told him. "You've done nothing wrong and you can leave. We'll get in touch with you later to take a statement. When all this has settled down. So you can leave now. Why don't you leave?"

"No. I want to know what is happening. This lady lawyer invites me here. She has a very big favor to ask and she knows only I can grant it. She wants her pretty-boy little brother out of jail because he's getting a sore ass. Yes, I can do that for her, but what's in it for me?"

"A dirty weekend."

"Why not? I am as safe here as in Tijuana. Maybe safer. My bodyguards here are not Mexican and everybody expects them to be Mexican. It fooled my lawyer friend here. We're in the same elevator and she doesn't know."

"She's just a lawyer."

"Yes. We are going to start with a nice dinner at a nice restaurant. Then she wants to stop first at this floor. She shows me an office key."

Donahoo looked at Catalina. He thought that she was such a bright lady. How could she be so fucking dumb?

Urquidez was compelled to get it all spilled out. "I am led to believe that her pants are coming off. But this bastard is waiting."

"It was a dumb thing."

"Yes. I agree." The Luger pushed harder into Marino's face. "To plot to kill Diablo? That is a very big mistake."

"You're okay. You're free to go."

"No. I want to know all the plotters."

Marino said, eyes closed, "Just me."

"And me," Catalina said.

Urquidez shook his head. "I don't think so. You, what is your name?"

"Donahoo."

"Donahoo. You're not in the plot?"

"No."

"Then why are you here?"

"I was hoping to stop him."

"And the girl?"

"She was hoping to stop him too."

"Really?"

"Yes," Donahoo said. "She is his fiancée. They are engaged to be married. So she was hoping to stop him too. She was hoping that he wouldn't be such a crazy idiot to try something this dumb."

Urquidez considered. He glanced at Catalina. "So it is the woman and you and the bastard who is praying?"

Catalina said, "Please. This man is innocent. He had nothing to do with it."

There was the wail of sirens in the street.

Urquidez turned to listen. "They're coming here?"

"Police cars," Donahoo told him. "They're surrounding the building." He kept trying to think of some solution. "I told you. We were trying to stop this. That's why the police are here. To stop Marino. Not to stop you. You're free to leave. Why don't you go?"

Urquidez looked at Marino. "What will happen to this man?"

"He will be punished."

"How?"

"He will go to jail. Maybe he will be executed."

"Maybe?"

"I think he will go to jail."

"I think maybe," Urquidez said. He prodded Marino with the Luger. "Come. I'm taking you back to Tijuana. You seemed to like it there. Maybe you will like it again. But I don't think so."

Donahoo thought Jesus Christ. He was going to say what he thought, that they'd never make it, but he didn't want to provoke Urquidez into something more rash. He was pretty sure Urquidez was going to take Marino to Tijuana or he was going to kill him in San Diego. He was going to do one or the other.

"Okay," he said. "It's your gun and it's his head. I can't stop you. So you can have him. He's the one who fucked up, so he can dance for you."

Theresa said, "What are you doing?"

"Shut up," he told her. Footsteps were pounding in the stairwell. He said to Urquidez, "We have a fake bomb scare in the building. Another way we had hoped to stop him. So you can leave in the panic and no one will notice you. I'll go along and make sure. Safe passage to my car." He was looking at Catalina. "If you let the women stay."

Urquidez glanced at Theresa. "That one, perhaps. You can let her go when we get to the car. But not my lawyer friend. I have plans for her."

"Okay," Donahoo said tiredly. He was going to push the elevator button for down and then changed his mind. He thought he might have a better chance in the stairwell. "She did this to herself. So she can dance for you too." He was looking at her. Catalina in her rose silk pleated dress that buttoned all the way up the front. Here for a dirty weekend. She had changed for Urquidez. She had worn the plain blue one for him, Donahoo, but had kept the all-those-buttons dress for the beast, Diablo. "They are two very stupid people. They think with their hearts."

Theresa said softly, "Jesus."

"Shut up."

Donahoo led the way to the stairs. They went in a tight bunch. Urquidez with his Luger at the back of Marino's skull now. Catalina and Theresa on either side.

"Keep your word," Urquidez warned. "You all die here if you try to betray me."

Donahoo showed his cellular. Punched in Lewis's number.

"We're coming out, Lewis," Donahoo told him. They were starting down the stairs. "Diablo, Marino, Catalina, me. Theresa. We're coming out with a gun at Marino's head. He's gonna die unless we get safe passage. Understand? Safe passage or Marino is dead."

"Where are you going?"

"Tijuana."

"Like shit."

"Lewis," Donahoo said. "Look at it this way. There'll be a ton of cops waiting there. An orderly transfer of a murder suspect from one jurisdiction to another. We have a history of cooperation with the Mexican cops."

Lewis complained, "But they'll be *his* cops!" and Donahoo told him, "Yeah, so you are *my* cop, Lewis. We're even."

Urquidez said behind him, "I like a man who knows how to stay alive. Would you like to work for me?"

"I already do," Donahoo said.

□ □ □

The rest went like a clock. They caught up to a group of people evacuating Mr. A's and they stayed behind them on the stairwell and then a second group caught up. They approached the garage level en masse.

Donahoo stayed on the cellular. His cut foot was throbbing painfully. It felt like he had a shoe full of blood. "Okay. Garage level. No cops. Diablo doesn't want to see one or it's all over. We'll be leaving in my car. It's an '84 white Toronado. Red interior. License plate 506NZQ.

Lewis said, "No cops."

"We'll be going south on Fourth. West on Elm. South on Second. The I-5 on-ramp at Cedar. It makes a turn around the Holiday Inn—Harbor View. No cops."

"No cops."

Donahoo didn't like the reluctance in Lewis's voice. He said, "Lewis. No cops." He was playing to Urquidez. "This guy is serious. He's gonna blow Marino's head off. He doesn't give a shit. He thinks he's got the right. Maybe he has."

"What the fuck are you saying?"

"I'm saying you're gonna get us all killed if we don't do this straight."

"Okay."

They reached the Toronado. Donahoo shoved behind the wheel. Urquidez got in the back with Marino and Catalina. Theresa got in next to Donahoo. He was going to tell her to get out but didn't think he had that right. He said, "You don't have to come," and she said, "I know."

"Let's go," Urquidez said.

Donahoo took the Toronado out of the building and turned south on one-way Fourth Avenue. No cops. He was experiencing a little déjà vu. He'd done something like this before. Run for the border.

"Diablo, this is how we're going to do it," he said. "We're twenty minutes away, huh? Plenty of time for your people to get into position there." He looked in the rearview. He could see Marino and Urquidez. Marino had his eyes open now. They were empty. Nothing showed. The vacant stare of a man who knows he is going to die. After he has suffered a lot. "I can call somebody there for you. Give me a number."

Donahoo turned onto Elm toward Second Avenue. Urquidez gave him the number. Donahoo broke the connection to Lewis. He handed the cellular to Theresa. She punched in the number. She gave the phone back.

"Uh," Donahoo said. He was looking around. No cops. "Do you want to talk to them? Or me?"

Urquidez reached over for the cellular. He kept the Luger at the back of Marino's head.

Donahoo made the left turn onto Second. Urquidez started talking rapidly in Spanish. Down one block and a quick right onto Cedar. Urquidez was speaking very rapidly and very loudly. Now Donahoo was merging with First Avenue traffic and circling around the Holiday Inn—Bay View. He was on the I-5 on-ramp. He had to speed up to merge and then he hit the brakes and everybody went flying forward and Donahoo grabbed the Luger as it went off with a large explosion but harmlessly to the right of and past Marino's head.

The Toronado scraped along the concrete wall of the Second Avenue overpass and spun around and stopped. Donahoo fought Urquidez for possession of the Luger. He got it twisted around and pointed into Urquidez's face. He thought maybe he could pry it loose from him. He wasn't certain. He pulled the trigger.

The explosion and the blood and the brains came at the same time.

Jesus Christ, Donahoo thought, because he hadn't known, hadn't suspected, that kind of decision was in him.

Catalina and Theresa were screaming. Marino was still staring like a condemned man.

Donahoo waited for the screaming to stop. Then he found the cellular. Someone was shouting in Spanish. He said, "Fuck you and adios," and switched off. He wondered what he was going to do. He had a few moments to work it out. They were hidden by the overpass. If a chopper was around, it probably couldn't see them.

Marino said, "I'm sorry."

"Yeah," Donahoo said. "And so am I. But I guess it's just a Mexican thing." He was trying not to look at Catalina. He was wondering what he would do if he had to make this call and there was not Catalina but just Marino. He said, "You decide what you want to do. You can stay or you can run. If it was me, I'd run,

Cruz. I can't protect you. You're gonna grow old in jail." He said, "Which way will you be running?"

"South," Catalina said.

"Okay. I'll tell 'em north."

"Maybe we will meet again?"

"I somehow doubt that very much."

He turned away. Catalina got out of the car. She ran back clear of the overpass and went up the berm and into the trees at the back of the Holiday Inn. He watched until she had disappeared, long legs stretching, leaping like a startled deer.

Marino and Theresa were looking at each other. Neither had said anything.

Now Marino said, "I'll always love you, Theresa," and she told him, "Okay, but you were right, you fucking idiot, I won't be waiting."

"It's all in the Bible," Marino said, looking at Donahoo. "There are holy wars. You slay your enemies."

"It's time, Cruz," Donahoo said. He got the pack of Pacificos. He took one and put the pack back. "Take care."

Marino nodded. He got out and started for the berm.

"You're staying?" Donahoo asked Theresa, and she said, "Yes."

Donahoo punched in Lewis's number on the cellular and got Cominsky. He was thinking he should have given Marino his watch back. That would have been a nice gesture. Marino was going to need a watch that didn't glow in the dark. Hiding in black holes, he wouldn't want a watch that gave him away, would he?

"Cominsky," he said, lighting the cigarette. "I'm glad it's you. This is all fucked up. I got forced off the road. There was some shooting and Urquidez is dead." He said, "Uh, listen, willya? Marino and the Mexican lady got away. They've hijacked a car going north on I-5."

Theresa was looking at him and faintly smiling. Donahoo thought that he had to give them a chance. He would have to give wrong descriptions and the wrong direction and let them go. He was glad he was talking to Cominsky. He had a pass with the guy. Cominsky wouldn't question him. Cominsky would never suspect that he, Donahoo, was breaking all the rules, letting them go.

"It's an Oldsmobile," Donahoo told him, smiling too now. He couldn't help it. He reached across and gave Theresa a little punch on the shoulder. "I think a Calais. Super clean. Maybe an

'89, '90." He said, "That's a four-cylinder, quad 4. So you oughta be able to catch it. I don't have the plate, but you're looking for a two-door, alloys."

"Sure," Cominsky said slowly, like he was writing it down. He sounded very wise. "But what color?"

Thirty-one

The best time to go to the San Diego Library's main branch Friends of the Library Book Sale was on Friday. The sale ran weekly Friday through Sunday and most of the good stuff was snapped up by Saturday and there was just crap left by Sunday.

This was Friday. Donahoo had picked up four volumes, 1 to 5, missing 4, of *Blackie's Comprehensive History of England*, along with *Best Detective Stories of the Year—1974*, as well as Michael Connelly's *The Concrete Blonde*.

Now he was negotiating the purchase of a paperback edition of the Bible. The reason he was negotiating was that paperbacks were priced at 25¢ each if fiction and 50¢ each if nonfiction. He had asked the lady at the desk if the Bible was fiction or nonfiction and he thought there must have been something about the way he asked because she didn't want to make that call.

"Hey, you tell me," he said. "How much are you charging? Is it fiction or nonfiction? Is it a quarter or fifty cents?"

She looked at him. She took it from him. Then she put it aside. He said, "What's that mean?" and she said, "It's not for sale."

He said, "What? That's how you're gonna settle it?", and she said, "Next?"

Donahoo was going to make a scene. He thought it was time he made a scene somewhere. It had been more than a week since he had killed Diablo and let Marino and Catalina go and he still hadn't made a scene with anybody, not even with Lewis, or even with Saperstein. They were giving him a pretty wide circle and he was giving them a still wider one. There just hadn't been a good opportunity for a good scene. But this looked like a good time with this old bat volunteer for Friends of the Library.

"Let me tell you what I think . . ."

"Sarge?"

He stopped. It was Cominsky. He turned around holding the

239

books he still had and hadn't paid for. The *Blackie's* and the *BEST Detective Stories* and *The Concrete Blonde.*

"They said I'd find you here," Cominsky said, pulling him aside. "The guys, you know, they're starting to worry about you, the way you've been acting, and they thought maybe I ought to talk to you."

Donahoo stared at him. Cominsky the geek. A tall, thin, gawky, birdlike creature in a yellow checkered suit with wide lapels. A really weird guy. "You?"

"Yeah. You gotta stop thinking any of this is your fault, Sarge. Okay, like you say, maybe you were posturing, always wanting to look at Diablo, and maybe it was a mistake to plant ideas in Marino's mind, but how could anybody know he was gonna act on them? Nobody could have predicted that. It's not your fault. You gotta stop thinking it is and you've gotta stop talking about going to Guadalajara to find that Marquisa. It's making everybody nervous. And you also gotta stop mooning over that lawyer lady. The one dedicated to fighting unjustice? Catalina? That's never gonna work. She's not your type. You need somebody laid back. Somebody who is gonna give you a standing invitation to lie down. And it's not that Theresa. Your life is not worth a nickel if you're going around with a girl a quarter your age. Her father's a cab driver. You hear me?"

"Yeah. And so can everybody in the fucking library."

Cominsky took him further aside. He took him past the elevator and the pay phones and past the sign that said EMPLOYEES ONLY. He took him into the little cubicle there before the doorway.

"Saperstein's got this theory," Cominsky said, his voice lower now. "He thinks Marino went south. He thinks he's that guy down there leading that Chiapas peasant uprising. He thinks he's Subcommander Marcos."

"No," Donahoo said. He glanced back at the old bat volunteer for Friends of the Library. She was looking at him suspiciously. "For Christ's sake. The timing is all wrong. Subcommander Marcos has been down there for fucking ever. Marino just got this bug up his ass."

"Okay. I coulda got that wrong. Maybe Saperstein thinks he's an assistant to Subcommander Marcos. There's a story in the paper this morning about some corrupt official being killed down there in Chiapas country and Saperstein said it had Marino's mark."

"Well, that is possible, all right," Donahoo had to admit. He was looking over his shoulder. He had to get back and pay for the goddamn books. "Juarez justice. Wherever it is found down there—maybe Marino had a hand in it, all right."

"Huh?"

"I gotta go."

"No. Wait. Lewis asked me to ask you a question. He wants to know what you think. What set Marino off?"

"They sold him a bum watch."

"Right. Now this is from all the guys. They're wondering why you cut the top off your Toronado."

"Because the roof liner was scuffed."

"Now you're starting to make sense."